To
ke:
You are my Sunshine

SINFUL PLEASURES

Never let Anyone Dim your light

Tanya
Johnsen

By

T.J. La Rue

Welcome to the world of T. J. La Rue. I hope you enjoy this Tantalyzing Journey from the Bedroom to the Boardroom

T.J. La Rue

ACKNOWLEDGEMENTS

Thank you Damon Johniken for remaining by my side every step of the way, never letting me lose sight of my passion. For understanding my long nights at the computer, I'd like to thank my children Damon Jr, Tiana and Teja Johniken

This book would not have been possible without the support and encouragement of my friends and family. Words cannot express my gratitude to Rysing Starr Edits for their professional advice and services. Andrea Pike and BJ Betts, thank you for your friendship and your immeasurable support.

TABLE OF CONTENTS

KELLY

Finding Friday

For some reason, she keeps getting the feeling like someone is watching her. Kelly James sits at the bar waiting for her friends to arrive. They are having their "Sisters' Fall Feast," so they've all decided to go to Friday's. For once, they were able to agree on something besides the fact that she's always late. That's exactly why her behind is sitting at the bar an hour early, just so those bitches can kiss her ass. She nurses her rum and Coke, not really feeling the vibe.

You should see all of the "special ones" trying to buy her a drink. Kelly calls them "special" because they are here chasing ass knowing their wives/girlfriends couldn't care less. They don't care as long as their husbands/boyfriends aren't bothering them. A real special bunch. After busting their bubbles, she excuses herself to the ladies' room. She needs to walk around and shake this feeling off. She decides to go to the ladies' room to make sure she was still looking flawless.

As Kelly stares herself down in the mirror, someone walks in scaring the shit out of her. She was so busy giving herself the diva's stare in the mirror that she didn't notice her walk in. Smiling, the woman asks if she's okay. Giving her the, "GURRL, I'm fine," replies as she tries to play it off. But it's as if she saw right through Kelly. This stranger will not let up. As she continues to probe her for answers, Kelly is in awe of the stranger's beauty. Her look is beyond exotic and completely enticing. Her skin was the color of honey. Her grey eyes looked as if they had the power of a storm and she knew something was brewing. It took all Kelly had to look away. Now don't get it wrong Kelly is far from being anything but beautiful. She is short in stature, but towers in her 6-inch heels. Her caramel complexion tastes as good as it looks, but nothing on Kelly compares to her.

After she brings her mind back into focus, Kelly fesses up, "I keep getting this feeling like someone is watching me and it's making me feel strange." she touches up her makeup trying to pull herself together. The stranger watches Kelly fix her lip gloss.

"What color is that?" she asks. Kelly tells her how it was specially made for her by a cosmetic artist that she knows. The stranger leans a little closer, telling Kelly how her eye shadow compliments her green eyes. Kelly tries not to blush as she thanks her.

The next thing Kelly knew, the stranger is apologizing for talking her head off. She tells Kelly the only reason she came in here for a breather. The guys at the bar are boring her to death with all of their pick-up lines. The stranger moves to the mirror next to her. Kelly's relieved that she stepped back a little. For a moment, there was a fire between them and she wasn't sure why. The stranger informs Kelly the string on the back of her shirt is tangled and offers to fix it. "Sure, that's fine." says Kelly. She steps over towards Kelly as she looks away avoiding her glance.

Kelly feels her gently pressing her body close. The stranger leans in, breathing on her neck. Kelly's body loses control and starts to shiver. She looks up, causing their eyes to lock. The strange's eyes are mesmerizing. Her hands feel so soft as she unties Kelly's shirt. It slips down a little and exposes her ample breast. Kelly's breathing quickens. She stands unsure what to do as the woman's hand glides down her chest. The stranger pulls Kelly's shirt back up slowly.

Once again, Kelly tries to turn away from her stare, but she caught her eyes in the mirror. Watching on as she grazed Kelly's nipple with her hand. Kelly let out a soft moan. She can't control herself. The stranger playfully whispers, "Oops, my bad," in Kelly's ear. Kelly looks away again; embarrassed and turned on as hell. Her pussy is throbbing. She didn't know what to do. Kelly is close to losing her mind. She tries to open her mouth to apologize, but the stranger has her finger up to Kelly's mouth.

Her shirt falls completely down this time, ultimately exposing both of her breasts. Stranger whispers that she was the one watching Kelly. She pulls her long, black hair to the side and kisses Kelly on the neck. Kelly continues moaning as the stranger presses against her. Feeling the stranger grinding on her from behind, Kelly wants to tell her to stop, but it feels too good.

"*What is wrong with you?*" she asks herself. "*I don't know why I am doing this with a woman and a complete stranger at that!*" Just then, the stranger slides her hands down towards Kelly's pussy causing her knees to buckle. Kelly turns around facing her and says, "We can't do this, not here, we are still in the bathroom." The sexy stranger tells Kelly she's staying at the hotel across the street. Part of her wants to go, but her friends are coming any minute now.

Her heart is racing, her pussy begs for more. "I can't go with you," Kelly tells her. Her fingers rolls Kelly's nipples as if they were clay. She grabs her ass and pushes Kelly towards the sink. Her mouth is sucking her breast while one hand is teasing Kelly's pussy through her pants.

Pulling Kelly's ass even closer, she looks at her with those stormy eyes and says, "Come with me."

Kelly don't think twice this time, *"Fuck it!"* she says to herself and informs the stranger that she will meet her out front. The stranger smiles and kisses Kelly.

The kiss tells Kelly she won't be disappointed. Kelly watches her stranger walk away. Even though she'd never been with a woman, Kelly knew she wanted her. She found herself craving this stranger. Finally, she turns around and looks at herself in the mirror. She realized her shirt is still hanging down. Kelly quickly fixes herself up. Kelly had to make sure she looked good enough to eat, because she was about to be the main course.

Back at the bar, Kelly rushed the bartender like a mad woman. The special crew asked why she was in such a hurry to get out of there. "Stay a little longer sexy." they all chimed. The offers of free drinks poured in from the peanut gallery. But she knew why, they wanted some of her goods.*"Too bad they couldn't do what she just did to me in the bathroom,"* she thought to herself.

Kelly had to give it to her, the chick had game. She laughed out loud as she sashayed her ass out of there. The thought of what was about to happen had her panties on fire. (Well, not her real ones because she doesn't wear any). She was standing outside waiting for Kelly. *"Damn, I didn't realize how sexy she was."* thinks Kelly as she walks up to her, unsure of what to say. "I didn't think you were coming and was about to leave, I wait for no one," her sexy stranger says. Kelly apologizes, telling her how sorry she was. The stranger laughs when Kelly tells her how the "pack" attempted to make her stay.

They made small talk crossing the street. Kelly didn't really know what to say. She was so nervous, but hoped it didn't show. They walked through the lobby laughing and joking like they were old friends. Stepping off of the elevator, heading to her room, Kelly could feel the hairs on her body raising. She wanted to turn around, but they reached the stranger's room. She turned to smile at Kelly as she slid the key in the door. When invited her in, Kelly knew there was no turning back.

Once inside of her room, Kelly admired the decor. The stranger locked the door and grabbed Kelly from behind. Kelly let out a surprising gasp. This time the stranger's intentions were clear and she got right to the point. She started kissing Kelly, telling her how sexy she was. "I watched you walk into the bar..." the stranger said, as she started undressing Kelly. Hearing her telling Kelly how she liked how her jeans wrapped around her ass drove Kelly wild. They stood there kissing for what seemed like forever. Stranger's lips were tender and sweet. She kissed Kelly's mouth as if it belonged to her. She walked Kelly over to the couch. She sat down and pulled Kelly on top. She forcefully grabbed Kelly's ass as she straddled her. Kelly winced in pain, but it made her want the stranger even more.

Kelly watched as the stranger admired her breast. They were round and firm. She takes them into her hands sending Kelly's heart racing. She carefully massaged Kelly's breast and toyed with her nipples. Kelly bit down on her lip as she felt the urge to moan. She loved when her husband played with her lady mounds. She use to think they were made just for him, but this stranger had Kelly thinking otherwise. Kelly's breast seemed to melt in her stranger's soft hands. She pulls them closer and strokes them with her tongue. She pauses for a moment and looks up at Kelly. A slight smile crosses her face. Kelly braced herself for whatever's coming next. She attacks her breast with a yearning Kelly never seen before. Her mouth felt so warm and moist on her breast. She couldn't hold back her sounds of pleasure any longer. Kelly grabs the stranger by the back of the head, pressing her deeper into her chest.

Kelly hears her moan as she is smothered by her breasts. Stranger's hands wrap around Kelly's waist, holding her tight.

Their moans turn into grunts as Kelly grinds her pussy on her stranger. Her hands start to run wildly all over Kelly, covering every inch of her body. Kelly fights the urge not to cum as juices ran down her legs. Stranger's pants were covered with Kelly's stickiness. On the verge of exploding, Kelly wanted more. She wanted to fuck her stranger. It was driving Kelly crazy, yet the stranger was sitting there fully clothed. The stranger tried to kiss Kelly, but she refuse to be toyed with any longer. Something changed in Kelly. She stood up and crossed her arms. The stranger looked at Kelly with confusion and a hint of annoyance. Even through that, the stranger couldn't hide her desire. Kelly was standing before the stranger, naked in a pair of her favorite CFMP's (Come Fuck Me Pumps). Stranger's eyes traced Kelly's body, unsure of where to look next. She was greedy and wanted to take all of her in. Kelly's hands ran slowly over the contours of her body. She stopped at all of her special spots to pleasure herself. Softly, she moaned as she spread her legs. Her kitty was starting to purr. She stroked her tuft of hair in small circles watching the stranger become hypnotized. Slowly, Kelly guided the stranger's eyes towards her love hole as she submerged her finger deep into her juices. She smiled devilishly as she moaned.

By now stranger is on the edge of her seat trying to move closer to Kelly. She refuses to let her stranger take control again. When Kelly took a step back, it went unnoticed. Stranger's turbulent eyes were still fixated on the way Kelly magically made her fingers disappear. Commanding full attention, Kelly made sure stranger wanted more just like she did. Allowing for plenty of distance between the two, she decided to make full use of the coffee table centered in the room. Stranger watched as Kelly sat on the table and parted her thighs, formally introducing her to clit. Kelly started to pleasure herself as stranger watched. Performing turned Kelly on, she stroked her clit until it was harder than any man's dick. Stranger reclined in her seat as Kelly worked her fingers in and out. Her pussy was soaking wet. Moving her fingers faster, her stranger starting talking nasty. "Work that pussy. Fuck that pussy." She said. She wanted to see Kelly cum. Kelly slid her fingers out of her pussy, placing them in her mouth. Stranger moaned as Kelly sucked her fingers, licking all of the creamy juices off.

Her tongue belonged on Kelly's pussy. Kelly had enough of this foreplay with her. "Do you want more?" she asked stranger, who replied "Yes", in a sexy voice.

"Take off your clothes!" Kelly demanded.

"No," the stranger replied. "I want to watch you some more."

It was right here that their play for power really began. Kelly sat straight up on the table tightly crossing her legs. "Do you plan on taking off your clothes?" she asked. "I really didn't have a plan about taking off my clothes," stranger informed Kelly. "You are really starting to annoy me," she continued, "I am not amused with your little game right now." She smiled trying to lighten the mood. "You are soo sexy; I would love to watch you cum first."

Her demeanor tempted Kelly. She pushed Kelly to her point. Sitting there with many emotions running through her mind, she was confused and horny as hell. "How did I end up here letting a woman toy with me like this? I have to get out of here."she thought. Her head was spinning trying to fight back the tears welling up in her eyes. Kelly stood up and began to angrily grab her clothes. She excused herself and quickly, put her clothes back. She raced for the door. As soon as Kelly placed her hand on the knob, she felt a hand on hers. In a quiet voice stranger said, "Don't leave me." Kelly picked her head up, steadying herself to face stranger.

A lonely tear trickled down her face while she yelled, "You are cruel and I will not allow you to use me like that!"

They stood face to face for a moment not saying a word. She pulled Kelly's hand towards her body. Kelly's hand recoiled when she felt her softness. Kelly stood there with her mouth open looking at her naked body. Distracted by her anger, Kelly didn't notice stranger had finally taken her clothes off. Kelly was paralyzed by her beauty. Again, Kelly found herself losing control of the situation. Her body started to tremble—only this time she couldn't hide it. Filled with embarrassment, Kelly wanted to leave and yet she still had to have this woman. "I'm begging you, please stay," says the stranger. With her hands on the back of Kelly's neck she eases her over. Kelly's hands fall to the floor. The stranger pulls her closer, kissing her wildly.

Kelly's hands are out of control touching all over stranger's body. It's impossible to separate their moans anymore. Kelly is thrown up against the door, pinned by the stranger's delicate flesh pressed against hers. Stranger grinds her body on Kelly. The sensation of her touching nipples send chills up Kelly's spine. Teetering on the edge of losing her mind, "Fuck me!" the stranger begs over and over again. The fury builds right before Kelly's eyes. Stranger's pleas become entangled with grunts. Kelly moans back, "I want you to fuck me."

This woman is driving Kelly wild. Somehow, they make it to the bedroom. For a moment, they stand face to face. Stranger commands Kelly with her eyes. Kelly willingly placed her trembling body on the bed. Overcome by her desire, Kelly gives in to her temptation. She reaches out and pulls stranger on top. As they lay on the bed, the curves of their bodies begin to blur into one. Stranger begins to moan seductively as they kiss and grind on each other. She tries not to feed her hunger for Kelly, but her moans become stronger and stronger. Unable to fight the urge any longer, "I want to taste your pussy," the stranger says, as Kelly traces her nipple rings with her tongue. Not one to give in so easily, Kelly tugs on them making her stranger moan even more. Kelly couldn't hold out any longer, her kitty was ready. She laid back and unlocked her treasure box. Kelly sees the look of excitement on stranger's face as she admires her kitty's beauty.

Stranger leans in to kiss Kelly, this is the quiet before the storm. She starts on her neck, leaving a trail of small kisses on her way down south. Kelly writhes with anticipation; stranger slows her pace, not missing an inch. She goes lower and lower. Her silky skin glides past Kelly's stomach. Her face is now close to Kelly's pussy, causing her to let out a soft, pleading moan. Wanting her stranger's mouth on her kitty so bad, Kelly begin to pant as her legs started to shake. She can feel her breath inches from her clit. "Don't do it, don't do it," she tells herself.

At this point, she's convinced that she's going to cum just from this woman near her pussy. Kelly tries to calm down before she loses it and ruins this crazy moment. Slowly, her kisses get closer and closer towards the desired center. Kelly's hands are all over her titties. Those big, brown nipples receive the wrath of her pleasurable anguish. She squeezes her nipples, causing them to squirt milk all over the place. Stranger continues with her slow yet hungered pace. She reaches the center of Kelly's Tootsie pop. Instead of diving right in and smothering herself into the pussy, she flicks the clit with her tongue. Kelly is moaning and squirting milk out like crazy. She wants more; she has to feel stranger's mouth devouring her juices. "Please!!" she begs her. "Please give me more!!" her stranger replies with a grunt that sent chills up her spine. Kelly was afraid of what was about to happen next. "Maybe I should have kept my mouth shut." she thought to herself.

At that very moment, all thoughts stop running through her head. She felt the stranger place her mouth on Kelly. *"Her mouth is on my pussy!"* Kelly screams in her head. She lets out a moan that sounded like the life was being sucked out of her. Stranger spreads Kelly's swollen lips as far as they would go and went to work on her pussy. She licked up all of Kelly's pussy juices. The more she licked the more there was. It is as if Kelly were a fountain because, stranger was certainly is thirsty for her libation. Stranger's entire mouth covers Kelly's enlarged clit while her finger disappears in and out of her pussy. Normally, Kelly is quiet during sex with her husband, but she's taking her to a point where that's not an option. The more she samples Kelly's pussy the louder her moans get. The more Kelly moans the more stranger sucks. She's thrusting my pussy faster and faster to meet her mouth. She has Kelly near the edge and ready to give it all to her. Kelly grabs the back of the stranger's head, she tells her not to stop, that she's about to cum. Kelly can feel it building. She tries to hold it back. She doesn't want it to end. She tries to push the feeling back, but stranger buries her face deeper. It feels so good, Kelly can't help it. Stranger grabs Kelly's ass lifting her up closer. She continues to suck her pussy.

That's it, stranger has Kelly. She is grinding her pussy hard on stranger's face. She lets out a deep moan as stranger makes her pussy explode. Her whole body starts to shake. Kelly's bucking like crazy against stranger's face. Kelly hears herself say, "OH, GOD! I'm cumming!" It feels like fireworks went off inside of her body. After it was over, Kelly lies there trembling. She feels silly and tries to cover her face, but she couldn't move. Kelly has no control over her body and stranger knows it. She sits back looking at Kelly with a smile on her face. Her face is dripping with Kelly's juices. Seeing this causes something to build inside of Kelly. She wanted her, she needed her. Slowly, stranger crawls her way over to Kelly and places her mouth on her. They start to kiss again as Kelly grazes her pussy with her hand. She loved how the softness feels. Stranger is neatly trimmed and has a small tuft of hair above her clit in the shape of triangle. A soft moan escapes her mouth as

Kelly runs her fingers over stranger's trap. Her hips wiggle slightly. She wants Kelly to pleasure her.

Never had Kelly done anything like this before, but she wanted her. she was now a woman possessed by another. She turns stranger over to admire her beauty. "Your breasts are so soft," she tells her, caressing them. Kelly teases both nipples with her teeth. Stranger's moaning sounded like music to Kelly's ears and she wanted to hear more of this symphony. Kelly places stranger's breast in her mouth. Stranger cradles Kelly's head as if she wanted her to feast off of her. Kelly happily obliges. Her tongue glides against the supple skin. Kelly craves her juices. She positioned herself so that she was face to face with her pussy. This was the first time seeing one up close. She'd heard guys say pussy is ugly, but stranger's wasn't. Covered in juicy nectar, this beautiful flower glowed amidst the darkness of the room. Stranger is so wet, Kelly had to taste her. She circled the outside of the pussy with her tongue, taking time to savor it's essence. It is so sweet. She paused at stranger's clit before rolling it around on her tongue, trying to unwrap it's pearl.

Stranger's moaning...she's whispering, "Yes, Mami, get my pussy." She's telling Kelly how good it feels. Hearing stranger's pleasure turns Kelly on. She pulls her pussy lips open, going face deep into the triangle. Kelly sucks on her clit driving her crazy until stranger gets louder and louder. "FUCK ME!" The stranger yells, "FUCK MY PUSSY!" Despite being unsure of what to do next, Kelly wanted all of her. Her tongue disappeared into stranger's love hole, slowly massage her walls. As she screamed, "YES, YESSS!"stranger crawled backwards.

Kelly grabs her and fervently says, "This pussy is mine, you're not going anywhere!" Stranger moans even louder. Kelly's in full control now. She has her exactly where she wants. Kelly submerges her face back into stranger's pussy demanding her to fuck it. Grabbing Kelly's hair, stranger begins to unleash her demon. Her wet pussy grinds up and down on her face. Kelly grips tighter; taking the pussy.

The sound of Kelly devouring her love juices drives stranger wild. She begs for Kelly to let her cum. As much as Kelly wanted her to, she didn't. She couldn't let this end, even though she had to. Kelly wanted to taste her sweet and sticky cum in her mouth. Stranger's leg starts to shake. Kelly works faster. It's close. She wants it. Kelly starts to finger her as she sucks on her pussy. It's too much for stranger. She tries to sit up to watch Kelly eating her pussy, but she is powerless as she starts to cum. She cums so hard. It's way too much for Kelly's stranger. Her liquid flows freely from its haven. Kelly savor this treat as it is nothing like she's ever taster before. She climbs up and lies next to stranger. Unsure of what's to come next, but still pleasured by what has happened. They hold each other for a moment, still humming the erotic tune they'd composed all night. Stranger looks over and gives Kelly a soft kiss. Kelly tries to stop her, but she can't. The kiss becomes harder and harder. Their hands are all over each other again.

She wraps her leg around Kelly's. Stranger climbs on top of Kelly and begins rocking her pussy back and forth across hers Stranger puts Kelly's arms behind her head, pinning them with one hand. She's pulling Kelly's nipples with the other. She starts pounding her pussy against Kelly's. She pounds harder and harder as she demands, "WHO'S PUSSY IS THIS?" Kelly is unable to respond. Well, it's not that she couldn't, she simply refused to answer. They end up back at their power struggle. "I'm not gonna give back what I just took from her." Kelly tells herself as Stranger pulls her nipples harder. Kelly tries to keep the moan in but it's difficult because the sensation Stranger's sending through her body is unbearable. Stranger lets out a mischievous laugh. "WHO'S FUCKIN' PUSSY IS THIS?!" she yells.

Kelly stares Stranger in the face and defiantly says, "MINE."

Stranger loved it. She smiled as she kept pounding Kelly's pussy; she started grinding on it. "WHO'S PUSSY IS THIS, BITCH?"

Kelly couldn't believe Stranger just took it there. Kelly loved being called a bitch when she's being fucked. Refusing to answer. "Please," Kelly begged of herself. "Stay in control of this moment."

She says it again.

This time Kelly couldn't hold it back. She hears herself screaming, "IT'S YOUR PUSSY, BABY. MAKE ME YOUR BITCH! FUUCK ME LIKE I'M YOUR BITCH." The words tasted so good as they left her mouth. Kelly knew she was in for it. Kelly had just given Stranger full power over her—again! Stranger kissed Kelly one more time before focusing again on Kelly's pussy. She grinds on Kelly like she's trying to break her into pieces. Stranger powerful hands reach behind Kelly, grabbing her ass. She yanked it up off of the bed and rode Kelly's pussy like she had a dick. Stranger was Kelly's cowgirl and Kelly definitely was her thoroughbred. At one point, Kelly couldn't take anymore and begged Stranger to stop. Every part of her body was tingling. She didn't know what was happening to it.

Even though Kelly begged for Stranger to stop, her body wouldn't. Kelly pushed back harder and harder, eagerly meeting each of Stranger thrusts. The sensation is truly mind blowing. Kelly didn't know what to make of it. Stranger rode Kelly faster and faster until she made her pussy go off. Stranger didn't move off of Kelly until her body stopped shaking violently. Stranger finally removed Kelly's hands from her capture and climbed off of her. Kelly couldn't move. This chick was paralyzed and damn near in a coma. She hears movement going on around her, but her mind can't focus on what's happening. She feels the blankets being pulled over her body. Slowly she drifts off to sleep. Kelly tries to open her mouth to speak but it won't budge. Stranger placed a kiss on Kelly's lips and then disappeared out of sight.

When Kelly woke up the room was pitch black. She sat up, unsure of where she was and what just happened. Shocked by her nakedness, she jumped out of bed. She stumbled her way to the desk. turning on the light, she calls out, "HELP!" She felt foolish doing so, because she didn't know the woman's name. She looked down on the desk and saw a note. "You've been kissed," with a set of lips on it. This set Kelly off in panic. She ran around the hotel room searching for the woman hoping that she was hiding somewhere in the room. Every part of her prayed she would jump out and say, "Ha! Got ya!" like an episode of Punked. But she didn't—she was gone.

"I'll never be able to see her again. I'll never have an experience like that again with her." Kelly thought as reality set in. She cleaned herself up and got dressed. She still had somewhere to be. To remind her of their time together, she grabbed the note on the way out the door. Kelly needed her and this note was the closest she would come to it.

As she walked back to the restaurant, Kelly prayed that she was there waiting for me. Instead, she found her "sisters" there being entertained by the "special ones." Disappointed, she joined them at the table. Pissed because she arrived there three hours ago and was still late. They don't waste any time scolding Kelly about her tardiness. Confused at this point, nothing they say enters her thought process. The waitress brought out their desserts and asks if Kelly wanted to see the dessert menu. "I already ate mine." she responds, turning to find the "special ones" eyeing her down. Their faces still filled with desire. Kelly laughed as she stared off into space replaying the rendezvous in her head. She will never forget her time with the stranger, she's her "Girl Friday."

***

Kelly pulled up thinking, "This has got to be the craziest shit I've ever done." Even with that feeling, this was the closest she would probably come to reliving that night with the one she nicknamed, Girl Friday. Her mind replays how things got to this point. The past five months have been spent chasing the infamous Girl Friday. She was like a dream and their time was nothing short of amazing. Sometimes Kelly can't believe that it happened. She if Kelly didn't have the letter Girl Friday left along with the tingle in Kelly's kitty every time Girl Friday crossed her mind. "*Damn.*" she said, as she exhaled. Deep down killed her knowing she wanted more of Friday.

She searched Nakedpeople.com and Swingerslive.com hoping to find her. Even though she knew her chances of finding the incredible stranger are close to zero, still she searched. Those searches aren't exactly met with disappointment. She became entertained by the people on there. Kelly tried to make a connection several different times with other female, but it always fizzled out. The reason was always the same, no one compares to who she needed them to be. Two weeks later, Kelly reluctantly decided to give it one more try. While was browsing Naked People's site, a posting for a private party caught her attention. Everyone on the site was responding to the post wondering how to get an invite. "*What the hell?*" she told herself. "*Why not see what's it about?*"

Though she'd hung out at a swinger's club in the next town several times just to watch, this was her first private party. Kelly found herself posting a reply, just like all the others, asking for an invite. Excitement ran through her body as her fingers connected with the keyboard. "*How does this all work?*" she wondered, clicking send. Her mind races. She can't wait to go to this party. Her mood seemed to be getting better for her that night—until she read the message in her inbox from the party hostess—then instantly she became annoyed.

"What kind of crap is this?" she asked herself aloud. They required a questionnaire to be completed before they would present her request for admittance to meet the one they called Supreme. *"These people are insane. I didn't need to convince anyone to put me on a guest list! Who the hell does this Supreme chick think she is?"* Kelly thought to herself. She sat at her desk for a while sucking her teeth; huffing and puffing. *"Do they know who I am? I don't need to put up with this crazy shit."* She continued telling herself. While all of this sounded insane, she filled out the questionnaire. After finishing with their questions, there was something else that required her attention.

Thinking about this party had Kelly all worked up. Quickly she logged off and headed upstairs to find her twin daughters neatly tucked away in bed. Watching quietly in the doorway as her husband, Sal, slept, a warm feeling overtakes Kelly's heart. Throughout their relationship, seven years of dating and eleven years of marriage, Kelly always felt that he was her true soulmate. Although they'd had a fair share of ups and downs, she loved that man more than anyone could ever imagine loving another. Slowly, Kelly took all her clothes off and climbed in to bed with Sal, snuggling up close to him so he could feel her hot spot. Her kitty was in a bad way tonight. Kelly was ready for him.

She started to grind on him from behind. This had Kelly so turned on that she wanted Sal even more. Her full lips placed tender kisses on his muscular back. Finally, Sal wakes up, realizing that Kelly's cookie jar was open for his sampling. But this fool must've been on a diet because he turned to her and said, "Not tonight. I have to get up early for an important meeting." She can't believe it! Sal loves pussy. She decides to try another route by stroking his member in her hand with hopes of making him want to join in.

All of her advances are met with, "Kelly, STOP! I hav early," and he pushes her hand away. *"Did he just say what I th* she asks herself. It seems he did because she was staring at his back. Again. Kelly's heated at this point—as bad as Kitty wanted it, too! She has no words, she's speechless. The entire time they've been married she can't recall him ever turning down her pussy. All Kelly could do was roll over and think to herself, *"They better send me my damn invite!"*

When she woke up the next morning, Sal had left a note for her on the pillow. Kelly yelled, *"Why do people keep leaving notes for me?"* Instantly her disposition changes when she read how sorry her husband was about last night.

He wanted to be with Kelly more than anything, but had a BIG meeting today. "I promise to make it up to you." Reading the note out loud made Kelly feel a little better. Smiling, she got up to get the kids ready for school and send them off for the day. With everyone gone, she pours a cup of coffee to drink while reading the morning news.

Sighing, *"Okay! Let's get warmed up. I gotta get some work done on this novel today."* Kelly situates herself at the desk to check her email first. She almost jumped out of the chair seeing saw what was waiting for her. It was a response from the hostess. "Dear Poster," it read. "Congratulations, you've made it past Supreme's questionnaire stage. We found your answers to be alluring. Please submit a photo of yourself in your sexiest attire for Vixen's consideration." Kelly immediately bolts up the stairs, tearing through her closets and drawers like a maniac. *"Ugggh, I can't find anything!"* she cried out.

Instantly, Kelly knew she had to go shopping. Grabbing her keys and purse, she hopped in the car and drove 20 minutes to her favorite "goody store", as she called it. They have everything you could ever need. Quickly, Kelly finds the perfect outfit and a couple of toys to spice it up. She races back home to get Kitty ready. She had an audience waiting.

"Baby let's get you ready your grand debut!" Kelly says, as she stares at the reflection in the mirror.

After trimming Kitty up neatly, add one final touch. One that would surely send them over the edge. Sitting on the bed she begins to massage scented oil all over her body. The oil moistens her skin. The more Kelly rubbed the slippery liquid, the more Kitty started to talk. She was excited. "Ummm," Kelly moaned seductively, sliding the sexy new outfit across her skin. She topped off the negligee with her CMFP's. Now that Kelly's makeup and hair are perfect, it's definitely picture time.

Kelly set the timer on her camera and laid on the bed. It felt kind of silly, so she started with simple poses. The more Kelly thought about it, the more it turned her on. She pulls out some of the special toys. A twisted grin crosses her face. She wanted to get a little bit naughty. *"I think I'll use this one."*

She places the vibrator in her mouth. Twirling her tongue around the tip, she began sucking it. Her mouth works up and down the vibrating dick, tickling the back of her throat. Kelly's other hand was being called to by her breasts. Her nipples were throbbing. They wanted to come out and play, too. Tugging gently on her nipples sends a chilling rush through her entire body. Kelly loved it. Her attention bounces back to the vibrator, rolling the tip around the rim of her mouth. *"No more teasing."* Kelly put the dick in her mouth, while pulling even harder on her nipples. Kelly's moaning grows louder.

She opened her legs, giving the camera full view of a wet pussy with its new diamond ring. *"Smile pretty, Kitty."* She purrs. Kelly trails the tip of the vibrator around her juicy pussy lips. You could hear it sliding up and down with all the juices. She had no intention of pleasuring herself, but it felt so good. Kelly had to put it in. Sliding it in far as she turns the vibration up to the highest setting. Arching her back, she began working the vibrator in and out of her slippery pussy.

Kelly forgot about the camera and really started working her pussy. She needed to be fucked badly. Kelly pulled out the cock to taste her own juices. Kelly grabbed the other vibrator. Yes, she needed two—one in her pussy and one in her mouth. Kelly sucked and fucked herself until she couldn't take it anymore. She had to cum. Her hips rose up slightly. Kelly worked her pussy even more while ramming that dick down her throat. She loved to be such a dirty whore. There was a fire building inside. Her legs started to shake. In and out, in and out; Kelly's rubbery, textured friend burrowed deep in her love hole. The pace quickened as the feeling overtakes Kelly from head to toe. Moaning loudly, she falls back on the bed. The vibrating sensation thrills her clit. She ride the orgasmic wave as it flows through. Her body sprawls out all over the bed, unable to move.

It takes a moment for her to get herself together. When she fully recovers, Kelly gets up and turns the camera off. She cleans away all traces of her self-gratification. She puts away all of her toys, making sure the bedroom looks as if nothing has taken place. Kelly takes the camera back to her office to choose a photo. The spread was amazing. She can't believe they actually turned out this nice. Kelly tried and tried but she couldn't choose just one. Fuck it, she decided to send all of them. Grabbing a pen, she scribbles a note saying, "I'm good till the last drop." Even if they didn't choose her, she still had a good time all by herself.

Several days pass and the thought of the party hadn't crossed Kelly's mind. When she received another response from the hostess, it completely caught her off guard. This one was different from the others. Kelly wasn't sure what to think. This one is delivered to her house. It arrives via courier wrapped in a beautiful box, topped with pretty ribbons and bows. At first, Kelly thought it was a gift from Sal. She looks inside the box and see an envelope. Still thinking it was from her husband, Kelly's heart warmed. *"He loves me. That's my baby."* she said, with a smile. Looking closer at the envelope, she notices that the words "TO MI AMOUR" are not scribed in my husband's penmanship. Tearing it open, Kelly sees that it is a formal introduction from the hostess named, Vixen.

"Mi Amour, thank you for sending the wonderful collection of pictures for my review. It is my duty to organize the parties. I also recruit new club members at each event I host. Based on your responses, I think that you might be interested in joining our group as we are interested in you. Each respective member is reviewed thoroughly, which is how we obtained your address."

Kelly was a little freaked out, but equally turned on by the thought of someone watching her. She read the enclosed directions to the event. She wasn't too familiar with the location, but this didn't matter to Kelly. She focused on the strict rules she had to follow. This "Vixen" and all of her demands annoy Kelly. Still this didn't deter her, she read on. "Rule No. 1, goes without saying. NO ONE is to know about this club, event or location. Rule No. 2, upon arrival you will be presented with additional rules to follow. You WILL do whatever is asked of you once you've walked thru the door. This is your point of no return."

Any normal person would have thrown this package away once they opened it. But not Kelly, she couldn't wait! She looked at the date on the paper and saw that the party was the same night Sal would be out of town for another one of his BIG business trips. This was crazy.

Everything seemed to come together. Kelly needed to do was find a sitter for the kids. She dialed her sister-in-law on the phone to ask if she wanted to keep the twins that night. "Are you okay?" Kim asks.

"Oh, yeah girl, I'm fine." Kelly replies. "I just want to plan some me time."

Kim loved spending time with the twins any chance she got. Kim's response wasn't a surprise. "Of course, I want my babies!"

Everything was set. All Kelly had to do was sail thru the next four days. As easy as that sounds, it doesn't go as planned. Her mind was constantly racing. Nothing went right. Kelly couldn't focus on anything other than the party.

***

The days leading up to Sal's trip were filled with chaos. His grumpy demeanor upset Kelly. She decided to do something to bring a smile to his face. Kelly threw in a new pair of my panties when she packed his bag. This time around, Kelly left him a note. "Sal, I love you so much…" It made Kelly blush listing all of the things she wanted to do to him when he returned. "This will definitely keep him thinking about me while he's away." she giggled.

The kids are bouncing off of the walls letting her know that Kim was there. Hell, Kelly even started jumping, too. Her fun was about to begin. Several hugs and kisses later and everyone was gone. Finally, she has the house to herself to start getting ready for tonight. Kelly laid everything she needed out and took a nice, long soak in her oversized tub. Kelly drifted off to sleep, a short time later she's startled by the doorbell. She jumps up and puts her robe on to answer the door. Looking out the window, she sees it's the same courier service that delivered the last package. Opening the door, Kelly is handed yet another box. This one is even prettier than before. Closing the door, she ran back upstairs with her latest package. She tore it up to find another letter from Vixen. "Mi Amour," the familiar penmanship read. "I would like for you to wear the outfit you displayed yourself in when you took your photos."

"Lucky for her, I washed it as soon as I took it off." Kelly thought to herself. It got under her skin that this Vixen was so damn demanding. She put her other outfit back and started getting ready in the one Vixen requested. Her body had to be just right for tonight. Kelly took her time doing her hair and makeup. Seeing that everything was just right, it was time to leave.

Kelly drove to the location listed on the letter. The drive there was nerve-wracking. Kelly wanted to turn around several times. In fact, she did once, but something told Kelly that she had to go to this party. Becoming frustrated, Kelly steered her car back to the party. Once she arrived, all Kelly could think was, *"What the hell did I just get myself into?"* Even though the interior of the house was lit with only candles, it cannot be seen from the road. Kelly spotted a single dim light outside, where she has to pull up and give a strange man the keys to her car. *"Oh, hell no!"* she thought to herself. *"I don't care how fine he is!"*

"Leave your jacket and your keys in the car." demands the "Adonis." Kelly's mouth forms the words, "HELL NO," but is met with his finger pressing against her lips. His finger reminds Kelly that she is to do everything that is asked. She removed her jacket and acted like it was normal to walk around with a skimpy outfit on. Well, it wasn't so skimpy from the front, but the back exposed her entire backside. A thong was the only thing that held it together. Still, Kelly seemed fearless as she stood in front of the entrance.

He instructed her to walk thru the door and wait to be received. Kelly opened the door and walked forward. The door behind her slams shut. She muffles a scream in attempts to hide her fear. She walked forward again, towards the next door as it opens. It's hard to see anything ahead of her. A figure appeared in the poorly lit entryway and walks through the door towards Kelly. The figure hands her a mask and demands, "Put it on and do not remove it!" They make their way forward. As they do, there are more candles lighting the way. This allows Kelly to see the guide's figure, as she led her to the garden. The guide's naked voluptuous body moved before Kelly as if she was walking on a cloud.

Too busy taking in the sexy display, Kelly looks up, confused about where she was. The look on her face sums it up for the naked guide. They are standing in front of a maze. The naked guide gives Kelly her instructions. "This is your final test. If you make it to the end, you will be allowed to enter the party. For every wrong turn, you will have to remove an article of clothing from your body."

"What happens if you run out of things to remove?" Kelly blurted out. The guide trailed her fingers across the material of Kelly's sexy attire and leaned in towards her ear. In a seductive whisper she replies, "You will not be allowed to enter until you perform for my hostess and redeem yourself." The guides words trail off as her lips, grazing Kelly's earlobe. Kelly bit down on her bottom lip as she entered the maze, knowing she'd heard enough from these smart-ass chicks. *"One more sarcastic comment and I'm gonna dig into these bitches."* Kelly laughed knowing that she was a beast at anything that teased her brain. Plus, she's a tad bit cocky. She would never let anyone beat her at any game she played. Friday was the only person ever to cause her to submit in such a way. Kelly was determined that no one would ever get to her like that again.

She started off into the maze turning left and right, making her way to the center, finding it is a breeze. Stopping for a moment to take in her surroundings, Kelly's heart beats faster and faster. Her mind fills with images of several bodies intertwined as moans penetrate her ear canals. The moans get louder and louder, a sign that she is getting close to the end. When Kelly walked out of the maze, she was completely aroused and shocked to see the naked, female figure waiting for her. "It's impressive how quickly you maneuvered through. I am greatly disappointed that you are still wearing that outfit." She stomps towards the house and demands for Kelly to follow her. Kelly smiles knowing the guide wants to see the rest of her body. Yeah, she's real cocky at this point.

"If she likes my ass, she would love my pussy." Kelly says to herself, as she taunts her disenchanted tour guide. Even in the darkness, Kelly catches the guide licking her lips. The guide refocuses her thoughts and continues to lead Kelly towards the house. Upon entry, Kelly is given a formal introduction to the hostess, Vixen. Kelly hears Vixen talking, but is taken aback by her beauty. Completely amazed, Kelly felt Vixen was way too beautiful to be standing here before her. Vixen wears a sheer gown that floats on top of her body. Kelly inhaled Vixen. She smelled like Jasmine. Kelly's mind and body are mesmerized.

It registers with Kelly that Vixen is laughing at her and she quickly apologizes. "I'm sorry, I have never seen a female as stunning as you are. As corny as it sounds, you look like a Goddess." Amused by Kelly's admiration, Vixen strokes her face. They strike up a conversation as she showed Kelly around. Vixen provided a little more history about the group and how they operated. Once a month the group hosts events and pick a new member. Vixen would not reveal any real details about the recruiting process. She just said that everything was covered and honestly, Kelly really don't care about it at that point. Kitty was getting excited. As they continued with the walk around, Kelly notices that there aren't any men, only sexy ladies. She had to admit, the'd done their homework. It was as if they picked the cream of the crop. Vixen informs Kelly that she is going to leave her to explore, but that she should know that the one they called Supreme was watching her closely. If Supreme felt Kelly was worthy of joining the club she would know by the end of the night. "With that, enjoy yourself." says Vixen and in an instant she was gone.

Kelly watches the ladies around her pleasure each other. She wants to join in, but she's afraid. Still unsure of what she's gotten herself into, she fell back into the shadows. All of a sudden, she felt someone come up from behind. There was a pair of nipples grazing her back. Kelly felt this person's breath on her neck as they started to talk. "Why haven't you taken your outfit off yet?" this person asked. "I'm still waiting to see the rest of your sexy body." Kelly responds. She turned around to see the naked figure from the maze. They stand face to face. The guide's body pressed against Kelly's.

The cocky version of Kelly replies, *"I don't have anyone to take it off."* and flashed a half smile. Kelly was astonished by the fact that she just challenged a random chick to undress her in front of everyone. The guide smiled back. She wanted to play along with Kelly's game. She turned Kelly around and threw her up against the wall. This caused Kelly to moan softly. She couldn't help it, she liked it rough. The naked guide drops down to Kelly's ass and unties her thong from the back, using her mouth. The guides tongue grazes across Kelly's ass as she pulls the string. Slowly Kelly's outfit falls down to her ankles. People around them stop to watch how the undresses Kelly. Raising one leg at a time, she stepped out of the skimpy outfit. Standing in only heels and chains, Kelly remained facing the wall. She's not ready to turn around just yet. Gearing herself up, Kelly mumbles under her breath *"She needs to work to see the rest of my body."*

The guide comes close to Kelly's body and lingers for a moment. She felt a tongue run up and down her spine. It made Kelly's body quiver. Fingertips run up and down her sides. Kitty is ready, the guide has Kelly purring. She wants more. The guide spread Kelly's legs open, allowing her fingers explore Kitty's wetness. She moans when she felt Kelly's spot.

The guide toyed with Kelly's clit until her ass started to shake. She fingered Kelly while slapping her ass making her moan loudly. At this point, the crowd is getting larger anticipating more. The guide turned Kelly around to face everyone. She wanted Kelly to see them watching their erotic episode.

She thought that would scare Kelly off. Instead Kelly got off on that shit. The guide began to play with Kelly's titties, pulling and biting on her nipples. Kelly couldn't get enough of it. The guide snakes her way down to Kelly's treasure chest. Kelly tried, but couldn't keep kitty hidden away any longer. The guide props Kelly's leg up on the chair next to them, letting everyone see all of the glory. Kelly was soaking wet. Her clit was throbbing. Kelly knew that the one she called the "Naked Guide" is fighting it. "She wanted me from the moment she saw me." Kelly tells herself. Kelly decided from the start that she was going to make her beg for the goodies.

The figure comes close and tried to kiss Kelly. With her finger placed against the guide's lips she says, "You must ask first."

The figure does as she is told. "May I kiss your lips?" she begs.

"You may." Kelly tells her, but makes her stop when she gets close again. "Not those lips!" Kelly says. She takes the guide's head and motions her down towards Kitty. Kelly wanted her up close and personal.

The figure didn't hesitate to go to work. She grabs Kelly's ass and buries her face deep in my spot. Her mouth was so soft and moist on Kelly's pussy. She was licking up all of her juices. The guide fucks Kelly's pussy with her tongue. She was driving Kelly crazy. Suddenly there are other females are all over Kelly's body. They were sucking and teasing her nipples while kissing all over her body. Someone had taken the figure from behind with a strap on. Every time they fuck her, she sucked

Kelly's pussy harder. This kept up for quite some time. They end up in so many different positions. Kitty purred all night long. Kelly lost count of the number of times she came. She tasted some of the best pussy there, until she couldn't take anymore. Kelly staggered away from the group of entangled bodies to find a quiet spot. She need a break.

Completely exhausted, Kelly feel asleep in a corner. When she woke up, she found herself back in the car with her coat on. She didn't recall getting there. She was only aware that her wrist hurt. She drove home and headed straight for the shower. As she finished showering, she heard the doorbell. It scared her because she was unsure who it could be at this hour. She looked out of the bedroom window and saw the courier truck again. There was another box being delivered. She grabbed the box and ran upstairs.

Opening the box, Kelly found her outfit and a note from the one they called Supreme. "Mi Amour," it read, "I hope you enjoyed your experience. I was amused by your show. I am delighted that you decided to join our organization to unite women from the bedroom to the boardroom. The tattoo you now have on your wrist is a symbol of the commitment the group holds for all of its many members."

Dropping the letter, Kelly looked down at her wrist. At some point in the night, she'd gotten a tattoo, but couldn't recall when. All she remembered was feeling like someone had scratched her. She did have drinks at one point in the night with the naked figure. Everything was hazy after that. *"I can't believe this shit!"* she yelled. *"What the fuck did I really get myself into?"*

Kelly pick up the letter and finish reading it. There wasn't much left, but one sentence said it all. "This membership is for life. You may never walk away or return to your normal life again." Filling with rage, she ran downstairs to the fireplace. Turning it on, she had to burn everything.

She had to remove any trace of tonight. *"First thing in the morning, I'm going to find somewhere to get this tattoo removed no matter how much it costs!"*

SAL

Sal and Selena

As Selena's plane lands in Vegas, she knows what happens here most definitely will not stay here. Her thoughts start to race with the things she is about to set into motion. *"I am going to spend the weekend making him want me."* Selena plotted. This is supposed to be all business, but she had her own agenda. He was at the hotel waiting for her when she arrived. He looked genuinely happy to see his assistant. Getting out of the limo, she could see that lines were definitely going to be crossed this weekend. Sal watched Selena step out of the limo. It took everything in him to hide the excitement in his pants.

She flashed an innocent smile as he drank in her long, sexy legs. She loved how her legs disappear up her super- ultra mini skirt. "Hell, I'm out of the office on my own clock in Vegas right now." whispers Selena. She was here to play her hand and it damn sure was her lucky day. She maneuvered her ass from side to side as she walked towards the rear of the limo. Normally, she wouldn't have helped with her own bags, but she needed to give Sal more time to take her all in. Looking back, she sees that the bulge in is pants has grown even more. Selena plays it off like she didn't notice as she tipped the driver. She gave him some time to adjust himself as she gathered her bags.

Once he's able to get a handle on his thoughts Sal helped her in to the hotel, giving some small talk along the way. "I'm already checked in," Sal informs Selena. Since this is his first time in Vegas, he tells her he can't wait to see the sights.

"Well I'm an old pro at Vegas," says Selena., "I know all of the sights. Maybe I could be your special tour guide. Besides, I'm a sight to see on my own," Selena continues, as she brushed past him to get to the counter. She looked back giving him an innocent smile. Sal just stood there unsure of what to do with what he just heard from his assistant. She returns with her room key and tells him that she will see him in a few. "I need to go to my room and change my clothes."

Before he can stop himself, Sal blurts out, "I don't see anything wrong with what you have on."

Stepping within his reach, Selena runs her hands playfully across his chest and replies, "I want to be at my best if I am going to spend time with you." Sal smiles and offers to walk Selena to her room. She accepts his kind gesture and appears to be completely surprised when they reach her room. It's located adjacent to his. "Well, let me apologize to you in advance if I make too much noise," says Selena informed. Sal looks like he doesn't understand. "Ummm," she moans, "Sal, when I come to Vegas, I like to get it in." Sal stands there with his mouth stuck open. Selena helps him close it and whispers, "It's okay, I'm a big girl and I like to play with big boys."

She turns to unlock her door. She fumbles with the key until he moves up behind her and takes it from her hand and tries it himself. It still won't open. Too bad he doesn't know the key he's fighting with doesn't go to this room. Selena slowly turns to face him, sliding her ass against his struggling manhood. She places her body up close to his, looking him in the eye. The fire burning in her eyes held his gaze.

"Thank you for being my knight- in- shining- armor." She plays up her helpless role some more. "Sal, if you weren't here, I would have to walk all the way back downstairs for help." She pretends to look away and rests her head against the door.

He's distracted when Selena starts to play with her long wavy black hair. Sal stops playing with the key card. She can feel his eyes roaming all over her body. Slowly, she caresses her body. She can feel his breath on her neck. Having him right where Selena wanted him, she slides the correct door key into her right hand and quickly turns around facing the door. She takes the key from his hand and says, "I think you've warmed it up for me. Let me try."

Magically, she opens the door and brings in her luggage. She left him standing there not sure of what just happened and not sure of what to do with his engorged dick. Selena goes into her bedroom and unpacks her bags. She takes one look at the oversized tub and decides to take a long, hot bath. "I needed to soak and clear my head," thinks Selena. All of the plotting that she was doing had her senses tingling. Her body was in need of some attention.

She tried to ignore it in the tub, as she ran her sponge up and down her long, honey colored legs. She was purposely avoiding the pleasure spot. Selena knew what she wanted, but she wanted Sal to do it for her. Selena's mind started thinking back to when her body was pressed against his. She could feel his desire growing in his pants. His dick was rock hard. She had given him a little grind just so she could feel all that he had. When Selena came out of her thoughts, she realized her hands were busy playing with her pussy. She started rubbing her clit faster and faster. The whole time moaning and playing with her breasts. As the warm water surged back and forth on her pussy, she imagined Sal standing over her. He watches while she played with herself. He shoves his dick in her mouth and grabbed the back of her head. He keeps fucking her mouth harder and harder. In her mind she can hear him calling He calls out her name and begging her not to stop. The more Selena imagined it, the more excited she became.

Before she knew it, her pussy was ready to cum. She was thrashing around in the tub as her orgasm overtakes her. She falls back in the tub and thought about really setting her plan in to action. She had to get this man. Selena wanted to be the one who took him over the edge. Her time to relax was over. Selena had a man waiting on her to show him the time of his life in Vegas and that's just what she planned on doing.

***

"Damn, I can't believe what just almost happened." said Sal. *"Am I losing my fucking mind?"* He had never cheated on his wife nor has he ever thought about it. But there is something about Selena that drives him crazy. Sitting on the edge of the hotel's bed, all worked up, fantasizing about Selena and how sexy she was.

From the moment she showed up for an interview with the company, Sal hadn't been the same. She walked in the door with a certain sex appeal leaving him wanting more. She was classy from head to toe. It took all he had to keep himself from falling all over her during the interview. If it wasn't for his partner, Jacob, being in the room with him, Sal would've looked like a fool. Jacob grilled Selena for over an hour about why he should hire her. She had more than enough confidence about herself, but not to the point that she was arrogant. She handled Jacob's interrogation and all Sal could do was focus on her features. Her complexion was that of a smooth pot of honey, her big brown eyes called out to hime. Her body was perfect. She was curvy in all the right places with a tiny waist.

After Jacob hired her, she set in to do her job and nothing else. She didn't mingle with the staff. She did her job and went home. Sal didn't think about her anymore, she was just another employee. Sal was really trying to put his all in to his relationship with Kelly. That was until he stayed late at the office one Wednesday. Surprised to see Selena still working, Sal asked, "What are you still doing here?" Pretending to be startled, "Oh, I came in late this morning and still had some work to finish before I left," she says.

He could see that she had shed some of her work attire. She quickly apologized when she saw him staring. She had removed her jacket and was only wearing a corset type top. She stood up to reach for her jacket, but as she leaned over the top of the desk her skirt rose up her thighs revealing the top of her thigh-high panty hose. Sal started to get hard. He tried to quickly adjust himself. *"I can't let her see me like this."* She turned around as he was trying to conceal his excitement. Selena tried to pull her skirt down and as she did her breast popped out. Sal's eyes went crazy. He bounced back and forth from her ass to her titties, unsure what to look at. Sal's perspective

For a second, Sal thought he saw her massage her breast. He told himself, *"It's just my mind fooling with me."* She grabbed her jacket and stood up in front of him—close enough for Sal to smell her perfume. She pressed the jacket against her chest to cover herself up, but she only pushed her breast up for Sal to get a better look. Her skin just melted into the large, brown circles that topped off her full breast. She said in a sultry tone, "I hope this doesn't affect our professional relationship."

Unbeknownst to both of them, Sal's hand was rubbing her arm as he told her, "This certainly would not interfere with our relationship."

She replied, "Good," and slowly licked her lips. Suddenly, Sal had the biggest urge to kiss her. He had to taste her lips.

She dropped her jacket and stood before him with both breasts exposed. He had never seen anything so beautiful in his life. She took another step closer to him. He took her face in his hands and kissed her. He moved his tongue in and out of her mouth like he was a high school teenager experiencing his a first kiss. He wanted to savor every drop she had in her mouth. He reached around and grabbed her ass, pressing her against his dick. She was moaning and speaking Spanish. Sal had no ideaI didn't know what she was saying, but he knew it turned him on. Her hand was stroking his manhood thru his pants. It wanted to come out so bad. She started to unbuckle his pants as he placed her breast in his mouth. He thought for sure he was going to cum the minute her soft hands touched his dick. She started jerking him off while looking him in the eye and continued speaking in Spanish.

Sal was close to bending Selena over his desk and filling her with every desire that rose inside of him. Unfortunately, he was interrupted by the ring of his phone. It was Kelly asking him to stop by the store for some milk. She apparently forgot to stop on her way home and insisted that out kids wouldn't make it through the morning without it. As much as he wanted to savor everything Selena was currently offering, flashes of his family photo across his home screen quickly "sobered" Sal up and reminded him of his marriage and priorities. He sent Selena away with an apology and a promise to never cross these lines again and made his way out of the office and to the store..

The discomfort and shame Sal felt as a result of his minor indiscretion caused him to have a restless night. Luckily, Kelly didn't pick up on it and the kids were already asleep when he got home. The next morning when he returned to the office, expected things to be awkward between him and Selena, but she acted like nothing ever happened. Something about her still fascinated him. He knew he needed to keep his focus on his job and his family. Selena was off limits—a forbidden fruit on a tree he could never pick from again.

***

Yet now here he was in Vegas, imaging what he would do to her if the chance presented itself again. His dick was hard just thinking about it. The noise from Selena's room carried over to his. Sal worried that something was wrong. It sounded as if she was in the bathroom. *"What if she was hurt."* he thought to himself. That was until he realized she was moaning louder and louder. Before Sal knew it, his hand was pulling his dick out. He stroked it up and down while listening to her sounds. Sal wanted to fuck Selena. He wanted to put her titties in his mouth again. He can hear her clearly now. She's going from English to Spanish. Sal kept stroking his dick, grunting deeper and deeper. Thinking about how soft and wet her pussy is. Sal starts to cum it shoot all over the place. He lies back on the bed and enjoys the moment he just had.

Just as Sal was about to drift off to sleep, his phone rang. He looked and saw that it was Kelly. He decided to let her go to voicemail. He had to get up to go shower and change. He had to be fresh in case anything happened tonight. Even though he was ready for it, he was surprised by Selena's behavior when they went sightseeing. She was on her P's and Q's. Selena did exactly what she said she was gonna do. She became the best tour guide ever and showed Sal all around the town. It was as if they were the best of friends hanging out. Sal was having a great time, so naturally he was very disappointed when they returned to the hotel. Selena headed to her room, "I'm going to turn in early." she said. Leaving Sal standing in the lobby confused as hell.

The afternoon's outing definitely had Sal's head spinning. Selena had to admit, it was harder than she thought it would be. The plan was to toy with his emotions. Playing Sal back and forth created a yearning After quieting her desire in the bath tub, she got ready for her afternoon out with Sal. That was supposed to be the easy part, simply to pretend like she didn't want him. Selena waited in the hallway for him. Fully into her character, she was excited about hitting the town. Perspective

Sal came out of his room looking sexy as hell, in a simple sweat suit and sneaks. She damn near dropped her panties. She had never seen him out of a suit. They toured the town and towards the end of their outing, Selena acted like she'd had enough and wanted to go to bed. "Sal, I think I'm gonna call it a night. This day was too much for me today. I think I need to lay down," whines Selena.

Disappointed that she wants to end their night, Sal asks, "Are you feeling okay?"

Sweetening her words as she reached out for his chest, Selena replies, "Umm, I think it was the flight. It may have been what was too much for me. I need to go rest up for tomorrow's meeting."

Hearing her mention work killed Sal's ego. He still held out some hope that they would finish what almost happened at the night they were alone in the office. Reluctantly, he says, "Good night."

Selena purrs, "Good night,." back to Sal. She walks away, and as she does her finger tips lightly claw down towards Sal's manhood. Stopping inches away from the part of Sal's body that is calling out for her. Focusing on a new agenda, Selena leaves Sal downstairs so she could do some dirty work.

***

She raced back to her room and freshened up. She changed into her special attire and wrapped herself up tight in a trench coat. Selena grabbed the other room key card and made her way to the 13th floor, where her beloved pet was waiting. Selena opened the door and there she was, on all fours, waiting for her. Selena didn't acknowledge her when she walked in. Selena knows her pet wants her to, but that's not how things worked.

First things first, Selena had to inspect the room to make sure there wasn't any mess. Her pet knew how her owner liked things. After Selena saw that everything was in order, she sat down on the couch and called her pet over. Pet placed her head on Selena's thigh. She missed her owner. She hated to be locked away while Selena went to work. Selena stroked her head and finally spoke, "You were a good girl while mommy was away." Her pet whimpered. She loved her owner. Selena continued to praise her adoring companion, "Since you were so good, I have a treat for you."

Selena stands up and removes her coat, revealing a leather corset and thong. Oh, how her pet loved seeing Selena like this. She really went crazy over the big, black strap on her owner was wearing. Positioning herself before her pet, Selena says, "Suck it like the dirty bitch, I know you are." Her pet turns her head to the side and looks as if she cannot understand the words that her owner is saying. Selena grabs her by her hair and rammed the rubber dick in her mouth. The pet gagged on it, but started sucking it as if she was feeding off of it. Selena pulled her hair as she sucked faster and faster.

"Bitch, get up on the bed," Selena orders. She had to punish her disobedient pet. Selena mounted her from behind without any lube. She wanted her to feel it. Selena shoved it in as hard and as far as it would go. The pet grunted like an animal when Selena entered her. She started to push her ass back against the rubber dick. The pet talked shit to Selena, "MAKE ME YOUR BITCH!" Her long, curly, black hair hung down to the small of her back. Selena reached out for it and wrapped it around her hand tightly. She pulled down on it and told her bitch to ride her dick till she came.

Smacking her ass, Selena commanded her pet to fuck her harder. She liked when the pet worked her ass on Selena's dick. This would cause the pet to cum. Being ever so obedient, the pet fucked her back until her whole body shook. She slid off of Selena's "dick" and laid on the bed. Satisfied with her results, Selena got up and took her strap-on off. She walked over to the couch and spread her legs open and pulled her thong over to the side. "Pet, get your ass over here and suck my pussy," demanded Selena. Without any hesitation, pet was on her knees in front of Selena. Her mouth covered with pussy, the pet started lapping up all of Selena's juices. She flicked her tongue on Selena's clit just like she was trained to do. Breaking a pet wasn't always easy to do, but this pet was her favorite. Selena reached down and held the back of her pet's head. She rubbed the pet's face in her pussy as she smeared cum all over her face. Pet cleaned Selena up so she could make her way back to the other room. Selena couldn't wait to get back to her room. This day was so draining for her. She was so exhausted that she fell out as soon as she hit the bed.

***

Sal's so-called business trip ended early. It was time to go back to his family, back to his everyday life. He knew that he would be forever changed after what happened in Vegas. Still, none of that mattered when he turned on to his street. He pulled up, happy to see Kelly's car in the driveway. He hoped to sneak in the house while his family was still sleeping and steal kisses from them. They looked like his little angels when they were asleep. Sal checked in the girls' rooms, but it was empty. A smile crossed his face. *"They must've slept in my bed."* Sal continues to smile from ear to ear thinking all of daddy's girls were together. He walks to his room and is not only surprised, but in awe of the view. Kelly was sprawled out on their bed wearing only her bra and thong. She was lying on her stomach giving him a full view of her round ass.

Normally, he doesn't get to see her like this since the kids are always around them; Kelly preferred to keep her body covered. Sal never understood why she did this. She had a body many young girls would die for. She was constantly getting hit on by men and women. Her skin was the color of a rich cup of hot chocolate. It was smooth like butter. She made him want to melt when his skin touched hers.

Her long black hair rested on the middle her back. Sal's eyes intently followed the thong as it disappeared in her ass. She moaned in her sleep. Every time he saw her, Sal wanted her even more. He grabs his dick to try and calm it down. Just seeing her woke him up. Sal was harder than he's ever been before. He wanted to make love to his wife. He wanted to be deep up inside of her. Taking his clothes off as fast as he could, Sal lays down next to Kelly. He starts by gently kissing her on her back. His hands instantly went for her ass. Holding back the urge to laugh he thinks, *"I don't know how she gets it in her jeans."* Sal moves closer so he could feel her warm body against his dick. His kisses have moved up towards her neck causing Kelly to moan in her sleep.

Slowly, Kelly awakens from her slumber. She was surprised to see her husband next to her. Her eyes were puffy. He could tell she had been crying. Things were crazy when he left, but Sal didn't think she would still be upset by it. Seeing the look on her face made him want Kelly even more. His wife had a sexy way of looking sad. Sal put her face in his hands. He lowers his mouth towards hers, smothering her pouting lips. He pulls her body on top of his, spilling her breast onto his chest. Sal moans when he feels Kelly grinding her pussy on his dick. She threw her head back letting him know she was ready. He knew it was time for him to devour her neck. She loved when he did that-, it was her spot. Sal kisses Kelly on her neck and grabs her ass pressing her harder against his dick.

His fingers fought with the clasp as he unfastened her bra. Once it was off, he sat Kelly up on his lap. He wanted to admire her beauty one more time. Plus, he loved looking at her breast. Her nipples were big and black. She loved when he played with them. She knew the rule, though.

Sal knew what she wanted, but refused to give her what she needed. She had to beg for it, though. She was moaning louder and louder. The material of her thong was soaking wet. Her juices were being held back by the thin piece of fabric. Say, "PLEASE," teases Sal. She looked him the eye and for a minute, Sal thought he saw the devil in his wife's eyes.

He knew things had changed when she took control of the situation. Throwing him down to the bed she puts Sal's hands back behind his head. She started by softly placing kisses on his chest. This led to sucking and biting. She was like another person. Sal heard himself yell out loud when she put his dick in her mouth. She went up and down on his dick, sucking it like she did this every day. Kelly never gives Sal head. Her tongue teased the head as her mouth wrapped tightly around the shaft. She went faster and faster, sucking harder and harder. He grabbed the back of her head and started fucking her mouth. It was as wet as her pussy. Sal wanted to cum in her mouth. He had to, but he didn't want to push his luck. "FUCK," he calls out. "Baby, I wanna to see my nut in your mouth."

He didn't expect her answer his request. He was happy to have his dick down her throat. When she said, "Come on, Daddy," he lost it. Sal fucked her mouth even harder, ramming his dick in and out. She was taking it all, grunting and moaning. She stared back at him like she was getting off having Sal watch her. She gripped his dick tightly with one hand and played with his balls with the other one. She never missed a beat. She sucked his dick like she was trying to take the skin off. Sal tried, but he couldn't hold back any longer. His body starts to curl up. It was as if all of his muscles were trying to force his cum into the back of Kelly's throat. Sal let out the loudest moan he could. Sal looked up to see his nut hanging from Kelly's mouth. She was smiling. She stuck out her tongue and hungrily lapped up the cum.

Seeing this had Sal hard again. He wanted to fuck the shit out of his wife. He couldn't wait any longer, he had to have her. Sal bent Kelly over, spreading her pussy open wide. Just when he was about to slide his dick in her pretty, pink pussy, he stops. He couldn't fuck her yet. Sal wanted to taste her sweetness. He fed on the rich juices flowing from her sweetness. Kelly started to grind on his face. She sounded like a wild animal being set free. She worked her ass faster and faster against his face, telling her husband to fuck her with his tongue. He started flicking her clit with it. She's yelling louder and louder; her legs start to shake. She can't take much more. Sal grabs her ass with both of his hands, pulling her back even more. His face is completely covered with her pussy. She screams, "FUCK ME, DADDY! FUCK ME!" She starts to shake all over.

She tries to move away, but he held her. Sal sucks faster and faster. Kelly's clit is nice and fat. She reaches back and grabs his head and winds her pussy up on his face. Sal feels her pussy explode all over his face. He turns her around to look at the mess she's made. Kelly starts licking her white cream off of his face. *"Damn," thought Sal, "I love this girl more than anything."* This was it, there was no more putting it off—, he had to fuck her. He wanted to make love to her insides.

Sal laid her down on the bed and spread her pussy open. Kelly's juices were still flowing. He teased the entrance to her love hole with the tip of his dick. She arched her back so she could receive him. He guided his dick into Kelly's tight hole. She braced herself against the headboard.

He stroked her pussy with his dick. Kelly was really getting in to it. She started throwing her pussy back with every pump. Sal loved how good it felt to fuck Kelly from behind, but he wanted to see her beautiful face filled with pleasure. He told her to climb on top of him. Kelly mounted his dick. She started off slow by gyrating her hips as if she were a belly dancer. Sal moans despite his efforts to hold it in. He couldn't help it. He was in a trance.

Kelly was sitting up on his dick, bouncing up and down. Her titties jumped with every move she made. His eyes following her breast the entire time. Kelly's tight pussy stroked Sal's dick. He wanted to fill her with every inch of his man tool. He pounded her harder and harder. She wrapped her hands around his back, pressing her body closer. She was moaning in Sal's ear. Her moaning turned him on even more. He went at that pussy harder and faster. Kelly moans in his ear, "Make me cum, daddy, I want to cum on your dick." He had to give her what she wanted. Sal starts rocking her ass back and forth on his dick, still fucking her like he's trying to go deeper and deeper. Her pussy is so warm and juicy.

"Baby, I love you so much," he says, "You are so beautiful." Tears are streaming down Kelly's face. He just keeps telling her how much he loves her until her face starts to twist with pleasure.

Kelly yells out, "I'm cummin', daddy! I'm cummin for you, daddy." Seeing her like that sends him over the top. She tightens her pussy around his dick and strokes every drop of cum out.

Sal reaches up and grabs her face and kisses her for what felt like forever. They fall back on to the bed. He couldn't let her go. Sal holds Kelly in his arms and they drift off to sleep. If his sister hadn't called to bring the kids home, he would still be holding on to her. Kelly jumped in the shower and Sal decided to join her. When he gets in, he instantly notices her tattoo. Sal grabs her arm and asks his wife, "Where did you get that? Why do you have that?"

Kelly looks at her husband, afraid to answer. She looks away and repeats the story she told the people at the tattoo parlor, "I went out with the girls Friday night and had too much to drink. Somehow, we ended up getting tattoos. Baby, are you mad at me for getting it?" asks Kelly.

Sal replies, "It just caught me off guard because I thought you didn't like tattoos. It's nice and no, honey, I'm not mad, just surprised." He plays it off and starts washing her back. Sal was glad his wife couldn't see his face while he lied to her about why the tattoo really surprised him.

KISSING KELLY

Kelly and Admiral

It's been months since the party. No matter how hard she tries to forget about it, it's impossible. Kelly is constantly reminded of the blissful event by her tattoo. She couldn't find a shop willing to remove it. She had finally come to terms with the fact that she was stuck with it. Her new plan was to immerse herself with family and finishing the novel she'd been working on. Those were the biggest obstacles in her life right now. Things between her and Sal had hit an all-time low. When he first came home from the Vegas trip, he'd made Kelly feel like things would be different. Somehow better, you could say. This lasted for a couple of weeks and had her floating on cloud nine. She even felt guilty about her actions at the party, but something happened. Out of nowhere, Sal pulled back. Kelly chalked it up to the stress from work. She knew how hard it was on him at times.

So, being a good wife, she left her husband in his own mental space. She started working on her novel again. Thinking that if she finished it would help ease some of his burdens. Sal always worried about securing multiple streams of income for the family. Kelly wanted to contribute to this, in addition to being a stay at home mother. She loved literature, so giving writing seemed to be a natural fit. At first, Kelly's writing flowed so easily. Then things took a turn. She hit a wall and couldn't write through it. She sat for hours at her desk trying to will her fingers to make the words appear on the screen. She got up and stretched. Maybe if she got the blood moving through her body it would jolt her brain. She stared out of the window, trying to let go of her frustrations.

Still unable to focus her thoughts, she thought that a change of scenery would help. Kelly decided to try out the new coffee shop not too far out of the way from her house. She pulled up to the shop. Instantly, something seemed to put her at ease. Kelly's excited as she walks in, thinking to herself, *"I'm going to get some serious writing done here."* She sat there and did a whole lot of watching instead of writing. This new environment captivated her mind. Kelly didn't realize how long she'd been sitting there smiling before he noticed her, but she saw him smiling back at her. She lowers her eyes and stares at the laptop like she's trying to work. *"Oh my God, I am so embarrassed,"* mouths Kelly. She still can feel his eyes watching. She looks up to see his face still smiling at her. She can't force herself to look at him.

Not knowing how to act, she just sits there with a silly smile on her face pretending to work. Finally, he gives up, she thinks. He gets up and starts walking in her direction. Kelly tries not to get flustered. He gets closer and closer. It's taking all she has to keep her composure. He reaches Kelly's table and places his hand on the empty chair. She wants to go crazy, but somehow, she manages to keep it together. He pushes the chair in and walks past towards the counter. Laughing to herself, Kelly realizes that she got all worked up for nothing. Just when she started to settle back down and focus, the stranger has returned. He's standing at her table. "Would you mind if I joined you?" he asks. Kelly doesn't know what to say. She stares into his dark brown eyes. "Is it okay if I sit with you?" he asks again, "I come bearing gifts." He places a cup of tea and a muffin in front of Kelly. Coming out of her daze she accepts his offer of company. At this point, she knows there's no way she's gonna get any work done. He introduces himself, "My name is Admiral."

"Yes, you are," Kelly says in her mind., "You are certainly worthy of such a name." She takes a moment to take in the handsome creature seated before her. His tall, muscular frame was smothered in dark brown chocolate. His big, brown eyes jump out at her when he spoke. She was glad Admiral asked to join her. Kelly had to get to know more about this brother. They started off with small conversation. "So, how come I've never seen you in here before?" asks Admiral.

"This is my first time here," Kelly tells him., "I was looking for a change of scenery to help me write."

She's surprised to see his face light up when she talks about writing. Smiling ear to ear Admiral says, "I'm a writer too!"

Kelly can't believe how taken she is with him and she doesn't even know him, yet. "Really? You're a writer? What kind of books do you write?" she asked him. Admiral took a moment before he answered. He was on his fourth novel, but he always blushed when he told others what he wrote about. Most people turned their noses up when he told them. Once, a family friend told him that his mother raised him better than that. Said he needed to get a real job instead of writing junk. She still asked him to sign her copy of PUSSY FETISH though.

When he shared with Kelly that he wrote erotica novels, she felt the heat rise through her body. Kitty seemed to have a mind of her own with this man. Kelly adjusted herself in the chair and tried to focus on having a conversation. Admiral laughed., "I guess you don't do that kind of writing, huh?"

What could she say? It was true. How could she tell this man with dirty thoughts that she wrote children's books? And how this was her first attempt at writing an adult novel minus all of his special topics.

They went back and forth talking about everything from writing, to life and nothing in general. Before they knew it, the two of them had spent well over three hours talking.

Kelly quickly packed up and apologized to Admiral for having to leave so abruptly. She had less than 30 minutes to make it to the other side of town and pick the kids up from school. If she was late, they would never let her hear the end of it. Admiral walked Kelly to the car, carrying her things. He was a true gentleman. He asked if she would be returning to do more writing another day. Kelly knew damn well that she shouldn't, but the smile on his face was so inviting that she had to see it again. *"What the hell?"* She convinced herself that it was all in fun. "Oh, of course I'll be back, especially since I got so much done today."

Admiral laughed and reached for her hand. He loved a woman with a witty come back. His deep voice thanked Kelly for spending the afternoon with him and providing him some much-needed inspiration. With that, he kissed her hand and walked away, leaving Kelly there to stir in all of Kitty's juices. She had to stand there for a minute to try and digest what had just happened and why the hell Kitty was out of control. Kelly jumped in the car and sped off to get her babies. *"Get your mind right girl!"* Over and over she says this to herself. She had to get her mind right. Breaking every speed limit set, she barely made it in time.

When she arrived, the kids were too busy playing to realize that their mother was late. Kelly was so glad they didn't notice. Normally, when she's late, they complain to Sal and it turns in to a huge an argument between them. He never understood why she didn't have everything done, even though Kelly technically doesn't work according to him.

She stopped to pick up dinner because, yet again, Kelly forgot to take something out this morning. She knew Sal would fuss, so she made sure to get his favorite takeout. Kelly and her twins went back to the house and started on homework. The kids breezed right through their work and wanted to play out back. While they did that, Kelly decided to do some much-needed housework. A couple of hours later, her husband, Sal, came home from work and was greeted by cheers from the kids. Kelly had dinner on the table waiting. She wanted to make sure tonight was a good night for the family. They needed one desperately.

He wasn't too pleased about having take-out, but was glad to see that she went the extra step and got his favorite. The dinner was going good up until the little reporters informed their father that Mom was late picking them up from school today. The twins and Sal talked about Kelly being late as if she wasn't sitting at the same table with them. Finally, Sal spoke to Kelly, "What were you doing that was so important that made you late picking up MY children? I know it certainly wasn't cooking dinner."

Heated on the inside, but determined to play the good wife role, Kelly says, "Oh Sal, you know nothing is more important to me than my family, but I went to a new coffee shop to try and help me write and lost track of time."

"Good," says Sal., "I'm glad to see that you are FINALLY getting some writing done. So, how far did you get with it today?"

Trying to make her outing sound productive she says, "I didn't get very far with my writing, but I did end up talking with some of the other writers and bounced some ideas back and forth." Sal wasn't pleased with how her day turned out and he didn't attempt to hide his feelings. Kelly couldn't understand why no matter what, her husband couldn't see her writing as anything other than a playtime. He never understood why she quit her job to become a stay- at- home- mom who wanted to write children's books. But, since she helped him through school, Sal felt obligated to let her chase her dreams. He just wished they weren't so foolish.

Somehow, they made it through dinner and everyone settled down for the night. As usual, Sal was too tired to do anything with his wife. Used to the rejection, Kelly just called it a night, too. She couldn't wait for the Sandman to carry her off to slumber tonight. Kelly was comforted by his familiar dark brown eyes. Tonight, sleep was her friend.

After sending everyone off the next morning, Kelly tried to write. Her thoughts kept wondering back to Admiral. She had to see him again even though she knew that it wasn't a good idea. That still didn't stop her from getting ready to go and see this man. Kelly arrived at the coffee shop looking much better than she did yesterday. She had on a cute little top and some capris with heels. Her make-up was light, but far from minimum. She didn't want to seem as if she was going overboard for him. When Kelly walked in to the shop, she tried to play it cool and found an empty table. Sneaking peaks around the shop, she didn't see him. They hadn't talked about what time he normally comes in; secretly she was just hoping that would be here.

Disappointed with his absence, she decided to try and get some work done. Kelly unpacked and got right to work. Her fingers were going a mile a minute. She was on a roll. Finally, Kelly was unblocked. She wondered who to thank for getting her past that wall. Was it Admiral or the coffee shop? Her question was answered about 20 minutes later. She felt someone staring at her. Looking up, her eyes meet Admiral's..... He greeted Kelly with his beautiful smile. It warmed her all over. He walked over to the table and for some reason she couldn't wait to give Admiral a hug. He wrapped his strong body around Kelly. His embrace made her long for more.

She shook it off and told Kitty to cut it out. She didn't even know this man. Besides, Kelly reminded herself, you are a married woman with kids. Admiral sat down and called for the waitress to come over to their table. "Would you like anything, Kelly?" he asked. Since she was pleased with his choice yesterday, she allowed him make today's selection as well. He smiled back at Kelly and asked the waitress to bring his usual and to make it double. His eyes never left Kelly's stare. He saw something in her eyes.

"I'll admit, I didn't think that you were coming back after yesterday."

Trying to lighten the intense mood, Kelly says, "I had to give the shop another try today since I was so rudely distracted by someone who wanted to talk my head off last time." They laughed and talked like they were old friends.

Admiral apologized if the comment he was about to make was a little forward, "Kelly, please forgive me if I'm a bit too forward, but you look very pretty today."

Kelly played it off like this was nothing to her. "Oh, I just threw this on since I had to go to something at my kids' school," lied Kelly.

"I didn't know that you had kids," says Admiral.

"Well, Skipper," she jokes with him, "there's a lot that you don't know about me."

With that, Admiral sat back and thought long and hard to himself. Kelly could tell that there was something more on his mind. Finally, he asked the million-dollar question, "Are you involved with anyone?"

"Damn." Kelly cursed under her breath. "Yes, Admiral. I am married with 2 kids, a set of twin girls." Admiral's face all but cracked when the words left her mouth. Kelly felt the same way. The direction of the conversation changed after that, but Admiral continued to sit with her and they had a good time talking. "Would you excuse me?" asks Kelly. "I need to go to the ladies' room."

"Oh, sure," replies Admiral. "Why don't you let me show you where it is?" He was so nice and it was refreshing to Kelly, but she needed to get to the bathroom. She needed to readjust her inner thoughts and shut Kitty the hell up.

"Damn it, girl, get back on track." says Kelly as she fixes her make-up in the mirror. Satisfied with the pep talk, she agrees that this man was off limits.

All that went out the window when she exited the ladies' room to find Admiral still standing there. "Oh! You didn't have to wait. I could've found my way back," she says.

"Kelly, my dear, a true gentleman always waits for his lady." He stepped closer to her side. His cologne overwhelmed Kelly's senses. She wanted to walk back to the table, but her body wouldn't move. Kelly just stood there as she watched him walk closer to her. His body pressed against hers, forcing Kelly on to the wall. He caressed her face as his mouth pressed against hers. Her hands reached for his body, pulling him closer. Kelly's nipples hardened and pressed against his chest. She ran her hands through his long, black locs, kissing him as if he was her lover. Kelly's body called for him, it needed to be received by him. His kisses sent her mind racing. She wanted this man with every desire in her body.

Just when Kelly was about to surrender, her phone rang. It was her husband, Sal, letting her know that he wouldn't be home for dinner again. Kelly stood there staring at the phone torn between her emotions.

Part of her wanted this man before her to make love to her body the way she knew he would. Meanwhile, the other part of her couldn't understand why her husband was spending so much time away from home. On the verge of tears, Kelly ran back to the table to pack her stuff up. Admiral came up behind Kelly and kept apologizing for what happened. "I'm sorry," Kelly said. "It's not you. I just need get out of here before my head explodes." Kelly ran out of the shop leaving Admiral standing there, never looking back.

***

It's been almost a month since the last time Kelly was at the coffee shop. Her incident with Admiral was burned into her mind as if it happened yesterday. It takes everything in her to keep that man off her mind. His kisses had her wanting more. *"If Sal hadn't called,"* thought Kelly, *"I don't know what would've happened."* Her mind wanders back to the moment that they shared. She'd never felt another man's hands touching her body. His hands were wrapped around her waist, holding her close. She felt his muscles as she pressed against him. Her mind wanders back to the moment that they shared. As much as she wanted him that day, Kelly is glad things didn't get out of control. *"Humph, let's just consider that Admiral's last kiss goodbye."* she convinced herself. Kelly would never see him again, so she thought she had nothing to worry about.

She threw herself back into taking care of the family and working on her book the correct way. It was for the best;, her relationship with Sal needed to be fixed. Her husband was still spending a lot of time away from home. Sal seemed to be swamped at work. Every time Kelly called him at work she could never get through., His secretary repeatedly told her, "I'm sorry Mrs. James, Mr. James is in another meeting" or "on an important phone call. Would you like to leave a message?"

Today was going to be different. Kelly decided that she would surprise Sal at work. She prepared a wonderful meal for his lunch. She couldn't wait to see him. *"Please, let things go as planned,"* prayed Kelly. *"Maybe we could have a nice romantic evening if this goes well."*

Walking into the office, Kelly felt like a queen going to see her king. Only her king didn't act as if he was happy to see her. "Hey, honey," says Sal, "What are you doing here?" Sal looks around nervously before he gave her a hug and a kiss.

Lowering her head Kelly says, "You're not happy to see me?"

"Of course, I am," Sal replies. "I'm just surprised to see you. I thought you'd be at your little coffee shop working on your story." Kelly melted.

"I love you very much and missed you like crazy. So, I decided to come show you how important you are to me." Sal looks at his wife. He can see the love she has for him. All she asked of him today, was to love her back. He could do that.

"So, my love, what is it that you have hidden in your basket?" asks Sal. Beaming from ear to ear, Kelly begins to unpack his lunch.

Just as he is about to sit down, the phone rings. A feeling of dread washed over him. He knew by the sound of the ring who it was. "Yes, Selena," he answers in a dry tone.

"Ah, Papi, que espero usted didn't se olvida nuestra fecha de la comida." purrs Selena.

"Yes uhh, please hold all of my calls. I'm in a very important meeting, and do not want to be disturbed." Kelly fixed his plate while Sal finished his phone call. She got excited hearing him put her first. Kitty began to tingle, tonight was going to be good and she knew it. Returning to his wife, Sal sat down and saw all the trouble Kelly went through. "Thank you for being such a wonderful wife. Sometimes I think I don't deserve you,." said Sal.

Things were going well despite the constant ringing of the phone. Kelly watched the hustle and bustle of the office while Sal kept telling his secretary to push his appointments back. A strange feeling crept up on Kelly. *Was she being watched again?* All of a sudden Sal got up and slammed the blinds shut. Just like that, his mood changed. "I've gotta get back to work. I'll have to eat this later. Besides, I need you to go home and start dinner, Kelly. I've invited a potential business partner. for a new business venture I'm interested in. He's not from the firm so this is an casual get together. We are going to have dinner and drinks while we talk "shop" and feel each other out."

She couldn't believe he had someone coming over and forgot to tell her until now. Kelly didn't want to argue about it, especially not here, and definitely not now that things were going so good between them. Kelly stayed in the loving wife role and kissed her husband goodbye. "Baby, I'll see you at home and don't worry, dinner will be perfect." Kelly left the office annoyed, but still feeling like someone was watching. *"There I go being crazy again,"* said Kelly, as she shook off the feeling. She made a quick trip to the market for tonight's dinner. Relieved that this wasn't one of Sal's clients from the firm, Kelly knew that tonight's meeting was slightly casual, which made it slightly easier to prepare for. Sal explained how he planned on investing money in this client's store. They planned on expanding and needed to discuss options. That was tonight's agenda. Since it was involved business, Kelly called her sister-in-law and asked her if she could pick up the kids and keep them for the night. She wanted to make sure Sal stayed focused on the meeting.

Time went by so fast, but Kelly still managed to get everything ready with just enough time for her to get ready. Sal came home a little late; glad to see that things were perfect. Kelly was in the kitchen when their guest arrived. Sal opened the door and greeted him. "Honey, can you come here for a minute?" yelled Sal. "I have someone I'd like you to meet." When his wife walked into the room, she damn near dropped the tray of appetizers when she saw Admiral standing there with her husband. Kelly couldn't control the thoughts running through her head. *"Why is he here? How in the hell does he know my husband? Damn! Look how sexy he looked."*

Admiral spoke as if he's never met Kelly. She wasn't sure what he was up to, but she had no choice but to go with it. She quickly made her way back to the kitchen leaving them to their business. She couldn't believe that he was *HERE*…in *HER* home. Kelly couldn't answer any of the questions running through her head. Lost in thought, she didn't realize how long she'd been in the kitchen. Sal peeked his head in and asked, "Hun, is everything okay?" She didn't respond, Kelly just continued to stare off in to space. "Kelly, are you okay?," asked Sal.

Coming out of her haze she noticed Sal talking to her, "Huh, oh yeah, I'm coming now."

She couldn't get past the fact that Admiral was in her home. Kelly had to let Sal help serve dinner because it took all she had to keep from falling out. Both men complimented her on cooking such a wonderful meal. She had to agree. Kelly went all out for tonight. The conversation at the table was nice. It surprised Kelly how well they both got along so well. Before she knew it, they were both filling her with compliments. Her mind was racing, her heart was pounding and Kitty was stirring. Kitty purred. She wanted to have both of them. She'd gotten greedy. Kelly had to leave the room. She couldn't take any more of this.

"Alright, guys, if you'll excuse me, I'm going to the kitchen and clean up."

That's when Sal's "bat" phone rings. "Admiral, excuse me for a moment, it's the office calling." And Sal left the room.

Kelly began to remove the dishes, thankful she had some time to get herself together. She was wrong. Admiral came into the kitchen carrying dishes from the table. Her knees buckled when she saw him. Admiral came rushing towards Kelly, catching her in one hand and the tray she was carrying in his other. He sat the tray on the counter and held Kelly close. She couldn't fight him. Her body melted in his chocolate arms. She laid her head in the crook of his neck. His cologne opened her insides up. He held Kelly even tighter. She could feel his muscles tightening as his body pressed against hers.

Finally, Admiral spoke, breaking the silence, "Kelly, where have you been? Why haven't you been back to the coffee shop?" He had a million questions to ask her.

Kelly looked up and said, "I didn't think that it was a good idea for me to return after our last encounter. I'm married and didn't want things to go any further."

All of a sudden Sal came into the room. He stopped in his tracks when he saw Admiral holding Kelly. "What's going on here?," questioned Sal.

"I'm sorry, I came in here to help while you were on the phone. But when I came in here, I saw your wife about to pass out and I ran to catch her."

"Yes, Sal, Admiral was helping me steady myself," says Kelly. Sal rushed over and offered to take her to bed. Kelly told him that she was fine and didn't want to ruin the evening. She told both men, more so Admiral, that she just needed to sit for a few and to go finish their meeting. Making her way to the front room, she rested on the couch for a minute. She must have dozed off because when Kelly went back in to the kitchen, Admiral had just finished cleaning and putting all of the food away from dinner.

"Where's Sal?," Kelly asked.

"Oh, he said that he had to run out and take care of an emergency at work and asked if I wouldn't mind staying with you until he came back."

Kelly sighed and said under her breath, "He always has an emergency at work."

"Baby, are you feeling any better?" asked Admiral.

Kelly lied and told him that she did even though her head felt like it wanted to explode. "You don't have to stay with me. You can leave." Truth was, she didn't trust herself alone with him. Admiral walked over towards Kelly. She was glad that she was sitting down. He couldn't see her knees shaking. Kelly didn't want to look at him, but her eyes were drawn towards him. His shirt was wet from cleaning her dishes, it clung to his body. He leaned down to face Kelly; his locs were tied back loosely.

"Kelly, I can't leave you. I'm drawn towards you and I want to get to know more about you," says Admiral. "I haven't stopped thinking about you after your last visit to the shop."

Kelly listened and creamed as he told her how thoughts of her consumed his day. His words drew her in. Admiral told Kelly how he had to know more about her. He wanted to hear her voice and listen to her words. Before she knew it, his lips were within inches of hers. She couldn't control herself anymore. Kelly grabbed his face and kissed him madly. The truth is she hadn't stopped thinking about their first kiss and he damn sure hadn't either. His lips smothered hers, kissing them with everything he had. He pulled Kelly up out of the chair and wrapped his body tightly around hers. His hands caressed her body. Kelly's skin was on fire from his touch. She felt his dick pressed against her leg. She could tell that Admiral wanted her. He held her close and kissed on her neck. Kelly grabbed the back of his head and pulled him closer. He's in her ear. He's calling, "Kelly, Kelly. I need you, Kelly! I want you."

"Fuck," moans Kelly. This man is driving her crazy. She knows she shouldn't be doing this. Not here, not now and not like this. Her body wants him. Admiral starts taking off her shirt and her bra. Kelly stands in the kitchen with her breast out with Admiral devouring them as if they were tonight's main course. "Ummm, pleaaase stop, Admiral." He grunted. Kelly begged again for him to stop. She needed him to stop. She knew that if he continued there would be no turning back. As much as Kelly loved the way he made her body feel, this was wrong. Regaining her composure, Kelly asked, "Admiral, can you stop? This is wrong and I can't do this anymore."

He looked Kelly in her eyes and said, "I'm sorry. You are right. You are a married woman and this is your home. I didn't mean for that to happen." Afraid to look at her, he picked up her shirt and bra and not moment too soon. As soon as she put her things back on Kelly heard Sal close the front door. She sat down at the table as Admiral finished putting the dishes away. She watched him, unsure of what to think about him. One minute he's all over her saying that he can't get enough of her and the next he's cleaning her kitchen in front of her husband as if nothing ever happened. Kelly, on the other hand, feels like she's about to die. Sitting there she is torn between her husband and this stranger that has entered her life.

"Honey, are you feeling any better?" asked Sal.

As soon as Kelly said that she was okay, Sal turned his attention away from her and started talking to Admiral as if she wasn't there. Frustrated with the whole situation, Kelly got up and went upstairs. She couldn't do this anymore. She took a shower and went to bed. She didn't know what time it was when Sal came to bed, but she was glad that he didn't bother her.

ADMIRING ADMIRAL

Mr. Right

"**D**amn!" cursed Admiral, "*I can't believe the woman I dreamed of day and night is married to the man I finally decided to take on as an investor for my chain of coffee shops.*" Admiral had several offers but selected Sal based on the numbers he was able to produce. Had he done a little more research he'd met Kelly sooner. Maybe he wouldn't be as smitten with her as he was now. This is the woman that made him smile. He could to talk to her for hours on end. Admiral wanted Kelly the minute he saw her walk into the coffee shop. She seemed so unhappy and uncertain in her life. But when they talked it seemed as if she had something special inside dying to get out. Admiral didn't know what to make of things after her last visit. He didn't think he'd ever see her again. After Kelly ran out of the shop, Admiral knew that was the end. Now, tonight, he was sitting in Kelly's home about to make love to her. If she hadn't asked Admiral to stop, her husband would've walked in on them. He didn't care who saw them. When Admiral left Kelly's house, he still longed for her. He wanted to talk to her. He wanted to hear his name float off her tongue. He did have her number, thanks to the store survey she filled out. He'd never intended to use it before Kelly officially gave it to him.

"I'll call, but I won't leave a message."

He tried to convince himself that this was the right thing to do. All the way home he fought with his conscious. What reason would he have to call his potential partner's wife after making out with her in their home? Pounding the steering wheel, Admiral knew what he wanted to do and nothing else mattered. He was afraid to call her before tonight. He was afraid she would reject him. After their time in the kitchen it was clear how she felt. Admiral dialed Kelly's number, but was relieved to hear her voicemail. As he listened to her voice on the message a chill went thru his body. Against his better judgment he decided to leave a message. "Kelly, this is Admiral. You went to bed before I could thank you for a wonderful meal. I know that you are married and I respect that, so I will not pursue you. I think that you are an amazing woman and I am here if you ever need me as a friend." Admiral left his number and asked Kelly to give him a call. He hung up hoping she would call soon. He needed to hear from her. There was a part of Admiral that had already fallen in love with Kelly. He would do whatever it took to have her in his life. Admiral knew this was the real thing with Kelly. Smiling all the way home, Admiral knew that he hadn't felt this good since his beloved Michelle.….

***

When Kelly opened her eyes, she prayed today would leave her feeling better than yesterday. As soon as she gathered her thoughts, they went to him. The way he caressed her body, the way his kisses ran through her had Kitty begging for some play time. She tried to ignore Kitty's demands. Checking her cell phone, Kelly saw that she had a missed call. She thought it might have been one of the kids calling. Kelly didn't recognize the number so she listened to the message. The sexy voice she heard put a smile on her face.

"Kelly, this is Admiral. You went to bed before I could thank you for a wonderful meal. I know that you are married and I respect that so I will not pursue you. I think that you are an amazing woman and I am here if you ever need me as a friend."

Hearing his words had Kitty purring and her nipples throbbing. Kelly hung up the phone and found the way to her little friend. She was soaking wet. Her fingers slid in and out of her pussy. Kelly started moaning and playing with her nipples. She wanted Admiral so bad. She had to have him all over her body. Kelly wanted to feel his long locks flowing freely all over her skin. She felt his tongue on her pearl lapping up all of her juices. He's sucking my pussy imagines Kelly, pulling her closer. She can feel Kitty about to explode; Kelly tries to hold back because she doesn't want this moment to end. She tries to move away hoping to calm herself down. His powerful arms lock on her. He holds Kelly close so he can receive all of the goodness about to pour from her. As she's about to release everything she has inside, Kelly begs, "Please, don't stop." He grinds his face all over her pussy, instantly sending her over the edge. She holds on to the back of his head. Startled when she feels a handful of curls in her hand. Kelly screams out his name, "Sal!"

Disappointed when she realizes that it's Sal, not Admiral, between her legs, but unable to control her emotions, she creams all over his face. Sal looks up with Kelly's juices all over his face. The tears are streaming down her face. He looks at his wife for a moment and a smile comes across his face. He says, "Damn, baby, was I that good?" Between sobs she says, "I thought I was dreaming and you caught me off guard." Trying to avoid any further conversation, Kelly hops out of bed to take a hot shower. She needed to focus her mind. By the time she finished, Sal had already left for work. It seems like work is his new home.

Since the kids are gone, Kelly decides to sit down and work on her book. The only words she can find to write are the ones about herself. The words flow freely until she'd reach the chapter about Admiral. Her thoughts return to him. Something tells her that she should call him back, but she can't. Kelly goes back and forth with this for a while. *"Fuck it,"* she says as she decides to call him. Answering on the first ring, "Hellooo, Mrs. Kelly," said Admiral. "Hiiii, Admiral," she purrs. Kelly giggles at how bubbly he makes her feel. "I'm glad you called." he says. "Are you okay, are you feeling any better?" Not sure where her sudden assertiveness came from, she replies, "I am now." They continue with this nervous conversation for a while until finally he asks the question. "Can I see you?"

"Admiral, I don't think that is a good idea," says Kelly. "I know that you are married and I respect that, but something in me aches for you." Kelly laughed at his reply. "That's your mean little friend that's in your pants aching." He laughed as well, "Yeah, that too. But, seriously Kelly, it's more than that. I want to spend time with you. I want to know everything there is to know about the amazing Kelly James." Seeing that he wasn't going to back down without a fight Kelly agrees. "Clearly, we can't be alone. I'll meet you in a public place," says Kelly. "Yes, a public setting," says Admiral, "I have just the place for us. What time can you meet me at my shop?"

"Wait, YOUR shop," says Kelly completely confused. "My shop," says Admiral. "The coffee shop." "I.....I.....I," stammered Kelly. She'd thought he was just another customer wasting time there like she was. She didn't know what to say at first, "I can be there in an hour. I just need to check on my kids."

"Take all the time you need," says Admiral, "I'll be here waiting for you." "Damn," says Kelly. Admiral wasn't making it any easier for her. After taking a minute to pull herself together, Kelly stepped back into her mom role. She called and checked on the kids. Her sister-in-law had a whole day planned with them and would call later to see what the plans were for dinner. It had slipped Kelly's mind that today was Saturday until she mentioned their dinner night. They spent every Saturday night together as family night.

Kelly tried to call Sal at work. She got his assistant again, but this time she didn't bother leaving a message. She'd try him later since he was busy. Kelly got dressed and drove to Admiral's shop. He had the biggest smile on his face when she walked in. The shop was busy. There wasn't an empty seat. She was surprised to see it so busy. She must've come in during the slow times. It was insane in there. Admiral came from behind the counter, "Baby, would you mind waiting a bit before we leave," he asked, "The shop is crazy and I can't leave them in a jam."

"Of course, I don't mind," she said. "Is there was anything I can do to help?" Admiral made a silly face at her. "What," asked Kelly. "I have you to know in college I was a Barista. And a DAMN good one at that." He smiled and said, "Kelly James, I'm liking you more and more." He gave her an apron and they got to work. They cleared out the morning rush and his assistant manager finally showed up full of apologies. He told her it was okay things happen. They cleaned themselves up and got ready for whatever he had planned for them.

Admiral insisted on driving, but Kelly told him that separate cars would be better. She was still trying to keep her distance with him. The thought of the two of them confined in a car just didn't sit well with her. He wasn't hearing it. Again, Kelly knew this was another battle with him she couldn't win. She tried to pout and get her way, but he wasn't budging.

"Wait out front for me while I pull the car around," said Admiral.

Kelly didn't want to relinquish control over to this man, but she did as she was told. She waited for him and when he pulled up, she tried to get in the car.

"Wait," yelled Admiral. "I'm sorry for yelling," he says as he ran around to Kelly. "A lady should never open her own door when a gentleman is around."

Kelly loved his mannerisms, yet that didn't stop her from being cocky. She tried to hold her smart mouth back, but couldn't resist. "So, do we have to stand here and wait for a gentleman to appear so he can come to our rescue?" He laughed and told Kelly to get her smart behind in the car. Kelly replies, but as soon as the words left her mouth, she wished she hadn't said them, "But, you like my behind." Completely embarrassed she looks away, "Damn, I can't believe that I said that." Kelly tried to keep this visit on the up and up, but she already took it there. Admiral gave Kelly a smile that let her know he was thinking something. Something she knew she would enjoy, but shouldn't have. They got in the car and drove to the other side of town.

On the way to the secret destination they rode past Sal's office and it seemed like no one was there, but Kelly's mind was occupied with other things. Admiral and Kelly talked the whole car ride. He told her about his past, his present and his future. He truly was an amazing man. He went through so much during his childhood. Here he stood as a man full of so many dreams. He wanted to know more about her, but she couldn't share that with him. Everything about who Kelly was entwined with Sal's life. She just wanted to enjoy her time with Admiral and continue having him share the details of his life. Completely engulfed in his conversation, Kelly didn't notice that Admiral parked the car. They'd reached their destination. Admiral read the look of confusion on Kelly's face when he opened her door. Taking her hand, he helped her out. He shed some light on where they where and why they were there.

"This is Pleasant Springs. My grandmother has lived here for the past couple of years. I make it a point to come here every Saturday and visit with her."

"Oh, no Admiral." said Kelly as she backed away. "I don't think it's a good idea for me to come in. I'll just wait in the car." Kelly rambled on, "This is your private time with her and I shouldn't intrude."

Showing off that smile that Kelly loved, Admiral said, "Baby, I would love to share my visit with you."

He grabbed a few things out of the trunk and waited for Kelly to join him. He was so persistent. She had to admit deep down inside she wanted to meet her. She wanted to know if this amazing man was always this great. She couldn't believe how nice it was in here. The staff and the residents greeted Admiral as soon as they walked in. He seemed genuinely happy to see them. Kelly had a feeling that she was about to see another side of Admiral. She was afraid it would be one that she would love.

They found his grandmother sitting out on the patio. She was beautiful. Her delicate features lit up when she saw her grandson. He hugged her and gave her several sweet kisses. Admiral loved his grandmother and it showed. He turned to introduce his friend, Kelly. Taking Kelly's hand, Grandmother said, "I am so happy to meet the woman who stole my grandson's heart." Admiral smiled and looked away. Kelly swore his chocolate face turn red. Not sure how to play this one off, Kelly says, "I don't know what stories he's told, but I hope they were good." Smiling, the Grandmother said, "Baby, if Admiral brought you here, they were all true." Kelly felt at ease with this woman.

They sat and had a wonderful visit. They laughed at all of the memories she told Kelly about Admiral's childhood. It seems Kelly was right about his character. He was an amazing person. Still, she wasn't ready for what came next. It seems every Saturday Admiral came and entertained the residents. Today he planned a 3-legged race and face painting. This man was crazy and they loved it. He had everyone involved one way or another. You could tell this wasn't an act that he put on just because Kelly was there. He really enjoyed what he was doing.

Before she knew it one of the residents had tied her leg to Admiral's and they were off running. They didn't work well together. They spent more time on the ground laughing than running. After all of the fun was finished, the two of them went to the kitchen to help serve lunch. Kelly thought to herself, *"I haven't smiled so much in one day in a LONG time."* It felt good being there. After lunch was served, they asked Admiral if he would perform.

"Not this time, guys," he said.

The residents wouldn't hear it. They wanted him to perform. Not wanting to disappoint them, he went to his car to get his guitar. This day was full of surprises. He chose a song unlike anything Kelly had heard before.

She stood there crying and didn't know it. The song was beautiful. Realizing that her eyes were pouring out all of her emotions, she ran to the bathroom before anyone could see. Kelly regained her composure and turned to walk out when his grandmother walked in. She told Kelly that it was ok and that she didn't have to hide her feelings. Kelly felt uncomfortable when Grandmother looked at the wedding ring on her finger. Kelly quickly shoved her hands in her pockets.

"No matter what you do, sugga, you can't stop love. If my grandson brought you here then you are special to him."

Kelly wanted to ask if Admiral had brought other "special ones" here. It was as if the old lady was reading Kelly's mind. Removing Kelly's hand from her pocket and looking at her wedding ring Grandmother said, "He's never brought anyone here...only you." Touching Kelly's face she said, "At the end of the day, love is all we have."

Grandmother walked out and left Kelly lost in her thoughts. She was crying again. Kelly couldn't understand how could this man have her like this when she didn't even know him. She took another moment and got it together. She walked out of the bathroom to find Admiral looking for her. He walked up to Kelly and put his arm around her and hugged her. As much as Kelly didn't want it, she needed it. He kissed her on the forehead and she hugged him back. They stood like that for a long time. Kelly didn't want to let him go. They might've stayed like that if Kelly's phone hadn't started to ring. It was her sister-in-law law asking if Kelly had heard from Sal and where they were meeting for dinner. In that instant, Kelly was brought back to reality. "Kim, I'll call you as soon as I get back to the house so we could discuss our plans." Admiral must have noticed a change in Kelly. He had a worried look on his face. He said, "I'm finished here and can leave whenever you are ready."

"Admiral, I would love to stay. I really enjoyed myself, but I do need to leave now," she told him. They said their goodbyes and started to drive home. "Kelly, thank you for sharing the day with me," he said. Sitting back in her seat Kelly said, "I really enjoyed myself. I wish that I could come back and spend more time." He told her that she was always welcomed and that he went there every Saturday. Deep down in Kelly's heart she knew she couldn't come back. No matter how much she wanted to. She sat back and enjoyed the ride home. Kelly was so relaxed with Admiral. She slept the rest of the ride home.

She woke up to Admiral opening her door. "Always a gentleman." As she stepped out of the car, he thanked her again and asked if he could see her again.

"Admiral, I don't know," said Kelly. "I need some time to think."

Hugging her one last time he said, "I'll be here waiting for you." Somehow, Kelly knew he was telling the truth. Admiral wasn't going anywhere.

She got in her car and pulled off. Feeling guilty, Kelly waited until she was out of Admiral's sight before she called Sal. Time after time she was greeted by his voicemail. She went home and called his sister to make their dinner plans. They decided to let the kids pick since neither of them could get a hold of Sal. They tried and tried, but he wouldn't answer. Kelly started to get worried. "Take the kids to dinner and I'll meet up with you," she told Kim.

Kelly drove down to Sal's office to see if he was there. She found his car in the employee parking garage. Beyond angry she stormed inside. *"I've been calling this mother fucker all day and he wouldn't answer. What if something was wrong with our kids?"* Her mind cursed Sal every which way to Sunday. Something told her to take the stairs. She didn't want to give him any kind of warning before he saw her face. Kelly reached the office floor and opened the door.

In the background she heard the faint sound slow music playing. Slowly, she walked towards the sound. Nothing would ever prepare her for what she saw. There were candles lit all around Sal's office. He was seated on the couch and a naked woman was straddle on top of his manhood...her manhood. Kelly's head started to spin. She stood there for a while and watched his little show. When she'd finally seen enough, Kelly turned and ran out of the office. She searched for her car. She lost her composure. She called her sister-in-law and told her that she wouldn't be able to make dinner.

"What's wrong," asked Kim.

"Nothing," said Kelly.

"Is Sal still coming," Kim was at a loss.

"NO," said Kelly, "Sal seems to be a little tied up at work."

Kelly drove around town with nowhere to go. She knew she didn't want to go home. How could she? Kelly just kept driving until she found herself parked in front of the coffee shop. This was the last place she needed to be, but the only place she wanted to go. Kelly sat in the car afraid to go in. She was afraid to face Admiral. More than ever, she needed his strong arms to hold her. Admiral saw Kelly sitting in the car. His face beamed with happiness. He motioned for her to come in. She couldn't do it. Kelly couldn't get out of the car, she was a mess. Not wanting to wait any longer, Admiral came outside.

When he realized something was wrong, he rushed around to Kelly's door and pulled her out. He held her and asked over and over again, "What's wrong? Are you okay? What can I do?"

She couldn't speak. She had nothing to say. She just rested her head on Admiral's chest. The only thing Kelly could hear besides her cries were his heartbeat. He pulled her face towards his and begged Kelly to talk to him. He was worried about her. He couldn't stand seeing her like this. She wanted to tell him, but couldn't find the words to tell him what she'd just seen. He placed her in the passenger's seat and ran in to the shop. He let them know that he was leaving for the day. He got in Kelly's car and started driving. She didn't ask where, she didn't care. Kelly just wanted to be with him. They ended up at his condo. It wasn't what she'd expected it to be. It was actually nicely decorated.

Under different circumstances, Kelly would've loved a tour. Instead, she threw herself onto his couch and continued crying. Admiral kneeled down on the floor next to her and begged her to talk to him. As hard as it was, she told him how she couldn't get in touch with Sal after she'd gone home. "So," said Kelly, "I went to the office," and with great pain she described what she saw. He sat on the couch next to Kelly and pulled her towards him. He held her and stroked Kelly's hair until she fell asleep.

When Kelly woke up it was in the middle of the night and he was still in the same spot. He had stayed with her the entire time. She sat up and thanked him for being here with her. He told Kelly that there was no other place he could be than by her side. She started to cry again. Admiral took Kelly's face in his hands and kissed away her tears. His kisses made Kelly forget how bad her heart hurt. After the tears, he kissed her. This time she didn't want him to stop. Kelly wanted him to kiss all over her body. She started to undress him. She had to feel his skin against hers. Admiral's body tangled with hers. Kelly didn't know what happened. Suddenly, Admiral jumped up and said, "We can't do this."

She couldn't believe what she was hearing. *"Now, not only does my husband not want me,"* she thought, *"Neither does Admiral."* She started crying uncontrollably. Kelly had to leave. She couldn't stay there any longer. She needed to be alone to sort all of this mess out. Admiral came over to Kelly. He tried to hold her, but she didn't want to feel his touch.

"Do you need a ride back to your car," she asked dryly.

Hurt by her sudden change, Admiral replies, "Nah, I'll manage. I'm more worried about you than my car."

"Oh, don't worry about me." said Kelly in full sista girl mode, "I'm good. Can I have my keys, PLEASE??!!!"

"Kelly, please don't do this," He begged, "PLEASE, DON'T GO! Whatever I did to offend you, I'm sorry. You can stay in the spare room."

"Wow," Kelly said to herself, "*This fool offered his spare room. As if I needed anymore rejection, he was giving me roommate status.*"

"CAN I HAVE MY KEYS!" said Kelly. Not wanting to make things any worse Admiral did as she asked. He knew she would leave once she got them, but what was he to do? She was married to another man. Kelly snatched her keys and stormed out of his beautiful condo.

THE SET UP

A New Kelly

After Admiral rejected Kelly, she went home. Home to the one man she knew still wanted her even though she now knew he was cheating on her with the girl from the office. Their marriage was strained, but she knew Sal still loved her. They had history. They were a family. Kelly prepared her body just the way her husband liked it. She'd forced herself to stop crying. Setting the mood, she placed scented candles throughout the room. Next, she took the petals from the flowers Sal gave her the other day and laid them out on the floor and the bed. Everything was perfect. Slow, sexy music came from the speakers. Kelly's mind was racing as she got ready for HER husband. She heard Sal's car pull up in the driveway. She positioned herself to be the first thing Sal saw when he opened their bedroom door. Kelly figured he'd be surprised to see her. The look on his face let her know that Sal was unsure about coming home. When Kelly watched him having sex in his office, she knew that he saw someone. Kelly ran out before Sal could clearly see that it was her. He now stood before his wife in disbelief. Kelly tried different ways to entice him with her body. He just started yelling at her.

Kelly couldn't believe what she was hearing. Her mind races, *"He missed our family dinner to fuck his bitch and now he has the nerve to come at me like this?"* She's boiling on the inside. She's hearing him yell about dinner and telling her how stupid she looked. Kelly was at an all-time low. "

Here I am completely willing to disregard myself and allow another woman to share my husband. And STILL I wasn't good enough for him," thought Kelly, *"He doesn't want me anymore. My husband wants HER. I was just here to keep his house and his children."*

Kelly realized that she was the picture-perfect wife all for show. She ran into the bathroom with tears streaming down her face. Taking the outfit off as fast as she could, she ripped it to pieces. Kelly climbed in the shower and turned the water all the way to hot until it burned her skin. She started washing away all of the traces of today's pain.

Silently, she vowed to herself that she'd never allow another person to take her to this point. There were no words to describe how low and empty she felt. Kelly was too exhausted to dry off after her shower. She climbed into bed soaking wet. Her naked body was comforted by the warmth of the bed. It's blankets wrapped around Kelly, holding her tight. The tears continued to fall from her swollen eyes. Soon those cries soothed her to sleep. When she woke up the next morning Sal was in the kitchen making breakfast. He seemed happy to see her.

"Hey, honey, would you like some breakfast?"

"This mother fucker," thought Kelly, *"I can't believe he had the audacity to expect me to sit here and break bread with him like this bullshit never happened."* Kelly looked at the wonderful spread of food. She was disgusted by it all. Her stare bounced back and forth from Sal and his food.

With a sour face she said, "NOT AT ALL, I have other plans."

She grabbed her iPod and took off out the door for a run, something she hasn't done in a while. Too busy worrying about Sal's needs, she forgot hers. It felt good to hit the pavement. With each step she pounded away the horrible thoughts of yesterday. Kelly didn't know where she was running to and she didn't care. She just ran until her lungs started to burn. She had no choice but to take a break. It took her a moment to realize how far she'd gone. She was four developments over near a park. Kelly walked towards an empty bench. Sitting there, she found herself watching strangers go about their everyday lives. She started wondering how many of them were truly happy and what happiness really meant to them.

Kelly wondered what made her happy. She reflected back to all the happy moments she's had. Kelly became conscious of the fact that she's done nothing to fill her own self with joy. She started jogging back to the house. It was time to get started on her happiness. The first thing she did when she got back to the house was call Kim. Kelly let her know that she was about to hop in the shower, then she would come get the kids.

"Take your time momma," said Kim, "They're still sleeping."

It took Sal a moment or two to notice that Kelly returned home. He beamed from ear to ear as he asked, "Do you think we could do something today?" The word, "NO." rolled off Kelly's tongue so fast, he almost missed it.

"I have other plans. You know what, Sal? YOU should enjoy your day because I certainly plan on enjoying mine."

With that being said, Kelly turned and made her way upstairs. He followed his wife begging her to spend some time with him. All of his whining fell on a deaf ear. Kelly was deep in her thoughts. *"There was nothing this trigga could say to make me love him again."* When they reached the bedroom door, she told him that his words were pointless because she did not want to be with him. Kelly went into the bedroom, locking the door behind her.

Sal stood there looking like a fun dummy until he eventually got the hint and went to his new bedroom. Kelly was showered and dressed in no time. She packed a bag of clothes for the kids to change into. Kelly grabbed her keys and hopped in the car. As she pulled out of the driveway Kelly saw Sal looking out of his bedroom window waving. She put her Dolce's on and drove off. The kids were excited to see her, but even more so when she told them they were going to the zoo. The weather was perfect and the zoo was one of their favorite places.

The one they were going to was 2 hours away in D.C., but well worth the trip. They sung to Kelly while she was driving to keep her entertained. Nothing could have ruined this moment for Kelly except the constant ringing of her phone. "You'd think that at some point, Sal and Admiral would get tired of being sent to voicemail," she mumbled. Kelly had had enough. She turned off her phone. It wasn't like either one of them had anything to Kelly wanted to hear.

They made it to the zoo. Kelly and the kids ran like they were the wild animals. She took pictures of the girls feeding and petting the animals. She wanted to remember this day. When they were finished, she treated them to dinner at the one place Sal hardly let her take them to…McDonalds. Just when they thought this day couldn't get any better Kelly ended the night with a movie of their choice filled with all the popcorn they could eat. They laughed and smiled so much that day. Kelly knew she was truly happy with her babies and nothing else mattered.

She wished this day didn't have to end. Tomorrow meant that they would have to return to their normal routine. She would have to face the reality of her life. Kelly drove home as slow as possible, not wanting to arrive a moment sooner. The girls were happy to see their daddy and tell him about all the fun we had. They ran and covered him with hugs and kisses. Both of them tried to talk louder than the other to tell their version of the day. Kelly could tell it hurt Sal to hear they'd gone without him. He loved his girls with all that he had. He'd give anything to make them smile.

"Ok, girls," said Kelly, "Now that you've given daddy and earful about our fabulous day it's time to get ready for bed."

"Awww," said the girls in unison. They started to whine. "But, we have more to tell daddy." "Come on, girls," said Sal, "Why don't I help you guys get ready for bed?"

The girls smiled from ear to ear. Jumping up and down, they cheered and pulled Sal towards their rooms. Before he disappeared upstairs, he told Kelly that a package came while she was gone.

"I didn't know of any delivery services that ran on Sunday's," said Sal.

A naughty smile came to Kelly's face when she saw the wrapping. It was that same wrapping that led her to that party. Kelly knew what that meant. She looked down at her tattoo. She swore it started to tingle. Kitty started reminding Kelly she'd had a good time.

The party was about six months ago and so much has changed since then. *"I couldn't wait to go and have them meet the real me,"* thought Kelly. She was intrigued by the contents of the box: a mask and a GPS unit with a note attached. The note said to follow the directions on the screen. They would only appear at exactly 10:45 tomorrow morning.

She'd have to be at the meeting by noon. As before, there were rules. They weren't what Kelly expected. It stated that regular attire was required. Now, the time didn't throw her for a loop, it was the dress code. The more Kelly thought about it, the less she cared.

Her mind was racing. *"What the hell am I going to wear,"* thought Kelly, as she tore through her closet like a crazed person. After she tried on every outfit she owned, she finally settled on her tried and true girlfriend outfit as she called it. It was her all-purpose outfit. She looked at herself in the mirror and loved how she looked in her pant suit. When Kelly wore her favorite suit, she felt as if it gave her superpowers. She took the pant suit off and hung it back in the closet and got ready for bed, leaving a mess of clothes on the floor. She was too excited about tomorrow to even think about putting anything back.

She climbed into her bed naked. The silky sheets glide across her caramel skin, sending tingles through her body. It takes her mind back to the night of the party. She relives the entire night right before her eyes. The soft sexy lines of the females tease her most inner thoughts. Kelly wished she could fall asleep, but the persistent purring from kitty became too strong to ignore. Her hands became restless and wanting. She sent them down to her desire with a mission to pleasure. Kelly's finger rubbed and rolled her clit until she couldn't keep quiet any longer. She kicked the blankets off and spreads her legs wide open with one swift movement. The sudden gust of air chills her warm and creamy center.

Kelly reached under the bed for her special box. Not missing a stroke, she continues to play with her pussy. Her moans travel over to Sal's new bedroom. He hears Kelly's sexy moans, wishing he was there. He turns over and tries to ignore his wife's sexy session of pleasure. Kelly pulls Chocolate Thunder out of her box. She needed something that could put in some serious work. Tonight, Thunder would get his fair share of overtime. She slid the massive cock inside of her. Her wetness guided it to her center. Her lips stretched as far as they could go, eagerly gripping it up as it entered her cavity. Between its size and the vibration, Thunder took Kelly's breath away. Her moans were caught in her throat.

When she was finally able to release the satisfying sounds of her motorized lover, it caused Sal to jump up outta his bed. He sat on the edge of the bed listening to his wife. Those were the sounds she used to make for him. She sounded so sexy. Sal thought about how she looked the other night. Standing before him offering her body to him. Sal leans back and reaches into his pants. His dick is hard. He wants his wife. He strokes his dick as he listens to Kelly fuck herself. He strokes faster and faster to keep up with her moaning. He tries to imagine that he is in the room with her. He is the one who is sucking on her breast in his mind. He grips his dick tighter wanting to feel the walls of her pussy as they brace for the impending earthquake.

Suddenly, he realizes that it's become harder to hear Kelly. Thinking that she was getting too loud and she didn't want to wake Sal, she piped it down. Sal knew she had toys, but never saw her play with them. It was their little agreement, so to speak. When Sal was home, he handled all of her sexual needs and when he was away on business, she had her box. Just as fast as she thought to be considerate and not wanting to disturb him, she said out loud, "Fuck that selfish bastard!"

She rammed Thunder deep inside her pussy. Her moaning resumed and this time became more animalistic. Kelly lifted her hips off the bed and thrusted her pussy forward. She was taking all that Thunder was throwing at her tonight. Sal kept stroking away to her music. Kelly had no clue he was sharing in on her private session. Kelly thought she was alone when it was time for Kitty to reach the top of the mountain, but

Sal was right there with her. Whatever she was doing to herself had Sal on the trip of his life.

No matter what they did, their lives were intertwined in more than one way. Kelly and Sal stroked out at the same moment. His dick was still throbbing for more after he'd shot his load off. He needed more. Sure, a hand job every now and then is nice. Nothing could compare to being with his wife. On the other side of the wall was a different story. Kelly tore Mr. Thunder away from her creamy center. She wanted to thank him for a wonderful evening. No date would be complete without a kiss. She let Thunder tickle her lips before she tongued him clean. Having tasted her own juices put her thirst for a special lady's libation at ease for now. Kelly covered up with her blankets and let herself be taken away by her dreamy eyes.

***

Sitting in his office, Sal wondered how his life got to this point. Staring out of his window, he watched his employees go about their day. Feeling like he was on the verge of losing everything, Sal slammed his fist on his desk. He knew what he had to do. He remembered what happened last time he tried. The day played back in his head like a nightmare. It was a Saturday afternoon he'd called Selena and asked her to meet him at the office. He needed to discuss something with her. Selena's sweet voice offered him some of her tasty treats, but Sal wanted to end things. He wouldn't allow himself to be tempted.

"Selena, I don't have time for games right now. Meet me at the office in 30 minutes. I have something to discuss with you."

She tried again to seduce Sal only to have her words heard by the dial tone. Selena made another phone call. She had to step things up. She couldn't let Sal walk away. He was part of her plan. "Hi, baby." answered to voice on the other end of the phone. "I need you," said Selena.

"Ummm, I need you too!" the voice replied. "We have work to do," ordered Selena, "It's time." Knowing what that meant, the voice snapped to attention. "When and where?"

Selena was already at the office waiting for Sal. He didn't expect her to be there when he arrived and he certainly didn't expect her to be sitting on his desk. Slowly, Selena spread her legs open, showing him all of her glory. She teased her clit with two fingers. Sal's mouth was moving, telling her how and why he couldn't see her anymore. The more Sal talked, the wetter her pussy got. Before he knew it, Sal was having a one on one conversation with her snatch. Her juices were smeared all over his face. Not wanting Sal to have the upper hand, Selena pushed him up against the arm of the couch. She unfastened his pants with her teeth. This girl was crazy. Sal moaned as Selena's teeth slid his zipper open.

Once Sal's pants were down, she stroked his thighs with her face. His dick jumped in anticipation of what was to come.

"Down, boy," he told himself, "I can't do this." ran though his head.

Catching Sal deep in his thoughts, Selena grabbed him by the ass. She shoved his dick completely in her mouth. Sal couldn't fight it, he reached for the back of her head pushing deeper. Selena twirled her tongue around the tip of his dick. Selena went to work on his dick like she never wanted to let it go. Sal felt bad about wanting to end things with her earlier. The more he thought about it, the more Sal had to have her. He pumped his dick in and out of Selena's mouth faster and faster. She took it all, never gagging once. Sal shook his head amazed at how Selena sucked the hell out of his dick.

Just as his head turned to the left, Sal thought he saw someone out of the corner of his eye. He thought it was Kelly. Sal wasn't sure. He couldn't focus. He looked again and thought he saw someone running away. Before he could do or say anything, there was a rush of pleasure. He's never felt like this before. Sal felt Selena's mouth on his dick and someone else's tongue on his balls. He looked down to see a girl on the floor between Selena's legs. All of a sudden, Selena started moaning. Sal looked again. He saw that Selena was riding the girl on the floor. The girl was fucking her while Selena was sucking his dick.

At first Sal was mad at Selena for setting him up, but his man friend told him otherwise. Sal was so turned on watching this strange chick fuck the shit out of Selena. She continued to suck Sal's dick. He couldn't hold back any longer. Sal grunted, "I'm about to cum." The girl on the floor jumped up to join Selena in savoring Sal's juices. She was just as sexy as Selena. Seeing the two of them naked in front of him with their mouths open made Sal shoot nut off everywhere. The girls had cum all over their faces. The strange girl turned and started licking Sal's juices off Selena's face. Her fingers were playing with Selena's pussy. Sal sat there for a while watching these two ladies lick and stroke each other. His dick was in his hand.

His man friend began to talk again. It was hard and telling him it was time to get some of that pussy. Sal got down on the floor with the girls. He eased his dick into Selena's tight pussy. She gasped as if Sal was pushing all of the air out of her body. While Sal was fucking Selena, the other girl sat straddled over her mouth. The girl sat facing Sal. The harder he fucked Selena the more she sucked this girl's pussy. The girl's titties bounced up and down. Sal watched the girl toy with her nipples and lick her lips. Sal pulled the girl to him. He kissed her, working his way down to her breast. Having Selena locked on her pussy and seeing Sal latched on to her bosom was too much. The girl exploded. Smearing her creamy juices all over Selena's face. Her body quivered uncontrollably. She climbed off of Selena and got down on all fours in front of Sal. Selena repositioned herself down in front of the girl.

Against his better judgment, he took the girl from behind. Her pussy was just as tight as Selena's. He had to force his way in. Once inside his dick drowned in all of her juices.

"Give it to me," the girl begged, "Fuck me now."

She wanted him to be rough with her. She pushed back and started grinding on Sal's dick. It was as if something took over him. He couldn't stop himself. Sal started fucking her like he was a wild animal. The girl lowered her head and went to work. Watching the girl eat Selena's pussy took his mind to the next level. Selena's face looked like she was in pain. He knew Selena; she was trying not to cum. This girl was attacking her pussy. Sal was so caught up in watching the two of them. He felt himself cumming deep in this stranger's pussy.

Sal didn't think that either of the girls noticed that he came. They were kissing and sucking each other all over. He sat back and just enjoyed their little show. This was a first for Sal. He'd never been with two women before. This was something he'd talked about with Kelly before, but she wasn't open to any of it. After Kelly refused, he never thought about it again. Selena had him where she wanted him. She took care of Sal when he was at work and satisfied all of his desires, even the desires Sal didn't know he had. Selena was beyond amazing. The two women were pleasuring each other. It took them a while to realize that Sal wasn't in the mix.

They slowly crawled their way over to him, still playing with each other's bodies. They tried to draw Sal back in. At first, he wanted to, but he couldn't. Once Sal realized what happened, he had to find a way to get out of there. Sal disappointed the ladies by declining a round two. The ladies tried again, but things came to an end. They said their goodbyes. Sal hopped in his car and sped home. He checked his phone and saw that he had over a dozen missed calls. His sister and Kelly blew his phone up. Sal checked his messages, but they all seemed to sing the same tune: "Where are you? How dare you miss dinner? Please call us back. We're worried something happened."

The last message had Sal worried. It sounded like Kelly was crying. The recording was too short. He couldn't really make it out. But Sal knew he'd heard enough. Enough to make him wonder if it was Kelly he saw. Sal was completely lost. His body was there, but his mind was stuck on his sexual nightmare. He could feel how dreadful it was going to be going home that night. Sal knew then that he could never live down what he did to his family. The "movie" continued to play in his head. All the lights were off in Sal's house when he pulled into the driveway. Once he got the nerve up to enter the house, he checked the kids' rooms, but they were empty. He heard the faint sound of music coming from room he shared with his wife.

When Sal opened the door, he was shocked. The room was filled with candlelight and rose petals. Standing before him was the most beautiful sight. Kelly was wearing one of her sexy outfits. Sal loved seeing her like this. Her body glowed in the candlelight. Her long silky hair was neatly pinned back. Her make-up was perfect as always. She stood before her husband. She wanted him. But Sal couldn't make himself want her.

"I can't give myself to her," thought Sal.

How could he? He felt so much guilt from his relationship with Selena. He carried the shame of what he just did with Selena and this stranger. Sal didn't know anything about the other girl he fucked without a condom. How could he touch Kelly?

Secretly, Sal hoped that the candles and rose petals masked the aroma of sex that oozed from his body. To hide his shame, Sal went off on Kelly. He scolded her for missing dinner with his sister and their kids.

Sal knew what her response was going to be before Kelly even said it, "Sal, I was worried about you. I couldn't stop crying. I thought something had happened to you. I was so upset, but didn't want the kids to see me like that." Kelly started crying, she kept saying over and over that she'd thought something happened to him.

Sal wanted to take her in his arms and hold his wife. He wanted to comfort her and tell her that he was safe and here, promising her never to leave her. Instead, Sal yelled at Kelly again, "Take off that stupid outfit and make up. You look like a whore!" Before Sal walked out of the room, he threw one more insult at her.

"Damn, Kelly, I don't know why you always feel the need to soak your entire body in cheap perfume. After a hard day at work you just gave me the worst headache ever. I can't even sleep with you. You got it smelling so bad. I gotta sleep in the guest bedroom!"

It killed Sal to say those hurtful things, but he couldn't lie next to Kelly knowing he'd been unfaithful. As Sal lay in the guest bed, he fell asleep listening to the sounds of Kelly's muffled cries.

A NEW DESTINATION

Taking Over

The next morning, Kelly jumped up out of bed. She was excited about the upcoming events of her day. She rushed into the girl's room. *"I gotta get 'em moving today."* she thought. The girls seemed to take forever in the mornings. Kelly couldn't afford to have her day thrown off schedule. Any other day she would have been pleasantly surprised at what she saw when she entered the twin's room. Today just wasn't that day.

Sal had them dressed and ready to go. Uniforms on and their hair brushed in two neat curly ponytails.

"Good morning, mommy," they cheered. Kelly smiled.

She loved her family. For a moment she forgot how much she despised Sal until he said, "Good morning, hun." Hearing his voice soured her disposition. Kelly knew at some point she would have to confront her husband. She wasn't ready to deal with it right now. Since

Sal was taking the girls to school, she decided to go write. She sat down to her desk and saw that Sal had left her a letter.

Dear Kelly,

For the past couple of weeks things between us have been rough. I know I act like it's your fault, but it's not. I'm the one to blame for all of our problems. Kelly you are the best wife anyone could ask for. I love you and the girls more than anything in this world. I haven't made the best choices, but I promise you, baby, I'm going to make things right.

Love, Sal

"Ain't that bout a bitch," said Kelly. "This mother fucker is crazy. He fucks some other bitch at his job, a job I helped him build, in an office I helped decorate. That bitch's pussy was on MY mother fuckin couch. He thinks a corny ass letter is gonna set shit straight with me. Nah, I'm about to show em how to do it!"

Kelly fumed as she sat at her desk. She logged on to her laptop and went to work on her new novel. She had a whole lot of new inspiration thanks to her cheating husband. She typed until it was time to get ready for her outing. She was showered and dressed in no time flat. She sat on the edge of her bed holding the magic box, waiting for it to chime. She was anxious and nervous at the same time.

Finally, the screen lit up, "HELLO, KELLY JAMES", the robotic voice spoke, "WELCOME TO THE PERSONAL NAV 2.6 PLEASE FOLLOW MY INSTRUCTIONS AND I WILL GUIDE YOU TO YOUR DESTINATION. WHEN YOU ARE READY PLEASE TOUCH THE START BUTTON, BUT, I MUST WARN YOU," said the box, "THERE WILL BE NO TURNING BACK."

A chill ran through Kelly's body. She was shook, but not shook enough. *"This adventure was just what I need,"* she said as she touched the start button. The box guided her to a location that was an hour away in New Jersey. Taking in her surroundings, Kelly was in what looked like an abandoned industrial park. There were no other cars. The buildings were unmarked and appeared to be vacant. This time she was scared. Had she taken things too far? She thought about turning around and going home. Her home life was screwed, but running away from it wouldn't make it any better. "Fuck this," Kelly said out loud.

It was as if the box heard her. "KELLY JAMES, WE HAVE ARRIVED AT YOUR DESTINATION. PLEASE EXIT YOUR VEHICLE AND HAND YOUR KEYS TO THE ATTENDANT AND ENTER THE BUILDING ON YOUR RIGHT. I MUST WARN YOU BEFORE YOU ENTER THE BUILDING, YOU WILL FOLLOW ALL RULES. AND KELLY JAMES," The box called out to her, "REMEMBER, THERE IS NO TURNING BACK!"

Kelly couldn't believe that she was scared of a battery powered box. She stared at it hard enough to burn a hole in it. This has got to be a joke, Kelly thought. Maybe some kind of new member initiation. Kelly took another minute to get the nerve up to get out of her car. She walked up to the door. A masked attendant greeted Kelly. She asked for her keys and the GPS unit. Kelly handed them over and proceeded through the next set of doors. The building might have looked abandoned on the outside, but it certainly wasn't the case inside. From the inside, you would've thought that you were at the home office of a Fortune 500 company. *"This is unreal,"* she thought. Kelly felt as if she were Alice entering Wonderland. At that very moment, she was in the presence of some of the most powerful female players from every industry. Kelly recognized some of the women from the supermarket tabloids, Essence, Jet and People. All and several more were sitting at her coffee table at that very moment.

"Hi, my name is Pandora Simone; I take it that you're new."

Kelly smiled at the woman that was speaking to her. She didn't understand any of what was going on.

"I know it's a lot," said the woman named Pandora. "Come on honey, let me get you signed in."

Mrs. Simone had a southern drawl. Kelly giggled a little when the country belle spoke, "Yes, shuuga, I tend to talk a bit different from y'all city folks."

"I'm sorry," said Kelly, "Your accent is so strong. Just hearing you talk puts me at ease." "

Awww, honey, now what's got you so nervous," said Pandora.

"I'm just not sure about what's going on today, I'm new to the group," said Kelly.

Out of know where, "KELLY, KELLY PALMER! IS THAT YOU?" Kelly turned to the direction of the voice. It's wall to wall women. Kelly can't make out who was calling her name. "KELLY PALMER, GIRL, OVER HERE!!" Finally able to put a face to the voice, "Savannah, girl, is that you? OH, MY GOD!" says Kelly as she embraces her old college roommate.

"I haven't seen you since graduation. How have you been?" The old friends spend some time catching up. "So, what are you doing here?" Kelly asked.

Remembering where she was and the night that got her there embarrassed Kelly. Her demeanor changed instantly. Her hand instantly goes to her tattoo while the rest of her body stiffened. Unable to look at Savannah, Kelly's eyes hit the floor. Seeing how uncomfortable her old roommate was, Savannah said, "Don't worry we've all shared the same experience. What's important is the reason we are here today.

Remember it's all about from the Bedroom to the Boardroom."
Savannah's words offered a little bit of comfort to Kelly. With a nervous
laugh she said, "Yeah, I guess you're right."

The announcer called for the meeting to begin. The ladies were
instructed to head to the convention room and to be seated. Kelly
appeared to relax as she spoke to the other women walking in the same
direction. Her guard was still up because she didn't know what to think.
Kelly decided to stay close to Savannah just in case. The morning was
filled with speakers on various topics. They all seemed to lead back to
one thing, empowering women world-wide. Kelly enjoyed hearing the
Leaders, as they were called, speak. The final Leader's words spoke
directly to Kelly.....

The Leader spoke about infidelity in a marriage. Kelly twisted in her
seat as the words continued to hit home.

"Ladies we are the backbone for our families. Why should you let
your spouse reap the benefits of your hard work, only to share them
with a jezebel."

A jezebel, that's who she saw servicing her husband." thought Kelly.

The speaker continued, "As a wife you have an equal stake in your
spouse's company. Do not allow them to short change you. Do your
homework ladies, sit in on the meetings."

Kelly sat up giving her full attention to the speaker, while in a
corner, Selena secretly watched on. She watched Kelly's mind slip
deeper and deeper into the lecture by Maliah. She was the top Leader.
An honor given by Supreme to the woman with the highest number of
recruits that earned a profit. Kelly began her transformation right before
the very jezebel she sought revenge against. The seminar came to an end

and the ladies gathered for a meet and greet. There were so many faces and names being thrown at Kelly. She smiled from ear to ear.

While Kelly was in awe of her fellow BTB members, Kitty was engulfed with desire. Kitty so badly craved the assortment of candy as it paraded before her. Kelly ignored the feelings simmering below. She surrounded herself with endless conversations. Her Kitty wouldn't take no for an answer. Feeling her juices soaking her pants, Kelly hurried to the ladies room. She entered the room urgently. Lucky for her, everyone was walking out at the same time. Kelly chose the last stall. Once she locked the door her hands immediately went to her breast. Her nipples we hard. They were throbbing. The pressure caused her nipples to rub against the material on her bra. She removed her jacket and her shirt. Cupping her breast, she raised them to her mouth. She kissed herself, gently at first. Kitty told Kelly she liked that, but she wanted more. Kelly stood on the middle of the stall and released her breast from captivity. Her mouth watered at the sight before her. She began sucking her own nipples. "Harder." Kitty begged.

Kitty wanted to play, but Kelly held her back. Kelly knew better than to ignore her desire. Her pussy was throbbing. Throwing herself back against the wall, Kelly eased her hand down to her center. It was so wet. She began to pleasure herself. Her fingers twirled her clit around. Kitty was so worked up; she didn't want to be teased. Kelly stroked her pussy. Her chest heaved up and down. Seeing her breast move excited Kelly even more. With her free hand, Kelly grabbed her breast and shoved it in to her mouth. She thought of how if felt when Admiral sampled her goods. "Damn......Admiral." Kelly whispered. She hated thinking about him. His name would have her so turned on. Kelly tried not to moan when the sensation tingled through her body. She wanted to hold it back. She didn't want to lose the thought of Admiral in her mind. Kitty didn't care what Kelly wanted. Kelly had no choice, the feeling got stronger and stronger. Before Kelly knew it her legs began to shake uncontrollably. She rubbed her pussy faster and faster, still whispering his name.

The juices from her pussy coated her entire hand. The warm gooey mix cause Kelly's hand to glide effortlessly back and forth. Kelly dipped a finger in and out of her love hole. Her hips bucking harder and harder. Her body trembled from head to toe. She gave in to the desire; waves of ecstasy tore through her body. Kelly bit down on her breast so she wouldn't scream out her pleasure. Just as Kelly finished, she heard movement in one of the other stalls. Completely embarrassed, Kelly fixes herself back up and flushes the toilet. *"Oh, God, maybe they won't know what I just did."* Mad at herself for what just happened, she washes her hands and tries to leave the building.

Before she can reach the door, she hears that southern accent calling out, "Kelly, honey, wait up. Kelly, honey child, wait up now." Just feet from the door, she stops to turn and face her greeter plastering a fake smile on her face.

"Oh, hey Pandora girl, you wanted me?" Pandora's innocent face played right along with Kelly.

"I wanted to make sure you were okay," she says as she tries to catch her breath, "How did you like our seminar?"

"Oh! It was great. I learned a lot," says Kelly, still wishing she was on the other side of that door.

Pandora reached over and gave Kelly a big old bear hug. Kelly closed her eyes and pretended she was somewhere else.

"Sis, I am SOOOOO glad that you came to experience the power of the BTB movement."

"Me, too," said Kelly playing along.

"Oh, before I forget," says Pandora, "the young lady that you were sitting with asked me to give you this."

She hands Kelly a folded piece of paper. Kelly opens the paper. It's a note from her friend Savannah. "It was so good to see you again. Please keep in touch. Maybe we can do lunch. I missed you roomie. Call me, Savannah."

The note also had all of Kelly's old roommate's contact information. Kelly smiled thinking back to her college days. She turned and thanked Pandora for giving her the note. Kelly was so happy she even hugged her goodbye. Kelly stepped outside and was greeted by another masked attendant. The attendant hands Kelly back her keys along with another note.

"PLEASE FOLLOW THE CAR PARKED AT THE END OF THE ROAD. IT WILL LEAD YOU BACK IN THE DIRECTION YOU CAME FROM. PLEASE DO NOT RETURN TO THIS LOCATION. WE WILL CONTACT YOU AT OUR DISCRETION."

Kelly wanted to tell these people what they could do with all of their damn rules, but she liked what she heard from them today and wanted to learn more. She conceded that she would be a willing student from this point on. Kelly got in her car and followed the car until she recognized her surroundings. The car exited the highway and allowed Kelly to continue on her way home. She wasn't the same person she was when she left her house that morning. No one would be ready for the woman BTB had created today.

Getting off the highway, Kelly headed to her husband's office. She needed to confront Sal. Normally, she wouldn't want to cause a scene in front others, but that was the old Kelly. She stormed into the building with such a commotion. Kelly held her head high as she stormed passed the employees.

"Hello, Mrs. James, how are you doi…?"

She marched on. One by one the employees continued to greet Kelly only to be ignored. She wasn't here on a social visit.

"May I help you," said the receptionist guarding Sal's office.

"No, you may not," snarled Kelly.

Her blood was boiling. Kelly wasn't sure if this was the harlot sleeping with her husband. She only saw her from the back. Something deep down told her that she was the one. Sizing her up one more time, Kelly dismissed the receptionist and proceeded to enter Sal's office.

"Ma'am, I cannot allow you to go in there," said the receptionist as she threw herself against the door blocking Kelly.

Everyone stood silent, watching the two women battle unaware of the true reason.

"I'm gonna ask you one time and one time only! MOVE OUT OF MY WAY," said Kelly.

Refusing to budge, the receptionist replied, "MR. JAMES IS IN A MEETING AND MAY NOT BE DISTURBED. NOW YOU MAY TAKE A SEAT IN OUR WAITING AREA AND I WILL COME GET YOU AS SOON AS HE IS AVAILABLE."

A unified gasp swept thru the floor. They all knew that today would be the last day for Mr. James' secretary, she'd gone too far. Kelly pushed her to the side and entered her husband's office.

"Hello, Jacob," she said as she entered. "I am sorry to disturb you two, but I have an urgent matter I need to discuss with my husband."

Sal stood speechless at his wife. Jacob quickly gathered his notes and left as Kelly asked. She turned to face her husband.

"Kelly, what in the hell is wrong with you" asked Sal.

"What's wrong with me?" laughed Kelly, "What's wrong with YOU fucking your secretary?" It was as if Kelly had kicked him in his throat, Sal stammered on and on trying to deny Kelly's accusations. "Cut the bullshit, Sal, I saw you with my own two eyes."

"What did you see Kelly? You didn't see me! Have you lost your mind?" Sal went on and on trying to convince his wife he was innocent. Kelly went and sat behind Sal's desk. She smoothed out the pile of papers he'd thrown all over.

"Now, I stood behind every move you've made and helped make you what you are today. You've fucked me over for the last time. From now on I run things."

"Kelly, I refuse to discuss this here with you."

"Good," said Kelly, "because there's nothing to discuss. You can either do things my way or let our lawyers settle this."

Hearing the thought of divorce hurt Sal. He never wanted things to get this far. He never wanted to lose his wife. Whatever he had to do to make this right he knew he had to do it. Sal fell back on the couch.

"Yeah," said Kelly "that's the position that got you in this mess now." Sal lowered his head and began to cry. "Don't cry, Sal," Kelly's voice mocked him without sympathy, "It's too late for tears. Besides they're useless. I should know I've cried enough over your sorry ass."

"Kelly can we please stop this," begged Sal.

"NO," said Kelly, "What you can do is get this nasty ass couch out of my office. I'll be placing an order for all new furniture. I don't want any traces of that nasty bitch in here."

"Kelly is that what this is really about," asked Sal. "I'll get rid of her. I'll fire her and we can move on. I promise I won't ever see her again."

"Oh no," said Kelly, "You're not getting off that easy. I want her to stay. I want her here to remind you of what you did. Now, get the fuck out of my office. I have work to do."

Sal stood there staring at this creature who used to be his wife. He wiped the tears from his eyes and faced the stares and comments from his staff. They were still standing outside hoping to catch a stray piece of gossip. All they knew was the bosses' wife was about to get the sexy Latina fired. Sal ordered them to get back to work.

Jacob pulled Sal to the side, "Man, is everything okay?"

"I don't know," replied Sal. "Kelly is going through something right now."

Jacob had never seen anything like this from Sal or Kelly. He knew something was up, yet he also knew enough to stay out of it. He went back to his office and left Sal to clean up his own mess. Sal directed himself towards Building Maintenance, he had to get that couch out of his old office. Deep down he was afraid of what his wife was going to do next, so he planned on doing exactly as he was told.

Selena tried to pull Sal to the side, "I need to talk to you," she said.

"Not now," Sal said dismissively.

She trailed on his heels. Sal stopped in his tracks, "I'm not getting into this now, Selena. Get back to your desk and get to work. We'll talk about this later."

Sal snuck off to the stairwell. He needed a moment to process what just happened. He put himself back together and headed towards the conference room. He had to get back to business.

Walking into the conference room, Sal saw Kelly sitting at the table prepared to meet with the prospective clients coming in.

"Kelly, I've had enough of this shit. I know I fucked up, but I'm not going to sit here and let you come in here and ruin my business. We will handle this between us at home. Kelly, you need to leave now!" ordered Sal.

"Look damn it," said Kelly, "I told you I'm here to work; I'm taking what's mine. So, sit down and let's go over your plan for signing these new clients."

The rest of the week continued like this. Sal couldn't win for losing. He caught hell from his wife while his mistress shot him the iciest looks ever. Work sucked and home life wasn't any better. The only thing bringing Sal joy was the time he spent with his daughters. Now that he wasn't seeing Selena anymore, he was spending more time at home. Kelly continued keeping her distance from Sal and making him sleep in the guest room.

MOVING ON

Summoning Selena

Selena spent the week at work fuming. She knew things were going to turn out this way. It's how things always ended, but this time it hurt. It hurt like hell. She played her part and got Sal to forget all about his wife and kids. Hell, he even forgot he was married most of the time they were together. Not all of it was an act for her. She cared about Sal. He was good to her and he was damn good to her body. Seeing him every day at work was torture for her. She needed to feel him inside of her. She tried to talk to him at work, hoping to convince him that he didn't have to put up with the crap Kelly was putting him through.

She could make it better for him. Instead, Sal ignored her and her calls. This made her want him even more. No one ever rejected Selena.

"Don't worry," she said to her vajayjay, "he'll be back."

Her body ached for a release. Since she'd gotten with Sal, Selena lost her pet, Vixen. She wasn't as loyal as Selena had thought. Vixen warned Selena about crossing the line and jeopardizing everything. Selena's face twisted as she thought about how Vixen ran back to Supreme and told her everything. Supreme was not pleased with Vixen's report.

Selena was ordered to appear before the Council of Leaders. The sisterhood would decide Selena's fate this coming Saturday evening according to the note card delivered with a beautiful bouquet of flowers on Tuesday. Selena cursed out loud when she saw the delivery man coming her way. She knew BTB wasn't having any upcoming events so this had to be bad. Every one of her female co-workers were jealous of the massive arrangement. Selena snatched the card and tried to keep her eyes from popping out as she read:

SELENA ALVAREZ :

YOU ARE ORDERED TO STAND BEFORE THE COUNCIL OF LEADERS FOR VIOLATING RULE # 96 IN THE BTB HANDBOOK. REPORT TO THE CHAMBER AT 9 PM SATURDAY EVENING.

Violating a rule normally isn't that big of a deal, unless it was rule# 96. That rule was created by the Sister Council to prevent the temptress from deviating from the plan. Selena knew she had messed up big time. She could recite the rules off the top of her head. In fact, she'd earned her rank for being so dedicated to following every single rule in the damn handbook. How could she allow herself to jeopardize everything? She'd fallen in love with Sal. She played him like a pawn in the beginning, but now she wanted to be with him. She wanted to protect him. She smiled thinking how Sal's face would light up every morning when he saw her waiting for him to come to work.

"I'm the one who makes him happy." thought Selena.

She knew she would have to find a way to get Sal out of this and Kelly out of the way. She was about to fight for her man.

***

Admiral sat staring out of the window at the coffee shop. Business had been good, but he hated going to work nowadays. At first, he hoped Kelly would come in to talk to him. He'd tried calling her but she wouldn't answer his calls. He didn't want to talk to her answering machine. He wanted to hear her voice. He needed see her, he wanted to touch her. He couldn't stand not knowing if she was alright. He slammed the cup of tea down on the counter. It was supposed to calm his nerves. On the verge of erupting, Admiral announced, "I'm leaving for the day. I'll check in with you tomorrow."

He left the shop and knew there was only one place he could go. There was only one other person who could make things right for him. His grandmother. She knew something was wrong the minute she saw his face. Placing her small fragile hands on her grandson's face she said, "If it is meant to be it will be, in the end she will need you to be her rock." Even though they sat in complete silence for the remainder of the visit, Admiral's grandmother eased the pain in his heart. Driving home Admiral decided that he would be patient, he'd wait for Kelly to sort through her problems at home.

While his mind told him that he needed to back off her, his manhood had a different plan. The image of Kelly standing in her kitchen exposed had Admiral's dick struggling to stay in his pants. He licked his lips thinking how good her lips felt on his. Trying to fight the urge not to, he picked up the phone to call Kelly. Even if she didn't answer he could still hear her voice on the outgoing message.

Kelly grabbed the phone out of her purse so she could turn the ringer off. She didn't want to talk to anyone right now. She'd just finished cussing Sal out for the umpteenth time. When she looked at the screen and saw his name, Kitty twitched. Kitty liked him, she liked Admiral a lot.

"Fuck," said Kelly. She couldn't keep avoiding him. "Hello," she said dryly.

He couldn't believe it, she actually answered. Admiral looked at the screen making sure he dialed the right number.

"HELLO?" Kelly said again.

"Hi" Admiral said as a smile spread across his face. "How are you doing sunshine?" he asked.

Kelly snuggled back in her chair and purred, "I'm good. How about you," she asked. She loved how he'd managed to make her feel all warm and fuzzy with just five words. "I'm glad you called." Kelly said.

Admiral laughed, "I've been stalking you, but all I could get was your voicemail. I was worried about you," said Admiral.

"I'm sorry, I just wasn't ready to deal with anything at the time," she said.

"Kelly, I wanted you so bad that night, I still do. But I want this to be what you really want," said Admiral, "You have a lot of things to sort out so I'll wait until you're ready. In the meantime, I'm here if you ever need a friend."

Kelly began to cry softly, hearing his words. His heart cringed with pain hearing her so hurt. "Whatever you need, no questions asked ok?" he said.

"Yes." said Kelly with her face covered in tears.

"Kelly, I care about you. I just want you to be happy."

"I will be." she replied.

"Good! When can I expect to put you on the schedule?" said Admiral.

"Huh?" Kelly replied, completely confused.

"Well, I'm in need of a little help at the shop and I heard you had some skills."

Kelly laughed so hard. It felt good to be her old self for a minute. Admiral liked hearing her like this. "I don't know if I can come show your crew how it's supposed to be done. I'm kinda busy taking over my husband's company right now," replied Kelly.

The bitch was back. Admiral didn't understand at all, so Kelly explained her plan.

"I was the good girlfriend, the good wife, in fact, the perfect wife. I played my part to better my husband and all he wanted to do was make himself better by hurting me. All he cared about was his company, never me. I was the one who helped him. I made it possible for him to become the man he is today and my thanks is that he uses me as his trophy while he goes off and fucks whoever. Well, I'll show him just what this trophy wife really can do. He wouldn't have any of this without me."

Admiral didn't like to hear her like this. He knew this wasn't the real Kelly. Trying to change the subject, "Why don't you come down to the shop, bring your writings with you. I'll show you mine if you show me yours," he teased her.

Kelly couldn't resist. Admiral had a way of getting to her.

"Fine," she said, "but I'm picking the muffins this time."

They set a date for Friday afternoon. She'd made sure her schedule was clear. She wanted Admiral to have her undivided attention. She couldn't wait to see him again and neither could Kitty.

Kelly seemed to be in better spirits after her conversation with Admiral. She was even a little nicer to Sal, just a little. In her mind she'd fast forwarded her week to Friday. She struggled to keep Admiral out of her thoughts. Somehow, she managed to make it to the end of the work week. She woke with a smile on r face. Her thoughts were on him, that man. Kelly wasn't sure what to call him. He certainly wasn't her friend. Even though he shouldn't be he was more than that. Kelly chose her outfit very carefully. She wanted to leave him drooling after he turned her down the last time.

Today they drove separate cars to work. Sal stayed off balance when it came to predicting Kelly's actions. Her attitude at work was laid back. The whole office seemed to be feeling her vibe. Today's going to be a good day thought Sal. He'd called his secretary, because that's all she was to him now.

"I need you to order lunch for me and my wife from Arinezo's, tell 'em to give you our usual order."

"The nerve of this fool," thought Selena, "I gotta order lunch for him and his wifey pooh. Now this nigga wants be all boo'ed up with her trifling ass. If he only knew how much of a whore she really was."

Selena couldn't stand how Kelly pranced around the office like she was the Queen of Sheba. She put all that aside and did what Sal asked of her, in the end it was all about him. When their lunch arrived, Selena took it upon herself to deliver it to Sal's office. She entered Sal's office bearing gifts.

"Honey, look what I have for you." she sang.

It was as if she were trying to hypnotize him with her sweet sounding voice.

"Oh good," said Sal as he jumped up from his desk.

He grabbed his lunch and looked puzzled.

"Selena, where's my wife's?"

It took everything she had to keep her eyes from rolling backwards.

"Don't worry, baby," Selena said as she wrapped her arm around Sal's neck, "I'm gonna take hers down in a minute, but I had to take care of you first."

Sal felt his nerves about to unravel. It had been a while since he was this close to Selena. She pressed her body closer and connected her lips with his. Sal didn't give in so easy at first. He was telling himself that this wasn't right. He knew better than to be doing this, not here, not now, hell not anymore. But he couldn't convince his body otherwise. He groaned as he began to kiss her back, harder than what she was giving him. His hands snaked around her tiny waist. Selena trembled from his forceful embrace.

"Damn, I missed this man." she thought.

Sal's hands began to search for her delicious ass. He squeezed it tightly. Her ass felt like putty in his hands. Selena moaned as she wound her body against Sal's. She was so turned on she couldn't stop herself from rambling.

"Maldiga a bebé que mi cuerpo le perdidó tanto…. No jamás déjeme…. Yo le necesito papi…. Te quiero papi….Te quiero papi."

Selena knew Sal couldn't understand what she was saying. But when she said what really was on her heart he knew. She felt his body tense once the words left her lips. She couldn't take it back even if she wanted to. It was how she truly felt about him. She looked him in the eyes bearing her soul and said it again..."Te quiero papi." Sal looked at her, her face was filled will love. He couldn't deny that he did feel something for Selena. Was nothing he could do about it. He had to save his marriage and get right with his wife. Just as he fixed his lips to tell Selena that there would be no more of this, Kelly flings the door open.

Seeing the two lovers entwined Kelly smirks and says, "I just came by to tell you I'm heading out to lunch. I see you're enjoying yours, so I guess I'll enjoy mine."

Kelly closed the door and left the building as if her panties were on fire. Sal tried to go after her but somehow, he couldn't get untangled from Selena. The more he tries to get away from her the more they struggle to stay upright. Sal lands on top of Selena, right where she wanted him. She lays there pretending to be injured by him falling on her, pinning her to the floor.

"Are you ok," Sal asked.

Wiggling beneath him she struggled between moans to reply, "Oh, baby, I think my hurt leg."

"Let me see," says Sal.

He looks down and realizes his hand is on her bare leg, her skirt pushed up past her hips. Selena's hem fell on the slope leading to her love box. Sal's hands followed the trail he's traveled so many times before.

Her softness called out for his body and he eagerly answered the call. He kissed her glossy lips. He tried to move in to her mouth. He couldn't get enough of her. His hands were still making their way to her box. She parted her legs to give him easier access. Reaching her area, he proceeded to search for her missing jewel. His finger-tips were slick with her dew. He brought his fingers up to his nose and inhaled her scent. His mouth began to water. He remembered the last time he buried his tongue deep inside of her. His dick was beating against his zipper begging Sal to let him out. He wanted to play with his old friend.

Sal thought one more time about walking away from the whole situation. Selena saw him in deep thought and began to unbutton her blouse. Her full breast we struggling to be restrained by one of the sexiest bras he'd ever seen. He nibbled on her neck, "Mmmm." purred Selena. Sal took his free hand and released her breast. He stared at them, shocked by what he saw.

"This is new," said Sal.

Selena just smiled at him. Now her perfectly round nipples each had a barbell. Intrigued by his discovery Sal wanted to explore her new addition. Carefully he ran the tip of his tongue around her thickness. Sparks shot through her body from the sensation. Her need began to grow. Her hips slowly moved in rhythm with the flicking of his tongue. She imagined him there. Sal placed his finger inside of Selena's warmth. She wanted him. His mouth watered as he thought about how good her juices tasted. He started kissing his way downtown. She spread her legs even more; she wanted him to taste all of her. Reaching the entrance to her love box, Sal rubbed his face against her delicate area. She rocked her hips, pressing her body closer to him. She wanted to feel the rush he gave her.

Sal looked up at her and licked his lips. It was time for his feast. He latched on to her clit and took Selena to her point mindless babble. Just as she was about to cum her mouth got carried away….

"Get your pussy, daddy. Don't let Kelly be the only one havin' lunch today!"

Her body began to shake. She let the feeling take over her entire body. She was oblivious to the fact that Sal was now staring at her wishing he'd never met her. Her words hit him right in the gut. He's never thought about Kelly being with anyone else before now. The image played in his head. Silently he said a prayer, *"God, please don't let my wife be with another man. Please show me how to save my family."*

"Selena, this ends now!" said Sal. "This thing between us should have never happened."

Sal stood up and adjusted his clothes. He extended his hand to help her up.

Smacking his hand away, Selena begged, "Baby please don't, you can't. Sal, I love you. You can't tell me you don't feel the same about me. I know you do."

She tried to pull Sal close but he stepped further away from her. "Selena, I care about you and maybe even to the point of loving you but it was wrong. I can't do this to Kelly anymore."

"Fuck Kelly!" said Selena. "Your wife is no better than you. She's a fuckin' whore and you're worried about hurting her...WHAT ABOUT ME! WHAT ABOUT US?"

"Selena, I'm sorry there's no more us." said Sal. "If it's going to be a problem with you continuing to work here, I can transfer you to another office if you would like but from here on out it's just business between us. Now if you'll excuse me, I need to call my wife."

Selena stormed out trying not to let her heartbreak get the best of her. She cursed Kelly and the air she breathed. Sitting at her desk she plotted the demise of the Great Kelly James. *"That bitch is gonna pay."* *Selena assured herself.*

Kelly had tears in her eyes as she walked out of the office. She'd laughed herself silly. Seeing the two of them was hilarious. She was close to actually believing he was truly sorry for his actions. Part of her wanted to believe that they could go back to the way things were. What she just saw told her otherwise. No, she wasn't mad at all. She didn't hate him. She didn't hate her. She didn't hate what they did behind her back. She didn't care. She felt nothing. Nothing for the man who was once her life. Nothing for the woman for who made Kelly wish to end her own life. She'd taken her life back. She was determined to never let another hurt her like that again. Today Kelly was ready to start new. She wondered if her new start included Admiral. There's only one way to find out thought Kelly.

She started up her car and headed for his shop. When she pulled up to the coffee shop, she saw that the curtains in the window were closed and the lights in the window were off. She went up to the door and tried to open it but it was locked. She wasn't sure what was going on. Thinking that he had stood her up, Kelly started to feel rejected again. But she knew how much he was looking forward to seeing her, something was wrong. Maybe something happened to his grandmother. Her thoughts began to run wild. She knew that whatever it was Admiral would need her and she wanted to be there for him. She pulled out her cell phone to call him as she ran back to her car.

"Did you change your mind about coming here?" Kelly turned around to see Admiral standing in the doorway.

That smile, that voice, that man. Relieved that he was okay, Kelly ran up to him and hugged him tightly.

"What's wrong, baby?" Admiral asked. Kelly couldn't answer.

She just hugged him tighter. He hugged her back and told her how much he missed her. He'd missed the way his body felt in her arms. He'd missed the way his insides fluttered every time he was with her. He'd thought about their last encounter and cursed himself for not being able to give her what she needed. He knew it was the wrong time for them. Admiral took in Kelly's trademark scent.

"Come on Kel, talk to me baby?"

She started to giggle. "I feel so silly." she finally said. "I thought something was wrong. I didn't know what to think when I saw the shop all closed up like this."

"Awwww, you were worried about me? Does this mean you care about me?"

Kelly looked into his eyes and replied, "Of course I care about you, you're a good friend to me." She could see the hurt in his eyes when she used the word friend. But how could she tell him how she felt when she didn't even know. She placed her hand on his face and kissed him on the cheek, "Admiral you are very special to me." He led her into the coffee shop. Confused by what she saw. She asked, "Where's everyone at?"

"I closed the shop to spend some time with you alone," he told her.

"That makes no sense, you're losing money."

"You're more important to me than money." he replied.

He leaned in and kissed Kelly softly on her lips. He stopped himself before he got carried away. Kelly didn't know what Admiral was up to all she knew was she liked being the center of attention for once. Admiral led her to a table and began to serve his queen. He'd prepared a wonderful spread for their lunch. Every taste bud in her mouth would be catered to today. They made small talk while they pretended to eat. The sexual tension in the room was thick. In the back of their minds their bodies tangled, submitting to each other's desire. Kelly's words brought Admiral out of his daze. Instead of responding to her question he just smiled.

"You're the best part of my day today." she told Admiral.

"Me…you must've had a bad morning." he said.

Kelly laughed when the images from this morning played in her head. She started telling him about walking in on her husband and his girlfriend/secretary.

"Kelly, I don't think that's funny at all. You need to do something about this."

Admiral moved closer to Kelly.

"I've said it before and I'll keep saying it. I care about you. Because of my feelings I've tried not to tell you how I feel about your situation."

Stroking her face with his hands he continues, "I need to know how you feel about me before I continue."

"Admiral you know that I think that you are a wonderful man. There is something between us I've never felt before. But I have a lot going on in my life right now, things that I'm not ready to sort out. There are things that you don't know about me. And I'm nowhere near ready to sort things out with Sal; I have the girls to think about."

Hearing the words come out of her mouth damn near killed him. She didn't out right say it but he knew she wouldn't leave her husband. Admiral felt foolish for hoping she'd say that she wanted him. In the end she was married and her loyalty laid with her husband regardless of what he's done to her and certainly regardless of how much Admiral loved her. Admiral got up and walked towards the bathroom. Once he was out of Kelly's sight, he leaned against the wall unable to take another step. How did he let things get like this? He'd been able to get his life back together and vowed that he's never to fall in love again. Now here he was all fucked up over someone who couldn't love him back.

Lost in his thoughts he didn't hear Kelly walk up behind him. She stood there watching him, knowing she'd hurt him. But how could she tell Admiral that even though she was married to someone else her heart really belonged him. She wrapped her arms around him and held him. She laid her head on his back. She listened to the rhythm of his heart. She held him tighter. His body relaxed in her arms. She found the courage to tell him how she really felt.

"The only reason why I don't care what he does is because of you." she said.

Still the words didn't really say what she needed to say. It was simple but was it worth the risk. Tears ran down her face. Her heart ached. She knew everything would change but she said it anyway....

"Admiral I love you."

***

Admiral felt her arms slide around his waist. He wanted to pull away but he couldn't. The feeling was so natural. They fit together perfectly. Her body was pressed against his. She was trying to make him feel better and he knew it. He'd heard her say it but did she mean it. Did she really love him? He stood there afraid to face her. *If her words were true and she did feel that way it would show on her face. What if they weren't.* he thought. How could he bear that? Kelly repositioned herself. She was now face to face with Admiral. His eyes darted from hers.

"Baby look at me." said Kelly. "I know the things in my life make no sense. The one thing I do know is how I feel about you. I love you. I need you. I don't know what will happen when we leave here but for now this is all we have."

Of course, he wanted more but in this moment nothing else existed.

"I love you too Kelly."

He kissed her. Her lips felt like putty being molded with each kiss. She felt it began to grow. Admiral hated that his body wouldn't keep his secret. He wanted Kelly more than anything. He pulled her closer, calling her name. Pressing her against the wall he kissed all over her body. Her heart raced. She loved how he made her feel.

"Admiral if we don't stop my buns are gonna be on your menu." Kelly said between breaths. They laughed and kissed and kissed and laughed. "I have to get back to work." she said.

"Come on I'll walk you out." he said stealing one more kiss.

She hugged him goodbye. "The girls have dance practice so I have a couple of hours to come by and help if you need me tomorrow."

He nibbled on her neck as he ran a finger down towards her hot spot… "I need you." he said.

Her hand was drawn to the bulge in his pants.

"Damn." she said.

"I know!" he said. "Go now or I won't be able to stop myself."

"Hmmm really?" teased Kelly.

"Kelllllyyy!" said Admiral.

"Okay, okay. I'm going now. I'll see you tomorrow."

Kelly drove back to work with a smile on her face. Pulling into the parking lot at work her smile disappeared. Once she went inside, she would have to face her problems. She hadn't planned on doing it today but she had to do something.

Sal was in Kelly's office waiting for her.

"What are you doing in here?" she asked.

"I was waiting for you, Kelly can we please talk?" begged Sal.

"Actually, I was thinking the same thing." Kelly replied.

"I'm sorry Kelly but what you saw isn't what you think it was." said Sal.

She felt her blood boiling. She wanted to beat the shit out of his worthless ass but she needed to keep a level head. This conversation was well overdue.

"Sal, I know what I saw. I know you've been seeing her for some time now. I saw you with her on more than one occasion. I watched you fuck away everything we had."

"Kelly I'm sorry," said Sal. "Can we please work this out?"

"Work what out Sal, you're sleeping with your secretary."

He pleaded, "What can I do to make this up to you?"

"Nothing," Kelly said as she sat down to her desk. "Look, Sal the bottom line is we are two different people now. The way we were is gone. We'll never get that back. We need to move on from here."

"That's exactly what I've been trying to say, baby." said Sal. "Good! Since you agree while the girls are at class tomorrow you can move your stuff out. If you need more time you can ask your sister to pick them up. She will need to keep them until you are done."

"WHAT," hollered Sal. "MOVE MY STUFF?"

"Sal, we need time apart to see where things really are between us."

"I'm not going anywhere," Sal roared. "I'm staying with my family. Damn it, Kelly we are going to work this out and that's that!"

"Sal you weren't with your family when you were bangin' your ghetto J-LO so don't worry about us now. I humiliated myself for you. I was willing to share you with that whore. I was so afraid of losing you that I lost me."

She couldn't hold back the tears any longer.

"I lost, Sal. I fought for us when I couldn't fight for myself. Do you know how low I felt? I laid in our bed alone and cried myself to sleep. Alone Sal. I'm not going to do this anymore. When I come home tomorrow evening, I don't want to see a trace of you there. Take all of your shit with you because anything left can be found at the Goodwill."

Sal begged his wife not to do this.

"I didn't do this you did Sal, now live with it."

Seeing that Kelly wasn't changing her mind he decided to talk to her again when they got home. He headed back to his office and replayed her hurtful words over and over again. Was she right? He did do this but were they beyond repair. Only time would tell. He would give Kelly the space she needed and prayed she would come around. The tears streaking his face eased some of the pain in his heart. Everything he'd ever done was for his family and now he'd managed to throw it all away. He hoped they could work this out. His family was all he had.

ONE MORE CHANCE

No Place Like Home

The tension was unbelievably thick that night at home. Sal had tried one more time to talk to his wife. He pleaded his case one more time, but she wasn't hearing it. "I'm sorry Sal you did this. We can sit down and talk to the girls about this after dinner." He never thought it would get this far. Not his babies.

"I'll stay in the guest room. I'll do anything but I can't leave Kelly. I can't leave my family."

"Like I said Sal, we'll talk to the girls after dinner. You know we need space and time."

That was it. There was nothing he could do to change her mind. He'd barely made it thru dinner. Watching the innocent smiles on his girl's faces broke his heart. They sat the girls down and began the dreaded conversation. Kelly started it off.

"Girls you know you daddy and I love you more than anything right." "Yes mommy." they chimed, full of giggles. Sal felt lightheaded.

His head began to ring. His stomach churned. "Your daddy and I have something we want to discuss with you. Go ahead Sal."

"I can't believe this bitch." thought Sal. He began to sweat, his body trembled. How can I do this? Looking at his angels he knew they didn't deserve this. He felt sick to his stomach. He had to pull himself together. If he stayed strong maybe they would take news much better than he had.

"Mommy's right." he said as he reached out to grab Kelly's hand.

Her body tensed up and a fake smile appeared on her face.

"We love you more than anything." he continued. "But mommy and daddy need some time apart."

"Oh, Daddy are you going on another trip?" they asked.

"Something like that honey." The ringing grew louder. "So, daddy is going away for a while, I'm going to stay somewhere else for a lil while."

"NOO, Daddy you live with us. You can't go!"

"I know sweetie but this is what's best and hopefully it will be just for a lil while, you'll still see me every day."

The girls couldn't understand. "Why don't you want to live with us anymore daddy? I promise I'll keep my room clean if you stay." "Me too!" begged the other, "I'll take out the trash."

"My babies." Sal said as he got down on the floor. "Come here." He held them as tight as he could, never wanting to let them go. They cried their little hearts out and he did too. "Daddy are you and mommy getting a divorce? 'Cuz Rashad's mommy and daddy got a divorce when his daddy moved out." Looking Kelly square in the eyes he said, "No honey no one is talking about getting a divorce. Mommy and Daddy keep fighting so we just need to take a time out that's all."

"Are we getting a new daddy? I don't want a new daddy."

Holding back his tears as best he could, "I love you two girls more than anything in my life. I will never leave you. I WILL ALWAYS BE YOUR DADDY YOU HEAR ME. No matter where I am. No matter what I am doing. No matter where I live. I'M YOUR DADDY AND YOU ARE MY DAUGHTERS." They held on to him for dear life.

"Okay ladies you have class in the morning so you need to take a bath and get ready for bed."

"Noo, mommy." they whined.

"It's okay girls. I'll come help you get ready for bed. I'll run you a bubble bath in the big tub and get out all of your bath toys."

"YAAAAYYY!" they sang. "I love you daddy." they yelled back as they ran upstairs.

Up on his feet Sal turned to his wife and asked Kelly, "Are you sure about this, it's not just about us?"

The words were caught in her throat but she nodded "Yes."

"Have you thought about them?" he asked as he pointed towards the ceiling and walked upstairs. As much as it hurt Kelly knew there was no other way. This was bound to happen. She just didn't count on the girls having such a hard time with it. She heard Sal and the girls upstairs having fun. She remembered how much fun they use to have together. *Those times are gone.*" she told herself as she poured a glass of wine.

Kelly felt strange sitting at the table watching the girls eat breakfast with Sal. She'd lost her appetite. She knew she was making the right decision it just hurt like hell. She was in a place where it felt like her life was spinning out of control. She had her secret desires that Sal knew nothing about and now there was Admiral. But that wasn't the root of her problem. Kelly was lost. She wasn't sure who she was anymore and she definitely wasn't sure who her husband was anymore. They both needed to sort out their issues. The girls finished breakfast and went to pack up for camp leaving Kelly and Sal alone at the table. Sal began to clear the dishes. Kelly got up to help him.

"I'd like to talk to you later this evening if your free." she said.

"No Kelly I'm not free or did you forget, its Saturday... family dinner night." he said sarcastically, "Even though you took my family from me."

"Sal, I don't wanna fight but I think there are some things we need to talk about and you're not the only one at fault for our problems."

"So, what are you saying Kelly you don't want me to go?" he asked.

"No, we need to be apart but there are some things we need to talk about. I don't know where we are in our relationship or where it's going."

He couldn't take it anymore. He threw the plates in the sink.

"Damn it, Kelly! When you know what the fuck you want let me know, cuz I damn sure know what it is that I want. I want my family, I want you! Is that too much to ask for?"

"No Sal, it's not but what I don't know is if it's too late for you to ask that of me."

"Kelly, I love you I'm sorry for what I did. I ended it and told her she had to go."

"I love you too Sal but sending her away isn't gonna solve our problems."

"But sending me away will?" he yelled.

"Uggghh!" she screamed, "I can't talk to you when you're like this. I'm leaving to drop the girls off."

Kelly pulled out of the driveway mad as hell. She'd tried talking to Sal, she wanted to come clean. It always had to be his way she thought. She wiped all events of this morning from her thoughts. She dropped the girls off and drove to the coffee shop. Sal sat down on their bed wondering how they'd ended up in another blow up. All they did was fight no matter who was right or who was wrong. He had no other choice but to go. Grabbing his suitcases out of the closet he decided to pack lightly. He was coming back home if it killed him.

ACTS OF BETRAYAL

<u>Chamber of Love</u>

Selena didn't know what was going to happen to her once she stepped foot inside the chamber doors. She still cursed Vixen for betraying her. Selena had taken Vixen as her pet only to earn brownie points with her other sisters. It turned out that Vixen wasn't as half bad. Selena actually grew quite fond of her. She'd made the mistake of getting too close to her. She heard the door slam behind her. The Leaders entered the chamber one by one. Their faces cloaked by the darkness of the dimly lit room. She lowered her head as she fell to her knees. Once she assumed her position of submission the sister took their seats. Selena's body trembled, her heart was beating rapidly. She was about to lose it. She'd never been called before the sisterhood.

"Calm down." she told herself. For what felt like an eternity the room was silent. The only noise was the crackling of the torches burning. With each crackle Selena was closer to snapping. Finally, the meeting was called to order.

"Sister Selena," Supreme called out, "You have been summoned to stand before your Council of Leaders for behaviors that do not promote the best interest of the Sisterhood. Do you understand the charges you face?"

"Yes, Mistress Supreme." Selena said "But I wasn't...."

"SILENCE!" Supreme ordered. "Your foolish ways have put everything we've worked for at risk. You've single handedly jeopardized every member's future here. Did you consider the time and effort that was put into this mission?"

"I didn't do anything wrong." Selena insisted.

Supreme stepped closer. Before she could speak Devine intervened...

"Have you no shame? You violate our most sacred order and you have the nerve to disrespect Supreme here in the chamber."

Vixen stood hidden in the darkness of the corner. She couldn't believe how well her plan had played out.

"Your honorable Supreme and my fellow sisters," said Selena as she rose.

"Please forgive me for any disrespect on my part, it was completely unintentional. Yes, it is true that I allowed my heart to become involved. Our mark responded to my advances in ways I wasn't prepared for. Deep down I know what is in the best interest of the Sisterhood and I would never do anything to ruin that. The Sisterhood is the only family I have." Selena fought back tears at the very thought of losing them. Her voice cracked, "Please give me the chance to make this right."

The Leaders gathered amongst themselves. Their voices conveyed anger, disapproval and finally compliance. Falling back in to their designated places the ladies awaited Supreme's final ruling. She stepped down from her post and approached Selena. The Sisters all gasped. Never before had they seen her do that. They whispered to each other questioning what she was doing.

"SILENCE!" Supreme ordered again this time to her fellow Leaders.

"Selena, I took you in to our order personally. Any act of betrayal is not only an act towards your sister but also a personal act against me. As much as we try to fight it, sometimes our heart leads us. It's up to us if we choose to act on those feelings. Remember our actions are for the greater good. I am giving you one more chance to finish this. Don't make this a decision I will regret."

Supreme adjourned the meeting and was followed out of the chamber by the remaining Leaders. Selena breathed a sigh of relief and was escorted out. Vixen stayed in the corner shocked by what just happened. She'd planned it perfectly. They were supposed to revoke her Sistership. How could Supreme allow her continue on with the task. This was Vixen's way of bringing down the inner circle one sister at a time. They would pay for what they did.

***

Supreme exited the chamber knowing her decision didn't sit well with her Sisters. How could she believe that Selena would do anything to harm their cause on purpose? Supreme turned and watched the girl with the troubled heart being escorted out. Supreme believed in her. In fact, she was the one who found her and introduced her to their world. *"She'll make this right,"* thought Supreme. Just as she turned back around to leave something caught her eye. She saw Vixen tucked in a corner. Chamber meetings were closed. Supreme knew Vixen was up to something and wondered what it was. From the moment Vixen joined Supreme had a bad feeling about her. She just couldn't put her finger on it. She didn't have time to deal with Vixen. Right now, she needed to worry about Selena.

The Sisters grumbled and groaned when they thought they she was out of earshot. They didn't know how far Selena had come.

"Ladies is there a problem with my ruling?" asked Supreme.

"No Mistress." they all sang.

They were pissed with her but they knew better then to actually say anything. She entered her office relieved that she was finally alone. She disrobed and relaxed in her oversized desk chair. She laughed when she thought how an everyday housewife could be the cause such an uproar.

Kelly James wasn't the intended mark that night at Fridays. Supreme was out scouting another potential mark when she walked in. Forgetting why she was there Supreme found herself wanting the beauty at the bar. She watched Kelly. She was getting a lot of attention from the guys. None of it fazed her. They all were given the same response...a hand to the face showing her huge rock, followed by...I'm married, sorry. Kelly never gave in. She was married and happy. Supreme thought it was sickening to be that happy and in love. Here this chick was sitting at the bar looking sexy as hell. She had the whole room after her and she wanted none of it. Supreme was so consumed with this stranger, she let her intended mark walk right out of the restaurant. She watched as Kelly played with her drink.

"Just give me a minute alone with her and it's a wrap." thought Supreme.

Her chance finally came when Kelly made her way to the ladies' room. Supreme was on her heels but she had to play her cards right, she knew nothing about this chick. *"What if she didn't like girls?"* she asked herself. *"Umm who doesn't like me?"* she whispered as she ran her hands over her body before entering the bathroom. The tingling sensation coming from her pants told her it was "SHOWTIME." Kelly's face popped into Supreme's thoughts. She looked so fucking gorgeous that night. She remembered how she had to tell herself to calm down. If she pushed too hard the girl might say no. Ever so helpful Supreme offered to fix her shirt. Of course, she'd let Kelly's top fall down on purpose. She wanted to see her naked from the minute she walked in.

Supreme remembered how soft Kelly's skin felt as she trailed her fingers over her breast. Supreme moaned not realizing that she'd started playing with her own nipples. She remembered how warm Kelly's mouth felt on her. Supreme opened her shirt and imagined Kelly in front of her. She loved how Kelly had straddled her, grinding her wet pussy on her leg. Just thinking about that girl's wet pussy had Supreme ready to explode. She unfastened her pants and inched her fingers towards her moist center. Supreme moaned when her finger tips connected with her clit. Damn she said feeling it throb in her finger tips. She drew circles around it, sliding in her own slick juices. With each pass she went faster and faster. Supreme arched her back and spread her legs as far as they could go. "Fuck!" she yelled out. She only got like this when she thought about Kelly. They were only together that one time. Supreme tried to act like the girl didn't matter to her. She was just another fuck. She'd left a note on the pillow kissing her goodbye. Supreme was almost out the door before she turned back to sneak a peak in to the girl's purse. It was only out of curiosity that she checked out the name and address on her license. She had no need for the girl named Kelly James who lived at 55 Devonshire Lane. Even in the elevator ride down, she knew she'd just told herself the biggest lie. *"I need her, I want her."* Supreme told herself as she approached her climax. She always came hard when she thought about that damn girl.

She regained her composure and prayed Selena wouldn't fuck this situation up any worse than it already was. Supreme had worked too hard to convince the other sister that switching marks was the best thing to do. At the time Kelly wasn't a good prospect. She and her husband didn't have the financials BTB was looking for. To be honest they were nowhere near close. For an average family they were sitting pretty but BTB only played with major ballers. Supreme had used a couple of favors some influential people owed her to build Sal's business. It was still below their standards but Sal had the potential to make this opportunity worthwhile. Supreme couldn't believe she'd done all this just for the chance to get close to Kelly again. If she did all of this how could she fault Selena for getting caught up with Sal. Because of Supreme everyone's hearts were all mixed up....

BLACKOUT

Bottom's Up

Sal's Saturday morning was spent doing whatever his little princesses wanted to do. They didn't have class so they were free. He loved spending time with his babies. He and Kelly hadn't been seeing eye to eye for the past month. It was as if they were in a constant battle. The one thing they'd agreed on was that the fighting had to stop. Until they could get a handle on things outings with the kids would have to be separate and his sister would be the mediator between the two. The family had enrolled in group and individual counseling. While he and Kelly worked out their own individual problems, working on the marriage was out of the question. When they first split Sal stayed at a buddy's house for a few days. His buddy's wife was out of town so it was like a boy's club hangout. All of that changed when the wife came back in to town.

Against his friend wishes, Sal checked in to a hotel suite until things got sorted out. The hotel was nice and the girls loved coming over, so it didn't hurt as much. One night sitting in his room all alone Sal began to miss his family. He missed his wife. He talked to her picture every night, begging her to forgive him. Tonight was harder than the others. He was at his breaking point. He just wanted to dull the pain. After he dropped the girls off to his sister Sal went to the liquor store. He grabbed all the fire he could carry out. Alone in his room he downed one drink after the other. He staggered from room to room, talking to his pretend wife. He practiced over and over what he would say to her if given another chance. Sal continued to drink his Grey Goose and lime juice concoction as if it were water.

He babbled uncontrollably while he staggered to the bedroom. His head hit the pillow and Sal prayed for sleep to overtake him. He closed his eyes but all he could see was his beautiful wife. Sal reached for his cell phone. She hadn't been at work all week. Even if she didn't speak to him seeing her let him know she was okay. He dialed the number not expecting her to answer. He just wanted to hear her voice on the outgoing message. Hello the sleepy voice on the other end answered.

"HEEYYYYY BABBBEE!" Sal crooned in to the phone.

"Sal is that you." she said. "Yes BABEE. Is something wrong?" she panicked.

"No BABEEE, I'm OKAAYY I was just thinking about you. I miss you. I miss u Kelly."

Sal heard her rustling around in the sheets. Thinking back to when she would sleep naked next to him made his dick ache. She would wiggle her ass back towards him. Once she was close enough to rest her ass on his dick, she would give him a little grind. He hadn't felt her softness in months.

"I want you." Kelly, he said.

"Look Sal."

"No!" he interrupted. "I've said it over and over I was wrong. What happened between me and her never should've happened. It's the only thing I've ever done in my life that I regretted other than hurting you. You're my life Kelly. Even though we are apart it hasn't changed. I would give my life if it would make all of this shit go away."

"Sal, please stop." she begged him.

He heard her crying. He hated it when she cried. "Baby I need you. Do you need me?" he asked.

"Yes." she said in between sobs.

"Do you still love me?" he asked her.

"Yes baby I love you."

"Good cause I love you too Kelly."

It hurt her to hear those words.

"Are you alone?" he asked her. The girls were supposed to be spending the night over his sister's house so he knew she was.

"Yes." she replied.

"I want to see you baby." he whispered. "Can I see you?"

"Yes baby." she whispered. She wanted him bad.

"You will have to come to the hotel baby. I can't drive I've been drinking."

"It's okay I'm coming baby, I've missed you so much." she told him.

His heart began to heal hearing those words. "I'm calling down to the front desk so they can give you a key. I'm gonna hop in the shower so I can be fresh for you baby. Imma tell em my wife is coming to see me."

She laughed hearing how silly he sounded. "I love you." she told him.

"I love you too Kelly."

Sal hung up the phone and called the front desk. "Hi this is Mr. James in Room 407. My wife is on her way over and I'm about to hop in the shower. When she arrives can you please give her a room key? I don't want her waiting for me outside if I'm in the shower."

"Certainly Mr. James. Is there anything else I can do for you tonight sir?"

"No thank you." Sal replied.

He sat up and reached for the cup he'd left on the table next to the bed. *"I need a drink to celebrate."* he told himself as he drained the contents. He hopped into the shower to cleanse his body. He had to be right for her. He was about to die without her. Smiling he stepped out of the shower. Hoping she was there he called out for her. The silence told him she wasn't there yet. *"Damn what's taking her so long?"* He'd purposely chosen a hotel close to the house incase anything happened and they needed him. Sal dried off and laid in the bed waiting for his love. His head started to spin. "Maybe I over did it." said Sal. *"I should rest my eyes til she gets here."* he told himself. *"Just for a lil bit."* he said before he blacked out.

She'd arrived at the front desk wearing nothing but an overcoat and 6-inch heels. Her makeup was flawless and her hair pulled tightly in a ponytail that hung down her back. Considering he'd only given her a few minutes to get ready, she was on point.

"May I help you?" the attendant at the front desk asked her.

"Yes, I'm here to see Sal James." she informed him as she leaned forward slightly. Her breast peaked out of her coat. It didn't hurt to give him a sneak peek at what he could never get. The attendant took one look at her and knew what was up. He handed her the room key.

With a wink he told her, "Have a good night."

She blew him a kiss as he directed her towards Sal's room. Using the key, she opened the door and called out… "HONEY I'm home!"

He didn't answer.

"Sal are you here?" she called out. She looked in the bedroom only to find him passed out naked. Seeing his naked body excited her. "Sal, Sal." she said trying to wake him. She sat next to him on the bed. "Sal are you going to wake up?"

She placed her hand on his chest. He moaned. She leaned over and started kissing him on his chest. He moaned louder. She looked and saw his dick starting to grow. Her mouth watered. She missed her old friend. She stood up and removed her overcoat. She grabbed his dick causing Sal to groan. He wanted her. She swallowed his dick in her juicy mouth. She worked his dick until her jaws were sore. She couldn't believe he hadn't opened his eyes. At first, she thought he was sleep. Once she placed her mouth on his she realized Sal was wasted. This made it even better for her. She reached for her cell phone. The camera on it was unbelievable. It was time for a photo shoot.

She fucked Sal every way possible. In his drunken stupor all he could do was lay there and grunt and groan. She didn't care as long as his dick stayed hard. She rode herself into an orgasm.

He mumbled "Umm Kelly baby you feel so good."

"The nerve of this bastard!" she said. She continued to fuck him. She had to get what she came for. She circled her hips as she tightened the walls of her pussy.

"UGGHH!" said managed to get out. She started talking shit. "You like this pussy daddy?"

Sal was reduced to caveman like responses. He continued to grunt and groan. She felt his body tense up. She slammed her pussy down on his dick harder and harder. His toes curled. The wave was starting from down below. She made his body give her what she wanted. She felt him shooting off deep in to her pussy. She climbed off his satisfied with her efforts. She put her coat back on and left Sal laying there balled up like a baby.

His head told the tale of one too many when he woke up the next morning. Everything spun so fast when he tried to life his head off of the pillow. He had the vague recollection of making love to Kelly. Was it true, had she been there?

"Fuck." he said as he tried to recall the events of the night before. He had to blame it on the Goose because he couldn't remember shit after he cracked that bottle. Sal was a light weight but his frustrations had caused him to drain the bottle. He grabbed his floppy member and looked at the stains of last night. He had traces of sex smeared all over it. He grabbed his phone to call Kelly to make sure she'd made it home safely when he saw the last number dialed. He didn't care about his headache anymore. When he saw the name of the last person, he called the screaming wouldn't end. The screen read….. SELENA ALVAREZ

***

"It had to be a dream," thought Sal. "There's no way I would've called Selena." His mind raced back and forth. Yeah, it was a dream he kept trying to convince himself. He'd gotten drunk and must've played with his dick a little too much. That would explain the dried up cum on it. He felt a little better with his story as he left the hotel.

"Good morning, Mr. James," said the desk clerk, "I see you're headed to work. I'm headed home myself."

"Good morning, Mike," said Sal.

"After a night like last night, I bet it is for you." said Mike.

"A night like last night." said Sal. "What do you mean by that?" he asked.

"Yeah, yeah come on." said Mike as he nudges Sal. "Mr. James you've been stayin' here for what now a month and I haven't seen you with any visitors come thru here until that hottie showed up here last night. Man, I know she ain't have nuffin' on under that lil coat of hers."

"What HOTTIE," questioned Sal,"Whaaat Sal, "Whaaat did she look like?"

Mike eyed Sal's wedding band. He laughed and said "OHHH okay Mr. James I got you! What Latin hottie? I get what you sayin'. Don't worry it's our lil secret." Mike dapped Sal bye and headed to his car.

Sal just stood there. He didn't want to go to work. He couldn't face Kelly and he couldn't stand to look at Selena. He couldn't go home. He had nowhere to go. He'd never felt so trapped in his life. Every time he tried to do what was right it always got messed up in the end. Sal was reaching his boiling point. Tired of being a victim he started putting his own plan together. Selena watched Kelly at work, shooting her dirty looks whenever she could. She played Sal last night but it wasn't enough. He still wanted his wife. After all the Selena had done to make him fall in love with her it wasn't enough. Kelly still was the love of his life. Kelly did no wrong in his eyes. She didn't want to do it but it was the only way he would see. She picked up the phone and called an old friend.

"Hello." the voice answered on the other end of the phone.

"Hi." Selena coo'ed in to his ear.

"Well I'll be damned," he said. "If it isn't my number one girl."

"Aww big boy." said Selena. "Your number one girl huh?"

"No one's as good as you baby girl." he told her.

"Well what would you do for your number one girl?" she asked.

"Whatever my number one needs, my number one gets." Selena smiled and brought her naughty friend up to speed.

CONFESSIONS

Out In The Open

Selena laid in bed feeling like a child waiting for Christmas morning. Tomorrow she would finally get to open her presents. She had everything all planned out. Finally she would get Sal back. She knew that he sisters would hate her for what she was about to do. But Selena knew that the way BTB lived their lives wasn't for her anymore. She wanted what everyone else had. She wanted a family of her own. She had a smile on her face as she drifted off to sleep.

Since Sal wouldn't return any of her calls, she had to have this conversation with him at work. She decided not to wear anything to sexy. Sal had to take her seriously. She didn't want him to think she was coming on to strong. So, she just had to let the facts speak for itself. Sal walked in to work feeling good for the first time in a long while. He'd taken the first step in getting his family back and he would keep on trying until things were finally the way they were supposed to be. His morning was ruined when he walked in to the office and saw Selena waiting for him.

"What are you doing in here?" he asked her. "I want you out of my office."

Selena quickly explained her reason for coming to him. "Sal you know how much I care about you. I know right now you don't want anything to do with me because you're trying to get back with Kelly." said Selena.

"What do you know?" he said sarcastically.

"I know I hate watching how she treats you. She acts like she's the victim when in fact she's no better than you. I mean really who is she to punish you when she's out doing the same thing. Sal, I love you and I know at one point you loved me."

"I LOVE MY WIFE!" yelled Sal.

"But does she love you?" asked Selena. "Look baby I never wanted things to end up like this. I don't want to show you this but this is the only way I can prove how much I really do care about you." Selena handed Sal the envelope containing pictures. She added some new pictures to the ones she was given by BTB plus the ones she had her friend take. "Baby I'm putting everything on the line for you. You know I'm here for you no matter what." Selena kissed him on the cheek and left Sal alone in his office. She would wait and let her plan go to work.

Kelly walked into the building determined to have the long overdue conversation with Sal. She lost her nerve last night. She thought about how good it felt to be in her husband's arms last night. For a moment it felt like things were back to normal. She put those thoughts out of her head and focused on what she needed to do. She went straight to Sal's office.

"Good morning." she said when she saw him sitting at his desk.

Sal just looked up at her. He gave her an evil look, sending chills up Kelly's spine.

"He's mad about last night." she told herself. "The girls really enjoyed having you over last night. I hope you come over again." she told him.

"I always enjoy my daughters Kelly." he said.

"Well like I said you can come over anytime. I mean it."

"That's nice of you," he said. "But, why are you here?" he asked.

Kelly was surprised by his sudden change in attitude. The tension was thick.

"Is something bothering you?" she asked.

"Nah, I'm good," he said. "How about you?"

"Well I actually have some things I want to discuss with you." said Kelly. "I wanted to sit down with you last night, but we kind of got caught up huh?"

Sal just stared at her. *"Just keep talking."* she told herself.

"I liked having you there, too. It felt like old times. Before all this mess got started. I wanted to tell you that you're not the only one to blame in all of this mess. I haven't been upfront with you and I've treated you badly during this whole ordeal."

"So, what the fuck are you saying Kelly?" asked Sal.

"Did I do something wrong? I don't understand where all this is coming from." she said.

"Nah, it's all good." Kelly tried to explain, "Look Sal I've done some things I'm not proud of. I let myself get mixed up with some people."

Sal laughed. "You're so full of shit!" he said.

"Excuse me?" Kelly asked.

"You heard what the fuck I said. For months you've made me feel like shit for cheating on you. You kicked me out of the home that I pay for. You took my girls away from me. And you wanna stand here all high and mighty because your nasty ass is done doing your dirt? Get the fuck outta here with that bullshit."

"Sal what are talking about? I came to you to see if we could work things out." cried Kelly.

"You wanna work things out huh?" said Sal as he walked from behind his desk.

"Yes!" Kelly said through her tears. "I want to try for our family. Sal I was a horrible person. I know we both did things that we regret but we can't change that. I just want to get everything out in the open and move on from here." she said.

"Oh, don't worry." said Sal. "EVERYTHING is out in the open. Don't worry you're pretty little heart. And things will be moving on."

Kelly smiled.

"I know everything Kelly!" he said as he flung the contents of the envelope at her.

Kelly watched as all of her indiscretions fell to the floor.

"I want your nasty ass outta my face. As a matter of fact, I want you and ALLL of you shit outta my house and my lawyer will contact you in regards to the girls…I'm filing for FULL custody. It's time to tell my girls DADDY'S HOME. I don't ever want to see your trifling face again…GET THE FUCK OUTTA MY OFFICE AND DON'T EVER COME BACK!"

Kelly grabbed the photos and quickly left Sal's office. She couldn't understand who in the group had set her up like this. And what they were to gain by ruining her family. Just as she reached her office, she found Selena standing outside her door. Selena handed Kelly a box, "Here bitch I think you'll need this." she said with a smirk plastered on her face. "Bye, bye baby."

Kelly Lunged for Selena, "YOU NO GOOD TRIFLIN HOME WRECKIN' LIL BITCH! IT WAS YOU!! YOU PLANNED THIS ALL ALONG!"

Selena laughed "You're so stupid. Everyone thought Supreme was wrong when she picked you. She was right you were an easy mark but I didn't think you were this easy. Don't worry sis, I'll take good care of him." Selena said as she showed her tattoo to Kelly. "I believe this is yours." She handed Kelly the box once again. "Now get the fuck out!"

***

"This can't real." she told herself. *"How can any of this be happening?"* Kelly tried to steady herself before her everything around her went black. She heard them calling her name. "Is she gonna be alright?" the other voice asked.

"Get her husband, Call 911! Kelly, Kelly honey are you okay?" Jacob called out to her. She opened her eyes and saw all of the faces crowed around her. "Kelly what happened?" asked Jacob.

"I guess I fainted. I didn't have breakfast this morning so I'm just a little weak Kelly?" said as she tried to get up.

"Where's Sal? Don't move Kelly. Did someone go get Sal?" Jacob asked.

"He's on a conference call. He said he'll be out when he's done." one of the employees said.

"No, I'm fine." Kelly said as she eased her way up from the floor. "Don't bother him. Jacob I'm sorry for any trouble caused. I'm going to go ahead and leave."

Jacob offered to walk Kelly out. He tried to hide how disgusted he was with Sal. He warned him in the beginning not to let things get out of control. Jacob walked Kelly all the way to her car. He ignored Kelly's protest. "I just want to make sure you are okay before you leave. I don't know what's going on and I don't care to know. All I know is two people I care about are having problems. You've always been good to me Kelly. And I promised myself I would always be there for whatever you needed. You have my number if you can't reach me you know Sharon will. I swear that woman must have a GPS lock on me."

Kelly laughed. "And that's why you love your wife she never lets you get lost."

"Truth be told Kelly," said Jacob, "I'd be lost without her. I mean it whatever you and the girls need whether it be an ear to listen, a shoulder to cry on or a place to stay we're here for you."

Kelly hugged her dear friend and thanked him one more time. He watched her get in the car and prayed she would be alright. Once she was out of his view, he stormed back in to the building to rip Sal a new one and fire that tramp he had for a secretary.

Kelly drove in circles. She didn't want to go to the place her heart kept steering her towards. "Not this time." she said out loud. "I have to do this on my own. I can't drag him back in to this." With nowhere else to go she drove home. Kelly looked at her watch. She had a few hours before the girls were to be picked up. *"Good I can go lay down for a while."*

Kelly grabbed her things and went to go inside. She fumbled with her keys. She wasn't in the mood. She tried to force the key in to the lock but it wouldn't work. She went around to the back of the house. She tried the back door. But her key wouldn't work their either. "SON OF A BITCH!" screamed Kelly. "I can't believe he changed the fucking locks!" She cried as she pulled out of the driveway. She drove in circles. She kept telling herself not to go to him not matter how much she needed him. Kelly pulled into a gas station to fill up her near empty tank. Not one for carrying cash she grabbed one of her bank cards. It declined the charge when she swiped it.

"The strip must be bad." So, she tried another one and got the same result. She went inside of the station and spoke to the attendant. "Excuse me, I don't think your machine is working properly. I tried to swipe my cards but it won't work." said Kelly.

The young attendant took Kelly's card and swiped it on her terminal..."No ma'am our machines work just fine...your cards been declined."

"That's crazy!" said Kelly. "I just used this card earlier."

"Whatever lady." said the attendant. "Do you have any money to pay for your gas? No, I don't." Kelly said as she stormed off. No home, no money she had no other choice. She went to him.

Her car sputtered when she hit his block. She'd made it there on a wing and a prayer. Now if only she could bring herself to face him. She wanted to be certain of the things in her life before she saw him again. Admiral spotted her car the minute she pulled up. They'd agreed that she needed space. Her world was too confusing right now. She must be here about the phone call thought Admiral. He was still a little pissed off about it but what could he do about it. The situation was done and over with. Kelly walked in to the shop with a troubled look on her face.

Admiral told himself not to get involved with any of it. She came in and sat at one of the tables in the corner. *"Fuck it."* he said as he grabbed a muffin and poured her a cup of tea. Who was he really kidding, he was already involved.

"Hey Kelly." said when Admiral sat down to the table. He handed her the muffin and cup of tea.

"You didn't have to." said Kelly.

"It's cool." said Admiral. "You look like you had a rough morning."

Kelly burst in to tears. He moved next to her.

"What's wrong?" he asked.

"Everything!" cried Kelly. "Everything is all messed up. All I wanted to do was make things better."

"What's all messed up?" asked Admiral.

Kelly reached down and pulled the envelope out of her purse. "This." she said as she handed him the envelope.

"I tried to patch things up with Sal and things were going good until this morning when he confronted me with those. He kicked me out of the house and froze all of our accounts. He told me I would hear from his lawyer." Kelly buried her face in Admirals chest and sobbed. "He wants to take my babies from me Admiral. I can't lose my babies."

He opened the envelope and looked at the pictures. They were shots of Kelly engaged in a sexual act. The images were a little grainy but the look of pleasure on her face was clear. Admiral tried to focus on comforting Kelly but the images stirred up his desire.

"Kelly you're beautiful." said Admiral.

Kelly laughed through her tears. "Is that what you think or is that what HE really thinks?" said Kelly as she pointed to him member. "Seems he wants to join the conversation."

"I'm sorry Kelly." said Admiral. "I don't know what I was thinking."

"Umm, I think I have an idea." said Kelly. "Just look at the rest of the photos. I don't think you'll like what you see." she warned him.

Admiral scrolled through until his face stared back at him. He was standing outside of the coffee shop. He remembered it clearly. Standing outside, saying goodbye to her. Promising to be the friend she always needed. He was letting her walk out of his life but he wanted to kiss her just one more time. He thought the moment was private. He didn't plan on anyone watching in the shadows.

"That's what his ass meant." said Admiral.

"Who meant what?" asked Kelly.

"Sal called me early this morning to tell me that our deal was off. He wouldn't be backing my expansion of the coffee shop." said Admiral. "When I asked why he said that he knew my secret and I better pray that he didn't have my license and permits revoked. I thought he was just trying to find a way to back out of our contract. But why would he go through all this trouble. He could've come and talked to me man to man."

"He didn't HIS BITCH, Selena did this." said Kelly. "Sal wanted to work things out between us. Selena couldn't accept that and wanted him back. The worst part is they played me all along."

"THEY who is THEY?" he asked.

Kelly filled Admiral in on the incident with Selena.

"So, you're telling me Supreme and Selena are in the same group that you were involved in."

"Yes, they are. And I'm afraid of what's gonna happen next." she said.

Admiral was quiet for a moment. "They never should've fucked with you Kelly and they damn sure shouldn't have fucked wit me. Come on baby get your things I'm taking you home."

"Wait," said Kelly. "I can't go, remember he locked me out." Admiral looked at her and said, "Baby you're going home with me!"

"Admiral I'm not so sure about this," said Kelly. "I shouldn't be here."

"Where else are you gonna go?" Admiral asked. "You can't go home; do you have any family here?"

"Other than Sal's sister, I don't. All my of family's down south. But Sal's partner did say I could come stay with his family."

"Baby it's your choice. I don't want to tell you what to do, but you're free to stay here." said Admiral. "I'll make up the guest room for you or you can sleep in my bed and I'll sleep in there. I don't care where you sleep just as long as you're here and I know you're safe."

Kelly didn't want to admit that she really didn't want to stay at Jacob's. Why did he always have to be right?

"Fine I'll stay but I need to make a call first." Admiral set the guest room up for Kelly while she made her call.

"Hey Kell what's up?"

"Kim, I need you to do me a big favor." said Kelly.

"What is it?" Kim inquired.

"It is possible for you to pick the girls up and let them stay with you?" asked Kelly. "Sal changed the locks and froze me out of our bank accounts."

"HE DID WHAT???? Mommy and Daddy raised him better than that. I know the two of y'all had problems but that ain't no reason for any of this bullshit. You want me to call him and talk some sense in to him?" asked Kim.

"No Kim, I just want the girls to be kept out of this as much as possible." Kelly thanked her sister in law before ending their call.

"No problem Kelly, I'll do whatever I can for you guys." said Kim.

Kim dialed Sal's number as fast as her fingers could dial. "Hey Sis." he answered.

"Don't you hey sis me! I heard what you did. How could you be such an ass?" Kim said. Sal didn't care. "Weren't you the one sleeping with your secretary?" Kim asked. "Look," she continued before he could respond." I try to stay out of your personal stuff. But this has been going on for far too long. You need to stop before you lose her, Sal. Everything you built you've had Kelly behind you supporting you 100%. No matter what has happened you two need to talk and get this resolved."

"I have NOTHING to say to that bitch." Sal yelled into the phone. "Anything she needs to say, she can say it to my lawyer."

Kim sat the phone in her lap. *"Lord, PLEASE don't let me snap on this fool."* She prayed silently. Putting the phone back to her ear she pleaded, "Brother I know you're in your feelings right now and don't mean it. Just give it some time."

"KIM HAVE YOU BEEN LISTENING TO ANYTHING I'VE TOLD YOU?" questioned Sal. "She's out fucking another man and doing all kinds of nasty shit with those women. You should've seen the pictures. It disgusted me to see my wife, the mother of my daughters like that. I just hope it was worth it because when I'm finished with her ass, she'll damn sure regret what she did to me and my girls."

Kim was displeased with the way her brother chose to handle the situation. "Sal, I don't know what to say to get through to you. Kelly only did what you did to her. So, don't sit here and act all high and mighty. Now as far as the girls, she's done nothing but be a DAMN good mother to them. Now Imma warn you--- Be an ass if you want to. Try to take those girls from Kelly and I'll be by her side fighting you the whole way. Remember you're not the only one with money!"

"Kim that's bullshit and you know it you're my sister!" Sal fired back. "You're supposed to have my back and support me no matter what."

"Baby bro," said Kim. "The day you said I do Kelly and the girls became your family. I'm only here to support you as a whole. Without her you're nothing. I just hope you see it before it's too late. Now with that being said, the girls will stay with me until this mess gets sorted out. They don't need to be around any of this mess."

"CLICK." Sal sat listening to the dial tone. *"I don't need her,"* Sal thought out loud.

"You're right babe,.," Selena replied walking in to his office as if he was talking to her. "I wish you would see that I'm all you need."

Sal rested his head in his hands. *"When will it end?"* he thought to himself. "Selena, I told you before. We're not like that anymore."

"I know but I just can't leave you all alone right now in your time of need." replied Selena. "I don't care how much you say you don't want me, I just can't turn my back and walk away because things get a little rough." Selena moved behind Sal's chair. She started massaging his shoulders. "I can feel how tense you are. Sal you got all of that stress weighing down on you. You're trying to take care of everyone else but who's taking care of you baby?" Selena asked as she dipped her fingers under the loosened collar of Sal's shirt. "You're a dayum good man Sal. You work hard to take care of your family and they turn their back on you. They need to appreciate you more." Selena tried to unbutton Sal's shirt. His hands stopped her. "Relax." she laughed. "I'm just trying to ease some of your tension away." Selena pulled his head back. Her voice softened, "Close your eyes and let me help you." She rubbed his temples. Sal wanted to make her stop but the way she worked her hands was like magic. Selena watched the rise and fall of his chest began to even out. *"Finally, he's giving in."* She thought. "If you were my man, I would appreciate you the way you deserve."

She eased her way back down Sal's shirt. "You're such a big strong man." Selena said, trailing her fingers over his chest. "A sexy man like yourself needs to be worshipped." Selena whispered in his ear while she tweaked his nipple. "You need a good woman to do that for you baby. You don't need a woman that will cause you any stress, no pain, somebody that you can trust." Selena kissed Sal on his neck. His manhood stirred. Sal moaned. "A good woman knows where all her man's spots are." She nibbled on Sal's ear. "Don't you want a good woman baby?" Selena asked. Sal shifted in his chair. "Let me be your woman Sal." Selena slid around the front of him. She climbed on Sal's lap and pressed her sex against his throbbing pole.

Sal looked up at Selena. She was beautiful. Selena loved to take care of him and he could talk to her for hours. Sal loved how she made him feel in and out of the bedroom. *"Maybe there could be something between us."* he thought. Sal grabbed her hips, grinding deeper against her heat.

"Can I be your woman?" she whispered.

Sal kissed Selena. "Yes." he replied. Selena climbed down off Sal's lap. "Take me home daddy." she said.

Sal thought about it for a moment. Home. Home was what he shared with his family, his daughters and his wife. But his wife threw it all away fucking around behind his back. Sal didn't know what hurt him the most, the image of her having sex with those women or Admiral fucking what was once his. Sal packed up for the day and left the office with the one woman left standing in his corner.

***

Kelly walked around Admiral's condo. For a bachelor he had great taste. Kelly wondered if someone helped him decorate his condo. She wondered if that someone was a woman. *"Now's not the time to be jealous, you've got other problems."* Kelly told herself.

"Admiral" Kelly called out.

"I'm in here sweetie." he said.

Kelly found him sitting behind a desk. It looked like he was looking over some paperwork. "You never stop do you?" she joked.

"For you I will. Come sit down over here." he said to Kelly.

"There's nowhere to sit." Kelly told Admiral.

"I guess you didn't see this STRONG lap over here waiting for you." he replied.

"I don't know about all of that." Kelly shook her head. "I think I'll pass and just stand."

Admiral stared at Kelly. She crossed her arms and pretended to be in a standoff with him. Admiral flashed her a cocky smile and untied his locs.

"It's not gonna work," she told him.

"Are you sure you don't wanna sit down, I make a good chair?" teased Admiral.

"As much as I want to, I can't. I'm here in your home because of this mess between me and Sal. Now I don't have a home for me and my babies to go."

Kelly started to cry. Admiral pulled her down in to his lap.

"Don't cry Kelly. You know I will do whatever you need me to do for you and your girls. You're welcome to bring them here and I'll stay at the shop in the back room or I'll get a hotel room for you guys. Whatever you want me to do I'll do it." he pleaded. "Just don't cry baby."

He held her tight. Her tense body began to relax against his. Admiral picked her up and carried her into his bedroom. He laid her on the bed. When he turned to leave Kelly grabbed his arm and said, "Don't leave me."

Looking down at her sad puppy dog eyes and said, "Kelly if I get in the bed with you, I might not be able to stop myself. I want to respect your space right now but everything in me wants to kiss you all over and make things better for you."

Kelly looked at Admiral. His locs hung down around his face as he leaned over to stroke hers. Kelly placed her hands-on top of his.

"Please don't leave me."

"Are you sure about this?" Admiral asked.

Kelly trailed her fingers over his hands and closed her eyes. He was afraid to move. He wanted her bad. *"But is this the right time?"* Admiral asked himself. Admiral looked at the door and then looked at Kelly. Sure, about his decision. Admiral climbed into bed and laid behind Kelly. *"Just hold her."* he told himself. Admiral positioned himself next to Kelly and tried not to give in to his growing desire for her. Kelly's heaving chest rested against his. Admiral's fingers soothed the loose stands of Kelly's hair. She closed her eyes. Being with Admiral freed her mind and soul. All she needed him to free her body. He kissed her eyelids.

"Beautiful." he said "I've waited for the right moment to be with you. I've waited for you to come to me."

Kelly opened her eyes. "I'm here." she replied.

"Baby you're here with me, but you still haven't resolved your home situation." Admiral saw the tears welling in her eyes. "No baby. No more tears. You've cried enough." he told her. "It's time for you to be strong. You need to stand up and fight back, okay?"

Kelly shook her head "Yes."

He wiped away her tears," Don't think that I don't want you. Because that's the furthest thing from the truth." He said pushing his evidence against Kelly. "Tomorrow we will talk about what you want to do with your situation. Right now, I just want to lay here with you in my arms."

Kelly wanted to tell Admiral to go to hell but she knew he was right. She needed to be sure of her next move before things went any further between the two of them. That and the fact that laying in Admiral's arms felt too damn good. Before long Kelly drifted off to sleep. Admiral eased his way out of bed. He went back to his office to finish the call he started earlier.

"Sorry about that." he spoke into the phone. "She was looking for me so I had to end our conversation."

Laughter came from the other end of the phone.

"Baby you should know by now I'd wait for you any day."

"I do baby girl, I do." Admiral replied. "Now where did were leave off at?" he asked.

"Are you sure you wanna go there again?" she questioned.

Admiral looked at the lump still trapped under his pants. "Yeah I'm sure." he said.

"Babe, you know once I start. There's no turning back. Can you live with the end results?" she asked. "I know what I want." he told her. "Somehow, I knew you would say that," Savannah sighed into the phone. "I just hope it's worth it."

WAVING THE WHITE FLAG

Hitting Below the Belt

The next morning Admiral watched the intense fight taking place under his sheets. "I don't think you're winning." he laughed. Kelly threw off the sheets.

"What's that supposed to mean?" she snapped back.

Seeing the crossed look on her face, Admiral decided to go easy on her. Waving the napkin in his hand, "I come in peace…please accept this delicious meal prepared especially for you, all mighty blanket slayer." he joked.

"Since you came bearing gifts, I guess I can spare your blankets from certain death." Kelly replied. After finishing breakfast, she showered and changed into some of Admiral's workout clothes. Standing there swimming in his clothes Kelly told him, "We have to stop past my house to see if I can get any of my clothes."

Admiral shook his head "I don't know how well that's gonna turn out. I'd rather take you shopping for whatever you need."

"No" replied Kelly, " You were right. It's time for me to fight back."

Kelly had a new sense of determination. She wasn't going to let Sal boss her around anymore. "Besides sooner or later this get up is bound to fall off of me."

Not one to argue Admiral asked, "Well can I at least drive you?"

"Sure, why not...I may actually need you." Kelly joked.

When she pulled up to the home she once shared with her husband, Kelly gathered her nerves.

"Everything is gonna be okay babe. I told you before we don't have to do this."

"Admiral, I HAVE to do this if I'm going to move on in my life." Kelly said. "I'm not thrilled about it. I just know it has to be done."

He didn't like it, but Kelly was right. *"It has to be done."* he told himself.

"I'll be right her waiting for you. But if you need me."

Kelly interrupted him, "I know you have my back if I need it. I can't thank you enough for being there for me."

Kelly took one last deep breath before heading up the walkway to her old life. She rang the doorbell and prepared herself for whatever Sal tried to come at her with. Nothing could have prepared her for what happened next.

"Well look who it is at MY door this time of morning." Selena chimed. Her face full of victory. Kelly wanted to jump on Selena and whoop that conniving slut for being in her house.

Kelly began to speak, " What...."

"What am I doing here? Oh, honey I'm here taking care of YOUR husband. I'm enjoying the life that I took from you." Selena continued, "Don't tell me you came to beg for him to take you back, because last night he was begging me not to stop. I doubt you can top that Martha Stewart."

Kelly turned to look at Admiral. He read the look on her face loud and clear. "I knew this was a bad idea." he whispered. He raced to Kelly's side.

"Is there a problem here ladies?" he asked.

"How cute you brought along your boy toy." Selena teased.

"Selena, I have nothing to discuss with you and could care less that you are playing house. Where's Sal?" asked Kelly.

Selena turned and called out "Honey something is at the door for you."

Sal came to the door smiling "What is it honey?" His smile left his face the instant he saw their faces. "WHAT THE FUCK ARE YOU DOING HERE?" Sal yelled.

"I told her not to even think about begging you to take her back baby. After last night you're mine...all mine." Selena giggled.

"I'm not here for either one of you. I'm here for my things." Kelly said.

"Anything here that belongs to you is trash, just like you," Sal sneered.

"Kelly I've heard enough." Admiral couldn't hold back any longer. "I know I promised you that I would let you handle the situation, but I'm not going to let this lame ass dynamic duo disrespect you." Sal took a step towards Admiral. Admiral gave Sal a quick flex. "Look here's how it's going down. Kelly's going in the house you share with HER and she going to get her things. What she can't take with her in this trip will be removed by the service I am sending. They will come in and pack up everything belonging to her and anything stated on the list SHE sends with them." Admiral continued, "If any of her property is damaged...even a scratch..." Admiral looked the two up and down.

Before Admiral could finish his sentence, Sal said, "Selena let her get whatever the hell she wants. As soon as she's gone, we can get back to doing what we do."

Kelly laughed at Sal's weak attempt to get back at her. "I'm sure whatever you do Sal, it won't be long." Kelly snickered.

She knew it was wrong but she had to get in one last jab. Kelly grabbed as many of her things that she and Admiral could carry. She informed Sal that she would contact the movers within the hour to collect the rest of her things.

"Sal let's keep this civilized. It's clear that this marriage is over and we both are moving our separate ways. Even through all of the pain, lies and humiliation we loved each other at some point. I will always love and respect you for being the father of my kids. I hope you have the decency to do the same for me." Kelly extended her hand to Sal.

"I can't believe you Kelly. How low can you be?" asked Selena.

"Enough!!!" barked Sal. He placed his hand in Kelly's. He knew his wife better than anyone. She'd never do anything to intentionally hurt him. She'd always put her family's needs before her own without ever being asked to do so. It just was how Kelly was. He knew her heart and it was pure.

Selena saw the look in Sal's eyes. Seeing the tension in his body release when he made contact with Kelly pissed her off. How could this woman still have such a hold over him? Selena stormed off recoiling for now. One thing for certain, Sal was going to pay for chastising her.

Ignoring the pounding of Selena's feet as she stomped her way upstairs Sal continued. "Kelly, your things will be here ready to be picked up whenever you are."

After a small exchange of words, they said goodbye. Sal closed the door knowing all hell was about to break loose behind it. Thankful for the sounds of the shower running from upstairs, Sal walked to the bar and poured himself a shot of Henny. He needed to feel the slow burn before he took on this demon woman. Sal turned to find Selena wearing nothing but her birthday suit.

"Selena I'm not pleased with the way you acted earlier." he said. "I'm sorry baby," she pouted. "I get so furious when SHE is around you." Selena started her water display. I know how much she hurt you with all of her cheating and lies. I just don't trust her so I can't be as forgiving to her as you are."

"I don't forgive her for shit!" Sal insisted. His rage started to return.

"Just seeing you touch her after she did all those nasty things made me think that you were falling for her again. I couldn't sit by and let her hurt you again." Selena looked him in the eye and vowed, "I'll hurt her before I let her hurt you again."

"I don't know if it's the liquor or all the blood being drained to down below my belt but I'm feelin it!" Sal thought to himself. *"More like feelin her."* He smiled. Sal pulled Selena to him and began to kiss her tears away. Selena moaned when his lips connected with the salty trails of her emotions.

"No one can make me feel the way you do Sal. I'm yours forever. I'll never betray you."

Hearing Selena pledge complete devotion to him made Sal growl. Selena saw a look of desire mixed with pain in his eye.

"Don't say it if you don't mean it." Sal begged of her.

"Sal, I promise you with everything inside of me, I will never leave you. I will never take you for granted and I will NEVER allow ANYONE to come in between what you and I have." Selena took a step back, letting Sal admire her in full glory. "I give all of myself to you."

Grabbing Sal's hand, she led him upstairs. Reaching the top of the stairs she pulled Sal past the guest bedroom they'd been sleeping in. Once Sal realized where she was headed, he pumped the breaks.

"Whoa, you know we're not going in there. My room is over here." he pointed.

"Sal, I'm prepared to give you ALL of me. Every inch of my body and soul. There isn't one part of my body that is off limits to you." she said. Sal's eyes instantly were drawn towards her posterior. Seeing what his eyes focused on, "Yes baby ALL of me. But yet you stand here and tell me that this room is off limits to me."

Sal replied, "It's not like that Selena. I lived in that room with my wife and all of her things are still in there. Once she moves all of her things out, we'll go in there."

Selena ran Sal's hand over luscious rump. Sliding it over the separation. "I'm here committed to you, ready to give you every part of me and yet you want to keep a shrine for that vile bitch? I've done everything for you. When are you really going to allow yourself to be free baby?" She pressed his fingers deeper and deeper into her divide. "Don't you want it all daddy?"

Most of the positions they tried last night in the guest bed, looked like a game of twister gone terribly wrong.

Sal groaned. "All of you?"

She leaned up against the bedroom door. "All of me, baby." replied Selena.

Sal opened the doorway to his marital chamber. Selena walked towards the bed, keeping full eye contact with Sal. Her fingers inching towards her hidden domain. Selena hissed when she made contact with her fattened clit. She backed on to the bed. Spreading her legs open, giving Sal full view. Her soaking wet pussy leaked all over the floral printed sheets. Rimming her pussy with two fingers, Selena lubed up her fingers before sliding them in her forbidden rear entry way. Breaking open her tight ring.

"All of me." she moaned.

Sal always begged Kelly to try anal but she always whined about the pain. Sal joined Selena on the bed. He kissed her swollen clit before he started lapping up the juices flowing from her love hole. Selena lifted her bottom up off the bed. Sal buried his face in her junction and sucked her clit.

"Like that baby, like that." said Selena.

The more Sal sucked the more she fingered. Selena loved the way Sal worked his tongue. Something about his tongue skills had her ready to cum at the drop of a dime.

"You about to cum baby?" asked Sal. As if it were her cue Selena felt her body rupture. Sal sat back to watch his "work" as he called it. The aftershocks tore through Selena. Sal stroked his dick and asked, "You ready for all of this?" Selena positioned herself on all fours, "ARE YOU READY FOR THIS?"

Selena spread open her ass cheeks, exposing her so called untapped treasure. Sal swiped his dick through Selena's slit to lube up his rod. Selena pressed her face against the bed. Sal tapped the tip of his dick against her hole.

"I've never done this before." He admitted.

"Neither have I." said Selena crossing her toes at the bold-faced lie. "I heard it's supposed to be the ultimate fuck. That's what I want with us."

Sal eased his tip in. Selena grunted at the anticipation of what was to come. Sal thrust his hips forward and pulled out slightly. Gasping with each stroke. The feeling was like nothing he'd ever experienced before. This hole was tighter than a virgin pussy. *"There's no way I'm gonna to fit all the way inside of her."* he thought.

"Deeper Sal." Selena pleaded.

"It's our first time I don't wanna hurt you babe." He replied.

"Damn," thought Selena, *"That's what I get for tryna play all innocent."* She had to push Sal. "I want all of you Daddy, fuck my ass hard pleasssseee. I want you to make it hurt." she begged.

Sal did just as Selena asked. He rammed his dick deep in her ass. While he stroked her ass, she played with her clit, wishing she had another dick or one of her toys in her pussy. The tingled stirred deep in Sal's core. He wanted to fight the urge to release the sensation building.

If there was a moment he wanted to savor, this was it. In and out, in and out, Sal stroked Selena to what he thought was the best orgasm either one of them had ever experienced. After uncurling his toes, he collapsed next to Selena.

"You okay baby?" he asked.

Longing for more than Sal had delivered, Selena hid her dissatisfaction when she replied in a syrupy tone, "Oh baby you made me feel so good. I'm just gonna go to the bathroom to clean myself up."

Selena made her way to the bathroom in two shakes of a tail feather. The fire still burning between her thighs begged to be extinguished. She turned on the shower. Finding the perfect temperature and adjusting the shower nozzle she climbed in. She took a couple of squirts of Kelly's fragrant body wash and lathered her body with the flowery scent. Her fingers glided with ease over her slick skin. Selena's body responded to her touch and begged for more. Her nipples called for her personal touch. She teased them until the desire couldn't be ignored any longer. Touching her spot caused her body jerked at the intense feeling. Lightly placing the tips of two fingertips over her clit, she trusted her body back and forth. The warm feeling made her nipples harden. Selena rested her head against the shower wall. The sounds of her oh's and ah's were quieted by the force full streams of water flowing freely.

"Why hadn't Sal made her feel like this tonight?" ran thru Selena's mind. She thrust faster and faster. Her momentum continuing to increase. Still barely touching her fully engorged clit. Her body kicked into overdrive. She bit down on her lip to avoid screaming out in sheer pleasure. She twitched and jerked uncontrollably as she teased her body to an orgasm. After composing herself she rinsed off and climbed back out of the shower. No sooner than she had wrapped the towel around her body, Sal entered the bathroom.

With a sheepish grin she asked, "Is everything okay baby?" Feeling much better after she handed what he couldn't do.

"The movers are here for Kelly's things. You can go to the guest room and get dressed so they can pack her things up." he said.

Inside Selena was screaming to the top of her lungs. She despised Kelly's bitch ass. *"Her day will come."* Selena secretly promised herself. She wouldn't be satisfied till Queen Kelly was completely knocked off of her throne.

Selena dropped her towel on the bathroom floor. Looking at Sal she said, "She can have that too." Selena walked to the guest room feeling the burn from the stares the moving crew directed towards her ass as she left the room.

***

Kelly and Admiral were amazed with how well things turned out with Sal. He drove to the coffee shop as they were talking. He didn't want to leave her side but Kelly needed to handle her affairs on her own. Admiral kissed Kelly goodbye and handed her the keys to his car.

"I shouldn't be too long. I just need to file some paperwork and check on the girls." Kelly told Admiral.

He went inside to his office and dialed his lawyer. "Is he in?" he asked the secretary on the other end. Without responding she connected Admiral right away.

"Hey I was just about to call you. What's up man?" Sam said.

"Cut the crap. We both know how you get down man." Admiral said sounding upset.

"Dude how many times do I have to tell you, the sad puppy dog act only worked for Michelle, not you."

Admiral sighed. Just hearing Sam mention her name flooded his heart with thoughts of his wife.

"It's been a while since you've gone to see her isn't it?" Sam asked. Not wanting to tell Sam he was right, Admiral remained silent. "Look A, don't feel guilty. I know she's a lot to handle. You need to be able to come to terms with this and live your life. You know there will never be any bad blood between us regardless what you do. You're family to me bro."

"I keep telling myself I should go see her. I just hate seeing her like that. I still blame myself for what happened. She went thru all of that just to try to make me happy." Admiral told Sam.

He laughed trying to lighten Admiral's spirits. "Nah man you know Michelle never does anything anyone tells her. She chose to do what she did because SHE wanted it. She wanted it for the two of you."

Admiral chuckled. "Yeah you right. But Imma get it together soon I promise."

Sam interrupted him, "In the meantime, I'm going to work on this problem thingy for your girl Kelly."

Admiral was glad that Sam was working on getting her situation resolved. But he didn't want Sam thinking Kelly was his girl. Again, Sam was in Admiral's head.

"Yeah, yeah, yeah...I know. She's NOT your girl. She's JUST a friend. Either way I'm on it."

Finishing his conversation, Admiral wondered how Kelly was making out on her own. He wanted to call her. He wanted to be near her and wrap her tightly in his arms. *"Let her have the space she needs. She'll call me if she needs me."* The last thing Admiral wanted to was be like her husband. Sal never gave Kelly the chance to breathe in life. Just as he decided not to bother her his phone rang. Smiling he answered the call.

"Hey babe, how's everything going?"

"Babe?" she replied, "Everything is working out perfectly babe." Kelly teased.

"I feel like such a sucker." He admitted.

"Don't. I have to confess I like hearing that." Said Kelly.

She quickly changed the subject and updated him on her day. She told him how she was able to meet with a few lawyers who were in the group BTB that she'd befriended. Instantly Admiral had a huge problem with that. Kelly sensed that he was upset but for the life of her she couldn't figure out why.

"Where are you heading to now?" he asked.

"I just pulled up at my sister in law's place. I can't wait to see my babies. I missed them so much. I hate this situation for what they have to deal with."

"How about this," he told her "Visit with your daughters. I'll catch a ride back to the condo. Come there whenever you are ready. And we will sit down and talk about making arrangements for you guys. I have another place the three of you can stay at until you get back on your feet."

"Oh, that's sweet but you don't have to worry. They also took care of that too!" She exclaimed.

Admiral grumbled. "Kellz do you think it's such a good idea to have them involved like that. Remember they were the ones who set you up."

Feeling like a child being scolded she became short with him. "Look I know what I'm doing. They're ok. They are fed up with everything the group is doing and hate what they did to me."

"Are you sure this is the right thing to do?" he asked.

"It feels good to finally be able to take charge and stop letting people just walk all over me." Kelly replied. "You seem worried. What's wrong?"

"Nothing. I just want to make sure you know that whatever you do I'm here for you."

"Admiral you have been there for me through all of my craziness 100%. I couldn't have asked for a better friend."

Kelly pulled the "friend" card catching Admiral by surprised.

"Friend." he repeated.

"Yeah," she told him. "If I didn't have you by my side, I would be a complete wreck. I won't ever be able to repay you."

"It's cool. Go ahead and get your girls. Don't worry about bringing the car back. I'll pull my Charger out of the garage. Keep it as long as you need it."

The conversation ended leaving Admiral feeling open. He realized that he was falling for someone that clearly didn't feel the same about him. He promised himself that he needed to pull back and see what this situation was really about. Getting back at those who took everything from him.

MAKING IT RIGHT

Family Matters

Kelly spent the evening being showered with love from her girls. She ended her night with a heart to heart talk with her sister-in-law. Kim remained silent while Kelly laid everything out on the table. *"WOW!"* was the first thing that Kim could say.

"I know." Kelly agreed. "It's a lot. I'm not proud of what I did. But I can't let the shame or guilt keep me from moving forward. I never wanted any of this to turn out the way it did. The reality is it happened and now I need to pick up the pieces."

"I can't believe either of you two. This entire situation is insane. You two know better than all this sleeping and sneaking around with those psychos!" scolded Kim.

Kelly shook her head. "Admiral isn't a psycho." she replied.

"No, you're right he's not. I feel bad for him getting caught up in y'alls chaos. He sounds like a good dude. I'm surprised he's not with a good woman like me." Kim hinted. "I mean like you keep saying you two decided to pump the brakes and just be friends. Is he seeing anyone?" Kim questioned.

She saw the irritation building under Kelly's skin. It reminded her of the same look Sal gave her when they had the very same conversation.

"Umm hmm. Just like my brother. Neither of you really want this situation to end."

"I'm NOTHING like your brother! Is that what he told you? What did he tell you?"

Kelly would've gone on and on if Kim hadn't stopped her.

"He came over to see the girls looking all sad in the face. Talking about how he still loves you. Misses you like crazy but too stubborn to admit it. Instead he's running around with that Rosie Perez wanna be. Do the right thing, Kelly, and fix this. Don't let that dried up tamale have what's yours."

Kim walked upstairs leaving Kelly speechless. "And send that Black God my way!" she said before she closed her bedroom door.

"She may be crazy as a bed bug but she's right about one thing. I'm not letting her have what's mine."

Kelly went to bed with Selena heavy on her mind. She wondered what made Selena so determined to ruin Kelly's life. She sent Sal a text telling him that she wanted to meet up with him tomorrow and talk about what was going on.

The message Kelly sent woke both Sal and Selena up.

"Who's texting you this time of night?" grilled Selena.

Sal's eyes focused on the name showing on his display, "WIFEY".

"Are you serious? THAT BITCH TEXTING YOU THIS TIME OF NIGHT!" She continued ranting in Spanish.

Sal was thankful he didn't understand a lick of it. "She's my wife and the mother of my children. She can call me anytime she wants." He informed Selena.

She crossed her arms and pouted. "Well what did WIFEY want?"

Sal rubbed his head and laid back down. "She wants to meet tomorrow and talk."

He closed his eyes and pretended to go back to sleep. He laid there like a kid waiting for Christmas. He wondered what Kelly wanted to talk about. He prayed it was about working things out. No matter what happened he loved Kelly. Selena moved closer to Sal. Convinced that her body would sway his thoughts back to her. Sal refused to respond forcing Selena back to her side of the bed.

Rising before the crack of dawn. Sal was showered and dressed, sitting at the kitchen table waiting for the right time of morning to reply to the text that barely let him sleep. He hurriedly sent his response when he heard Selena stirring around upstairs. "Kel I'm all for meeting up to discuss things. If you want we can meet at the office. My schedule is clear today. If the office isn't good for you name the place and I'm there."

He hit send, grabbed his briefcase and made a mad dash for his car. Today he needed to stay clear of the temptress that sent his world into a tailspin. Kelly read Sal's message as she got the girls ready for school. She was impressed at how well he was still handling things. She was curious if he would remain to do so after hearing what she wanted to discuss. "Your office is fine." she replied. Their pending conversation floated around her thoughts while she fed the girls breakfast. She dropped the girls off at school and made her way to Sal's office.

"DING, DONG." The doorbell rang out. "FUCK!!!" cursed Selena. She was rushing to get out the door. "First that bastard sneaks off without me this morning. Now some asshole is at my door." she grumbled "WHAT?" Selena barked as she swung open the door. Her jaw dropped when she saw the face staring back at her.

"Did you think we wouldn't find out sister?" Selena gasped for air as she tried to shut the door.

Sarge shook her head. "Is that how you treat a guest?"

"Get out of my home!" Selena demanded.

"Your home." Sarge giggled, "Last I checked YOUR home was sum lil run down shack that Supreme handpicked for you."

Selena started to cry. Thinking of her days on the street running from foster home to foster home. That "run down shack" was the only first Selena ever felt safe in. Now she had the house of every woman's dream. Even if she was living in the shadows of someone else's life, it was now hers.

"We all told Supreme you were no good from the start. But she insisted there was more to you than what we saw. She was producing results at the time so we stood behind her decisions. Somehow, you two lost sight of the big picture. All because she wanted a piece of this man's wife, while you thought you could slip in and replace Kelly. When things started going wrong, we told Supreme to reign you in. We told her if she didn't handle that she'd pay the price for your mistakes. So, guess what sweetie I'm about to put an end to your little fantasy." warned Sarge.

"NOOOO, please don't do this." begged Selena. "Please just let me have my family. I'll walk away from the group and you'll never hear from me again."

Sarge couldn't understand. "Family? What family? When she found you, you were living on the street. You had no clue who your real family was since you were given up for adoption at birth."

Selena pleaded, "Sal needs me and I need our baby." Selena said as she held her stomach.

"You stupid bitch!" Sarge said as she slapped Selena. "Do you know what you've done? Do you know how badly this will end now? Wait until the Sisters find out." Sarge couldn't wait to report back to the circle.

Selena begged again, "Please don't. Please just give me time to make this right. You guys can still walk away with everything we talked about. Just give me some more time."

Sarge knew she was supposed to report her finding back to the others. They were discussing voting Supreme out and punishing Selena for violating the group's sacred rules. If this happened that would mean the assignment would be scrapped and no one would profit from Sal's demise. All the Sargent saw was money.

"I'll give you two weeks to sort this mess out. I'll hold the girls off until then, but after that I'll have to tell them everything. So, fix it NOW!"

Storming into the office, Selena looked for Sal. She needed to keep his marriage on the rocks. She overhears Jacob telling Sal how he needs to work things out with his wife.

"Jake you have no idea how happy I was when Kelly said she wanted to talk about all of this mess. I'm so ready to put it to an end. This was the worst mistake of my life." replied Sal.

"You mean to tell me if that devil of an assistant came up in her now throwing her cookie up for grabs, you would pass?" Jacob asked.

"I'll be honest the sex was great at first you know." Sal admitted. "It was something different for me but in the end she's not my wife. There's no other way to say it other than I love Kelly and I want my family back. Nothing or no one else matters really outside of that."

It made Jacob proud of his friend hearing how he finally was putting this whole saga behind him.

"Your family should have been all that mattered from the start. But hey we all stumble along the way. I can't wait to tell Sharon you guys are doing better." Jacob headed to his office to get started on the day.

Selena remained crouched under her desk hidden from sight. Tears streaming down her face. Afraid everything she worked for was starting to fall apart. *"Get yourself together chick."* she told herself. *"I gave Sal the chance to end things on his own. I'll be damned if I let Kelly come back now. It's time to play dirty."* Selena went to the ladies' room to clean herself up.

"Just the person I wanted to see. Funny how I run into you." laughed Selena.

Kelly shook her head. "Not right now Selena. It's too early for any B.S. from you. I'm just here to talk to Sal and then I'll be on my way." Kelly warned her.

"I'm sure you want to have a conversation with Sal, but I have some things I need to say to you." Kelly tried to leave the bathroom.

Selena blocked her, "You hate me for all the wrong reasons Kelly. I'm not the one you should be mad at." She continued. "I was put up to this. She's been worked up about you since the day you two met."

Kelly quickly dismissed Selena. "I have no clue what you're talking about. Nor do I have any time for your games. I'm here for my family. So, move outta my way."

Kelly put her arm out to push Selena out of her path. Selena grabbed her wrist.

"Oh, sure you do. She couldn't stop bragging about you. She told us all about how she knew you were hers from the moment she laid eyes on you." Selena stepped in closer. Lowering her voice, she whispered, "She told us all about picking you up in the bar. She could tell you'd never done anything like that before. She gave us all the details of that night blow by blow, or should I say more like lick by lick." Selena twirled Kelly's hair. "She made your husband's business grow. Allowed your family to become wealthy and completely distracted. She invited you into our fold, sending me in to steal your husband. She wanted you all alone. She needed you to be vulnerable. Like that shy timid woman, she met in that bathroom. You were greatly underestimated." Selena chuckled.

"Leave me alone." begged Kelly. "Leave my family alone."

Selena reached down to her stomach.

"No!" Kelly exclaimed as she backed away.

Fighting off hysterics she tore through the office searching for Sal. She didn't see Jacob turning the corner.

"Whoaa girl, something's got you in a hurry this morning."

Kelly tried to smooth over her composure.

"Good morning Jake. I'm sorry. I'm kinda I'm a rush this morning."

"I can understand why. I just finished talking with that husband of yours. You guys have had a rough patch but it's finally coming to an end. I know you're happy things are turning around, huh?" Jacob asked.

Afraid to look him in the face Kelly lowered her eyes, "It was good to see you again." she said politely before sliding away.

Sal saw Kelly approaching his office. Trepidation filled his core, beads of sweat gathered on his palms. *"Come on man, get it together!"* he told himself. All Sal wanted was to have his family back. He hoped Kelly felt the same.

"Good morning." he said with a leery tone. Unsure of her mood, he gave her a half smile.

"Hello Sal." Kelly weakly replied.

The two passed pleasantries back and forth like two teenagers avoiding the topic at hand. Unsure of how to continue they stared awkwardly at each other. Sal tried to will the feelings rooted deep in his heart to Kelly's mind.

Selena sat at her desk praying for this "talk" to end. She jumped when Kelly walked out of the office.

"I'm finished with all of you so do me a favor and leave me alone!" demanded Kelly and stormed out.

Selena's eyes tried to apologize. *"If things are going my way, why do I feel like crap."* she wondered. Suddenly Sal opened the office door. Surprised to see the reason for all of his turmoil staring him in the face.

"What are you doing here?" he snapped.

"You, you left without me this morning honey."

"Selena I can't go thru this with you anymore. This episode with you cost me my family." Selena tried to interject. Sal waved her off and continued.

"This here..." he pointed back and forth between Selena and himself. "It's over. We are officially done. I'll make arrangements to have you and you stuff moved to where ever you choose." he turned to leave.

"WAIT SAL!" she cried.

"What?" he asked. "What else is there left to say?"

Swallowing hard she said, "I'm pregnant."

Sal thought Kelly was the storm sending his world into a tailspin. Sal snickered. Things couldn't be any clearer. Selena was the black hole sucking every good thing out of his life.

"I mean what I said! I want you out."

Her heart dropped, "What about...what about the baby?"

Sal shook his head. "If it's mine, we'll work about an arrangement."

Selena's blood boiled, "Is that what I am? An arrangement now. Your whore of a wife calls you one time and you go running back? I was the one giving you what you needed. Was I an arrangement when she was sneaking around with your potential business partner?"

Sal opened his mouth but Selena stopped him.

"Let me answer that for you. I was your woman and now WE are your family. I won't let you just push us away."

None of that mattered to Sal, "I mean what I said. I want you out. We have never nor will we ever be a family. If this baby is mine, I'll handle that," he spat. "You don't have to work today, there's nothing here for you to do. I've cancelled all of my appointments."

***

Kelly cursed herself for ever becoming involved with this that chick, Supreme, she said her name over and over full of venom. *"If I saw her right now, I would KILL her."* Suddenly it clicked in her mind. *"I need to find her. She's the only one who can stop all of this."* Kelly pulled into a parking lot. Rummaging thru her purse for her phone. She searched every email in her inbox until she found the one she needed. *"This is where she has to be."* Following a hunch, she drove to the house with the intricate shrubbery. This time when she pulled up there weren't any torches lit and gone was the Adonis standing guard. She parked her car and looked around. Checking to see if anyone was watching before she retraced her steps into the labyrinth. With every step of the way flashbacks of that night filled her veins. The fear she had then returned. Stepping back into the unknown was dangerous, yet enticing. The sensation of at least a dozen warm mouths pleasuring her body came back. *"You don't need that anymore."* she told herself. She peaked in the window once she reached the house. It appeared to be empty inside. She walked around until she found the door that once before lead her into their inner circle. Seeing it in the daytime, everything appeared normal.

Making her way to a lower level she found where she needed to be. "They can't hide everything." she said out loud.

"Who's in here," a familiar voice called out from another room.

Kelly ran for a closet. *"I can't get caught before I confront her."* Kelly thought to herself. Her heart raced. Panic set in. Heavy breathing made Kelly lightheaded.

The voice searched from room to room, "I know you're here... Show yourself!"

Close to jumping out of her skin, Kelly gave up. She opened the closet and stood face to face with the voice.

"What are you doing here? You were told to never return to this location!"

Kelly stared back blankly. She didn't expect to see the person she came for glaring back at her.

"I tried to talk to your flunky, but she wouldn't listen. You've really gotta get better control of her."

Kelly started to feel bold. She stepped out of the closet.

"You set her loose on my family. My marriage is ruined and I've lost everything,"

Kelly screamed at Supreme, unleashing a verbal attack. Pent up emotions finally boiled over. Supreme looked on in disbelief. Tears raced down Kelly's face.

"I'm sorry," she whispered over and over.

"How could you do this to me!" cried Kelly.

Supreme felt guilty to an extent. "Kelly, I hate seeing you hurt like this. This isn't what I wanted. I never intended any of this for you. After our time together, I couldn't stop thinking about you." Her fingers brushed against Kelly's arm. "I remember the first time I saw you at the bar. The center of everyone's attention, completely unaware of the power you owned." Touching Kelly again she said, "I knew then I would have you. I wanted to tame you and unleash everything within you." Shyly, she looked away and whispered, "I wanted you for myself."

"You ruined my life because you wanted me?" The words flew out of Kelly's mouth faster than she could think.

"No, not to ruin you. I wanted you to be mine. I needed you. At first I craved your desire. When we watched you for our research, I fell in love with you from afar."

Before Kelly knew it, she was wrapped in her arms. Supreme's hands were all over her body. "*No! No! No!*" her mind pleaded while body screamed otherwise.

"Yes! Yes! Yes!" Supreme nudged Kelly back into the closet.

Desire cursed through Kelly's body. Images of their encounter danced through her mind. Supreme's fingers slid between the spacing in Kelly's pants.

"Ummm, no panties just like I remembered."

Kelly hated that her body continued to betray her.

"Can I have it," asked Supreme.

She knew that she could easily have her way with Kelly. But, this wasn't how Supreme played this moment out in her head. Her hands recoiled. Breathing heavily, she placed them on opposite sides of Kelly.

"Baby, tell me I can have it," she begged, "Tell me you've thought about me and everything we did that night."

Kelly was silent. Supreme's heart ached to hear the words she desperately longed for. Wanting fingers trailed the hardened lines on Kelly's face.

"Tell me please." Trepidation crept in slowly.

Kelly reached up and caressed Supreme's face. "I've thought about you here and there."

Supreme's face instantly lit up.

"That day in the hotel was the first time I've done anything like that." Her mind wandered back to that very moment. "You gave me the rush I never knew was missing in my life. But I learned the hard way that such a rush comes with a price. Now it's a debt my family has to pay." Kelly said sadly, "That's why I'm here with you. I'm begging you, please leave my family alone. We need to repair all of the damage this mess has caused." Nudging Supreme to the side, "Now if you'll excuse me, I never want to see any of you again."

In that instant Supreme's world crashed down around her.

"I never wanted to hurt you or your family. I just wanted you to be a part of my life. I've never had anyone care about me. People always feared me so being a part of BTB was natural for me. I found women who were just like me. I gave them the freedom to fight for what they deserved. I gave them power when all others tried to take it away."

Kelly shook her head. What she was hearing completely blew her mind.

"You can't make people love you any more than you can make me wanna be with you," Kelly reiterated her plea, "Leave me and my family alone."

Supreme watched part of her heart walk out the door. She knew Kelly was right. Supreme fell down on her knees and crawled up in the corner.

"It's over," she told herself as she decided to send a text out to the group. Supreme hits send on her phone.

"It's done. " she told herself. BTB was her baby. The thought of being a part of it in hopes of finding that one true person, was over. She thought Kelly was the one. In fact, she knew Kelly was the one. Too bad Kelly didn't feel the same. *"I'll make it right."* she promised Kelly in her head.

MATTERS OF THE HEART

Letting Go

"BANG, BANG!"** The gavel echoed throughout the chamber. Nervously, Selena stood before the Leaders of the Sisterhood, her fellow BTB members looked on. "Let's not waste anytime beating around the bush. We all know why you are here. I know many may wonder why it took so long to formally acknowledge your wanton-behavior," Supreme took a deep breath before she continued, "I selfishly put my desires before the best interest of our group. I allowed my desires to impede my better judgement. I apologize to each and every one of you. I promise to correct all of my wrong doing that has taken place. For now, we must address the young lady standing before me." Supreme pointed to Selena, "Do you have anything you care to say before we continue?"

Selena lowered her head. *"Fight back."* she told herself. She looked Supreme square in the eye.

"I violated our sacred trust. I fell in love." Her heart ached thinking about her feelings for Sal. "Whatever you decide my punishment to be, I will fully accept."

In the past when others in her position crossed that line, they were let off with a warning or placed on suspension. There was always a hefty fine to pay. Selena prepared for all of this. Slowly, she stashed funds away while her love grew stronger and stronger.

The Leaders read thru the list of charges. Selena stood in complete silence. They took a few moments to weigh out all of the possible scenarios that could arise due to Selena's actions.

"This is the only way." Supreme convinced the other Leaders, "Selena Alaverez, please come forward and stand in the inner circle for your sentencing."

The others let out a loud gasp. The inner circle was reserved for the most heinous actions.

Now shaking, Selena made her way to the circle.

"As determined on this day by your Leaders, your actions are in direct violation of our most sacred rules. You showed little or no regard for your sisterhood, therefore, your punishment should mirror your actions."

Tears formed in the corners of Selena's eyes.

"You are ordered to terminate your pregnancy, IMMEDIATELY."

The crowd erupted.

Selena screamed out loud. "Noooooo! Not my baby!"

She was grabbed as she tried to run away.

"Take her to the back." Supreme demanded.

Selena was taken to the medical chamber. The Leaders were serious when they voted for an immediate termination. The room was transformed into a full surgical center.

"Have a seat on the bed," said the doctor.

Tears freely fell from Selena eyes. Sparing Selena an audience, she dismissed the guards.

"Don't do this," she begged.

It broke Dr. Stanton's heart hearing her plead for the unborn child.

Lowering her head, she replied, "I'm sorry my child. I MUST do this." She unlocked the rear exit. "I have to go in the back to prepare for your procedure. It will take me almost an hour. You will have plenty of time to do what is best for you and your baby."

Dr Stanton gave Selena a knowing look.

"Thank you," cried Selena.

In a voice barely audible, Dr. Stanton replied, "I'm not a killer."

Selena crept out the back door. If the doctor hadn't let her out, things would be different right now. Even though the doctor let her go, Selena wasn't free. She was still on the heavily guarded compound. She made her escape through the labyrinth. With every twist and turn, she recalled how her path crossed with Supreme's. Selena was just a teeny bopper, still cracking her bubble gum like she knew it all. One day, Supreme handed her a package. She told the young girl, "I've been watching you run this lil street game of yours for weeks now. When you're ready to step up to my level follow these instructions." Today was the first day Selena ever regretted opening that box. Supreme took her in and became that much needed mother figure.

Selena wasn't the only one who regretted that day. On Selena's 18th birthday her "mom" introduced her to the Sisterhood. From that day on everything changed. *"What was I thinking?"* she asked herself. That day replayed over and over in her head. "She's not ready." Supreme snapped at Sarge.

"Let me have her. I promise you, I'll make sure she's ready." Sarge promised.

She ran to the parking lot. She climbed in to the first unlocked car she found. *"Yes!"* she exclaimed when she reached in the glove box. Most members would leave their car keys there when coming to a meeting. Selena sped off, promising to make everyone pay for what they tried to take from her. Word spread like fire through the Sisterhood.

"Supreme, you have to call her," Vixen implored.

She shook her head no.

"She's not safe. You HAVE to warn her," Vixen pleaded again.

"She said she wanted me to stay out of her life."

"Supreme you did this to her. You placed Selena in Kelly's life. Don't leave her...them out there alone," Vixen corrected herself.

"Them?" Supreme questioned.

"Kelly and Selena, they are both in this situation because of you. I told you trying to get rid of the "evidence" would change anything. Save them before anyone else gets hurt."

***

Admiral's jaw dropped when she walked through the door.

"WHAT ARE YOU DOING HERE," he asked Supreme.

"I need your help," she explained.

Admiral laughed, "You've got to be fuckin' kidding me!"

Supreme reached out to touch Admiral.

"Keep your hands off of me. You make my skin crawl." he told her.

"You didn't think so at one point if I remember correctly," She teased.

Admiral lunged at Supreme, but caught himself just shy of reaching her.

"I told you that was the past! I'm done with you and your sick friends."

Supreme waved her finger at him. "Not so true, sir. You're NOT done with ALL of my friends. In fact, that's why I'm here." Her tone became serious. "She's in trouble and it's my fault." She explained how she'd met Kelly some time ago. Admiral nearly lost it when she admitted her whole elaborate plan to have Kelly for her own. "You have feelings for her, too, don't you?"

"Stay away from her and stay the hell away from me, too!"

Admiral had enough. "GET OUT!"

Supreme shook her head no, "I need your help. I'm afraid Selena's after her. I tried to force Selena to get rid of the baby and she escaped. She blames me and Kelly for the way this situation turned out. I don't want anything to happen to Kelly," she confessed.

Admiral's hands were dying to wrap themselves tightly around her neck.

"Admiral, I'm sorry about what happened to Michelle. I told them that she wasn't strong enough to come into our world, but they didn't listen."

He couldn't believe his ears.

"She was strong enough until you sick fucks tried to destroy everything that we built. Have you ever stopped to think about the people you really "bring" into your so-called world? You make them your slaves. You take away any hope of a normal life. All Michelle wanted was to be normal again. She did what she did to set me free from you guys, I owe her everything. And here you are doing it again to another good person, all just to get your rocks off," he snapped at Supreme.

"It's more than that with Kelly. Admiral I love her, even though she's in love with you," the words hurt Supreme, but she knew it was true. "Can we please not fight? I just want to save her." she pleaded with tears forming in her eyes.

Admiral put everything in him aside. *"This isn't about Michelle."* he told himself, "Where is she?"

Supreme filled him in on her last conversation with Kelly. "I cause more drama every time I'm involved. I'm not expecting you to clean up my mess, I just don't see how I can help," she said.

"I'll definitely need your help. Just stay behind the scene like you always are." he said sarcastically.

Admiral might've agreed to be on the same team but he wasn't letting Supreme off that easy.

"I'll let myself out now," she replied.

"I'm still a gentleman. Follow me." Admiral scolded leading her to the front door.

Catching him off guard, Supreme turned and hugged him. "Thank you for everything. And again, I'm sorry for what I've done to you and your family."

Admiral hugged Supreme back not knowing that Kelly was watching from the car. She waited until Supreme left. Just seeing her made Kelly's skin crawl.

"So, you're a part of this too?" she asked trying to control her emotions.

"It's not what you think," Admiral replied.

"All this time I've been crying my heart out to you, while you're reporting it all back to them!" Kelly started pounding her fist against Admiral's chest.

"Kelly, I swear I haven't. Please believe me," he pleaded.

Kelly grew louder and louder. Her fist continued to connect wildly with his muscles. By now, the onlookers stared on with little regards on not being obvious. Admiral took notice. He wrapped his arms around Kelly's waist. He picked her up and brought her inside the shop. He closed the door with his foot. He removed his hands from her waist and brought them up to her face. Cupping her beauty in his hands he again tried to explain.

"She came to me because she fears you are in danger. You told her to stay away from you. Kelly, she's doing just that. She knows I love you and would never let anything happen to you. Please, baby can you understand that."

"You lied to me! You know all about her," she cried.

"Baby, I never lied to you, but you're right, I know her. I'm not happy about that. Every day I want to forget her and everyday I'm reminded how she will always be a part of my life," Admiral confessed.

Kelly broke free. "I can't take this anymore. I want ALL of y'all to leave me the hell alone. I'm filing for divorce and moving me and my girls as far away as I can! You people are sick," She stormed out. Admiral called out after her but it was pointless. She climbed in the car and sped away.

True to her word, she filed papers to end her marriage immediately. She filed for a quick divorce stating that she only wanted support for her girls. Sal would keep the house and everything else they acquired together. The court date came quickly due to this fact. Sal tried to protest and offer support for Kelly, but she declined. They worked out an amicable visitation schedule.

"I'm moving closer to my family, Sal." she told him.

"I wish you would stay. You're taking my girls away from me." replied Sal.

"I need to be closer to my family right now." was her reason.

Sal understood. "I'm still here if you ever need me, Kelly," he told her.

"I know Sal, but I need to do this on my own. I'll keep you posted on when we are going. I want you to spend as much time as you can with the girls." replied Kelly.

***

"It's been a while since we've seen you here, Admiral. Has something changed since your last visit." asked Nancy.

Admiral smiled, biting his tongue. "Nancy, I see things haven't changed with you."

Nancy gave him a knowing look. Admiral shifted his feet, uncomfortable with her glare.

"Everything's still the same here. I'm sorry I haven't been around much. I've been handling a few things," Admiral apologized. "How is she, Nancy,"

"I pray for her every day. She's so sweet and her heart is pure. It hurts my heart thinking someone would want to harm her." Nancy shook her head.

That was the only time Admiral and her could agree on. Michelle didn't deserve this.

"Can I go see her?" he asked.

Nancy nodded her head. "You know where her room is, or did you forget?"

He snapped, "I know where it is, Nancy!"

Even though Nancy gave Admiral a hard time, she felt bad for the man.

"Admiral," she called out.

He stopped in his tracks, sighing heavily before he turned around. "I'm the charge nurse on duty tonight, stay as long as you like." Nancy replied sympathetically.

"Thank you," he muttered.

Admiral stood in front of Michelle's room. The room was decorated with pretty pink and purple flowers. Very few things moved Admiral to tears. Seeing Michelle like this did.

"She was...no IS my wife." he would remind himself.

Michelle once was a beautiful woman. She possessed beauty beyond compare. What attracted him to her the most, was her heart. Michelle loved and cared about everyone. There are times when being so caring can cause more harm than good. Michelle crossed paths one day with a woman looking help her "spread the love". This woman woo'ed Michelle with promises of empowering women, building families and riches more than one could imagine. Michelle believed in this new group of ladies. He recalled the day she burst through the door with the news.

"Admiral baby, I met the most amazing women today. They have this group just for women who want to help others. I finally found people who are like me and it feels great!"

Admiral didn't was to ruin her happiness.

"Just be careful," he warned.

Standing in the doorway of a small child's room, he kicked himself for not saying how he really felt back then.

"Aviral!" Michelle cried out.

His face lit up seeing her joy. "Hi 'Chelly Belly," he replied smiling.

"Why you no come see me?" she asked.

Even though she had the mentality of a child, Michelle could piece together moments of clarity.

Those small and random moments gave Admiral hope. Hope for his wife to return to her former self one day.

"Pway wif mee," said Michelle.

Admiral took a deep breath. *"You can do this."* he prepped himself.

He read all of her favorite books and played all of her favorite games. Michelle curled up in his lap. Sleepy eyes stared up at him.

"Be happy, Aviral." she told him.

"I am, Michelle," replied Admiral. She shook her head "No, you're not happy when you see me. I make you sad."

"Oh, baby that's not true. I am happy here with you," he reassured her.

"I want you happy here," Michelle said pointing to his heart. "Go be happy. I'm okay here."

Admiral's eyes stared back in disbelief.

"Michelle what are you saying?" he asked.

These coherent moments kept him hanging on.

"Michelle, I'm happy and you are getting better slowly." he smiled.

"No, Avie, I not get better. Chelly wants you to go. Go bye bye." she waved at him.

"Okay, baby, I'll go. It's getting late. I'll come back and see you soon." Promised Admiral.

"No," she told him, Let me go. I wub you but, Avie has to go bye bye."

Admiral started to cry. She gently wiped away his tears.

"No be sad, Avie, be happy. Bye bye good for you."

"Don't say that, baby. I'm not leaving you. We'll get through this. I love you so much, Michelle." he cried.

He held her tight. Michelle hummed softly. Her tune eventually turned into a song, "Our day is through, our jobs are done. We did some work, we had some fun. We worked really hard and played as friends, but Avie can't come back again."

She repeated her tune over and over. Each time growing louder until she became hysterical.

"You go bye bye Avie."

Finally understanding, he gave in. "Okay, baby, okay. I'll go. If you ever need me, I'm always going to be here."

He walked away, but glanced back one more time. Michelle was happily coloring in a giant coloring book.

"I wub you Avie." she whispered.

Admiral silently cried in the hallway. Nosey Nurse Nancy rolled by with her push cart.

"People don't give her enough credit," she said pointing towards Michelle's room, "that woman might have the mind of a child from time to time, but she has a heart of gold. She gave her life to make things right. Now she's giving you all of her love and setting you free," she told him.

"What?" snapped Admiral.

"I know you think I'm some old annoying lady who's always in your business, but I care about that girl right there."

Admiral tried to stop her.

Nancy continued, "I know about her past and what happened. Sad to think they could prey on her like that. You, too. Destroyed y'alls family. She wants you to be happy again. If I can see your pain, so can she. Michelle's accepted her fate and has moved on. It's time for you to do the same."

"I love her," was the only this he could say.

"I know, baby. And she loves you. Don't worry, I'll be here. If she ever needs you, I will call you. Go on and be happy, son." Nurse Nancy made her way back to the nurse's station.

Admiral sat in his car crying his heart out. He had to figure out how to pick up the pieces of his life without the women he loved. He walked around for days just going through the motions. His phone rang nonstop. Each time he pressed ignore. This time when it rang, it wasn't going to be any different. That was until he saw the name on the caller id.

"Yes," he answered. The voice on the other end simply replied, "I need to see you." Admiral knew he needed to go. "I'm on my way."

When he reached the caller's location, his burdens felt lighter. The two sat in silence for some time. Finally, his grandmother spoke.

"They need to be free, baby. More importantly THEY need you to be free."

"How do you know about any of this," he asked.

"You're way out here, but know more about my business than I do!"

Grandmom laughed. "It's my job to know about you. You're my baby. Besides, if I waited on you to tell me," humph she grunted, "I'd know nothing."

Admiral laughed. "You're always what I need."

"I know. Now tell me what the hell is going on," she said.

Admiral filled her in on the situation with both ladies.

"Kelly loves you, but she has so many issues to clear up before she'll be ready for you. Now Michelle, that's a strong woman right there. She's sacrificing herself for you again, baby. Don't let it be in vain. Talk to Kelly. Don't give up on her. Everyone in her circle has been false because of these women. How do you think she felt seeing you talking to the ringleader," she asked, "Shhh, I don't want an answer. I want you to think about it and put yourself in her shoes. She's scared."

Admiral told his Grandmother all of the things Kelly said.

"Save her baby. In order to save yourself, you have to save her. Now, if you'll excuse me, tonight is bingo night."

She hurried Admiral off. He had to leave before he inquired further about where her information came from.

***

Sal's heart stopped when he opened his divorce papers. *"It's official. My marriage is over."* Sal thought. He reached for the phone to dial Kelly, just as Selena called. Sal sent her directly to voicemail. He tried to reach Kelly again.

Afraid something was wrong with the kids, Kelly answered his call, "You've called me twice. What's wrong?"

Sensing her panic, he quickly responded.

"Nothing's wrong, babe. I just wanted to talk to you."

Kelly breathed a sigh of relief, "Sure, what's on your mind," she asked.

"Not over the phone," he told her. "Can we meet?"

Reluctantly Kelly agreed. If they were to make this co-parenting thing work, now was the time to start.

"Sure, just tell me where and when."

They worked out the details in such a friendly manner that Kelly didn't realize Sal's agenda. Sal's heart paused when Kelly entered the patio dining area.

"It's nice to see you smiling again," Kelly said as she greeted him.

"It's good to see you. You look beautiful honey."

His sugary sweet words floated past Kelly's ears.

"What did you want to meet about Sal?"

"Well, I see you want to get right to the point. I thought we could sit back enjoy our surroundings and have a wonderful meal. We use to come here all the time back when things were good," Sal replied.

Kelly grew annoyed, "So much has transpired between us since the last time we ate here. Those times are long gone. Again, what didn't you want to discuss Sal?"

Sal would always beat around the bush, making Kelly drag out information bit by bit.

"That's just it. I wanted to talk about the good times we use to have," he reached out to grab Kelly's hand. "I miss this. I miss us."

Kelly couldn't believe her ears.

"Us? What us? Us ended the day we both decided to step out of our marriage."

Sal wouldn't back down. "Kel please, we've been through far too much. We're good together," he pleaded.

"We WERE great together. You were my rock and I was yours. But somewhere we went wrong. We can't go back and change what was done. All we can do is move forward and I'm moving on without you. We will always be parents together, but that's where this ends."

Kelly left Sal sitting alone at the table. He wanted to beg Kelly not to let it end this way. Deep down inside, Sal knew it was a waste of time. There was no chance of undoing all of the wrong. It was time to put his marriage in the past, focus on being a father to his girls and deal with the situation with Selena. Her pregnancy wasn't going to magically go away, or would it?

WHAT YOU ASKED FOR

Chance Encounters

Admiral watched her slowly cross the parking lot. His heart ached. He longed to feel her touch. He wanted to call out her name. The feeling in his gut knew she was still angry with him.

"Why did I put off shopping until the last minute?" he cursed.

Turning around and leaving like he wanted to was not an option. This was his favorite place to "one stop shop." He waited, giving Kelly a head-start before entering the store. The plan was to let her make her way through the store while he secretly picked up his items without being seen. Every direction he headed, she was already there. This shopping trip would take longer than he initially planned. Doubling back down the aisles and hiding from Kelly was wearing Admiral out.

"Are you going to speak or just continue running around here like a lunatic," asked Kelly.

Standing face to face with the woman he loved deep down in his heart scared him. Their last encounter didn't end well.

"I wanted to give you space. After all, you were clear when you said you didn't want to see me again."

Admiral reached for the shelf and pulled a package towards his cart.

"I don't want to hurt you so that's what I'm doing. I hope all is well with you, Kelly. And it was good to see you again." he quickly said.

"You're just going to walk away like that," Kelly blurted out.

She knew she would regret her loose lips. She had just stopped craving his body. The way he held her tight as she slept lingered on the edges of her curves. Admiral stopped. He was afraid to look back. He couldn't bear to see the look in her eyes. She needed him but was too stubborn to admit it.

Still refusing to turn around, "You wanted this, Kelly. I'm giving you exactly what you want."

His words stung. Her natural instinct was to snap back, but how could she. Admiral was only doing what she told him to. She watched him walk away. Tears pooled in the corner of her eyes.

"Admiral, I'm sorry," She called out.

The words fell on his back, as he disappeared down the next aisle.

"Was that Kelly I heard in the background?" Sam asked.

"Yeah." Admiral sighed heavily.

"So, you two are back talking again?" Sam said, happy for his friend.

"No, I just ran into her for the first time since our blow up. One minute she loves me, one minute she hates me. Sam, I don't know if I'm coming or going with her. Sam, all of this has my head spinning."

Sam tried to comfort Admiral.

"This will all be over soon, I promise you."

None of it mattered to Admiral anymore. He'd lost Michelle and now Kelly.

"I hate to see him like this." Sam said out loud as he hung up the phone.

"It won't be much longer," Savannah reassured her husband. "We just need to let this play out."

Sam turned to his wife "I hope you're right Savannah, I really do."

Kelly finished her shopping trip, buying everything that wasn't on her list. Her mind still wandered back to her chance encounter with Admiral. Deep down she knew Admiral cared for her. He would never do anything that would cause her any harm. In all of the craziness, she found herself caught up in he was the only person she could truly trust. She went home and unpacked her purchases. More and more she tried not to think about him.

"UGGHHH!" she roared.

No matter how much she fought it, Kelly missed him. She decided to go pay her friend a visit and finally hear his side of the story.

She waited until the girls were out of school. It was Sal's week but she wanted to confirm that he picked them up on time before she made any plans. She grabbed a chilled bottle of wine out of the fridge. She grabbed her keys and headed Admiral's way. Kelly wasn't sure what was louder, her heart beating or her pounding on the door.

Admiral rushed to the door. It had to be an emergency, "WHO IS IT?"

He asked as he flung the door open. Kelly jumped back. Startled by the deepness of his voice, Kelly thrusted the bottle of wine at him.

"Here, this is for you. I'm sor..."

Her words were cut off mid-sentence. Kelly stumbled and lost her footing on the steps. Admiral reached out and grabbed her with one arm. He snatched her up like a scene from a grocery store novel. He inhaled her scent. Admiral missed being this close to Kelly. For Kelly, the feeling was mutual. A low moan escaped when she felt his body against hers. Admiral became conscious of the stares they were receiving from his neighbors.

"Come in." Admiral said to Kelly.

It was more of a demand than an invitation. Admiral pulled Kelly inside before she could move her feet.

"I'm sorry for the way I acted." Kelly apologized.

"Kelly you didn't know. I was just about to fix dinner. We can cook together and clear everything up then."

He led her into the kitchen. Seasoned steaks and chopped vegetables we spread out on the counter. Kelly asked, "All of this was for you?"

"I'm a big man, I like to eat," growled Admiral. Kelly watched as Admiral's tongue trace the outline of his succulent lips. She felt a tingle in the back of her knees.

"*Stay calm.*" she told herself.

Admiral placed the food on a tray and headed out the back door. Kelly followed. She wanted to see where he was going with the food. She saw the biggest man grill she'd ever seen in her life.

204 | T.J. LA RUE

"You're cooking on this thing?" Kelly said referring to his beast of a grill.

"Certain things a man needs to go big on. A grill is one of those things," he joked.

Kelly sat back and watched as Admiral moved with ease. Grilling calmed his soul. He was peaceful. At least that's what's Kelly thought. Admiral really was nervous being around her after everything that went down. He fought the feelings that started stirring the moment he laid eyes on her.

His mind wondered, "Why is she here?"

"Come and sit with me," said Kelly, "let's talk."

This is the moment he dreaded.

"Sure, what do you want to talk about?" asked" asked Admiral.

"What's new? We haven't spoken in weeks. I know a lot has changed with me. I filed for a divorce from Sal."

Admiral couldn't believe his ears. A smile tugged at the corners of his mouth.

"How did he take it," he asked.

"He wanted to work things out. We've lost all trust and the fact that he is having a baby with Selena, well, let's just say, I want no parts of that girl. In the end, my heart isn't there anymore." she replied.

"Where is your heart," Admiral asked in a soft tone.

Kelly leaned closer, "I'm still looking for it. I think I know who may have it." she teased.

Admiral leaned in towards her, "Do I know who this person is?" he asked.

"Maybe."

Admiral did his best to fight off the urge to go any further with Kelly.

"She still has a lot of unresolved issues." he told himself.

He hopped up and checked on the food. He fumbled around on the grill and avoided Kelly as long as possible. Finally, he headed back to his seat. Kelly reached her hand out and motioned Admiral over.

"Closer." she told him.

Admiral hesitated.

"I won't bite." Kelly assured him. "On second thought, I'll bite only if you want me to."

Admiral dragged his feet.

"Umm mmm, nope," Kelly shook her head, "closer my friend."

Left with no other choice, Admiral finally gave in. He hung his face close to hers and asks, "How can I help you?"

Kelly nibbled on her bottom lip. "I'm hungry," she whined.

Admiral let out a sigh of relief. "Oh, well the food's almost done."

Before he could say another word, Kelly cut him off. "I'm not hungry for food." She tugged on his shirt repeatedly. Each tug brought him closer and closer to her face. Kelly placed her lips on his. She started with quick, tender kisses. Her body fluttered. She thought it was crazy how after all of this time, Admiral still had an effect on her. She pulled him closer yet, Admiral was determined to keep some sort of distance between the two of them. Kelly caught on to the fact that Admiral was playing it safe. This turned her on even more. She became aggressive.

Kelly ran her hands around Admiral's neck. She sought out the collar of his shirt. The soft cotton material easily wrapped around her fingers. With one forceful tug, Kelly managed to separate the front of the fabric into two. Admiral growled. Kelly wasn't sure if was a sign that Admiral disapproved or that he was aroused. Nevertheless, she continued. Her trembling fingers danced across Admiral's chiseled body. Admiral stared down at Kelly intensely. Everything inside of him was boiling over. For so long, he'd fought the urge to take things to the next level convincing himself the time wasn't right. *"She's got too many issues."* he told himself. At the end of the day, though, he had the same issues. Kelly wasn't that different from him. Only difference was she had the balls to take her life by the hand and get what she wanted. And right now, she wanted him. Admiral's conscious spoke loud and clear, as his dick pressed against the zipper of his pants, *"Fuck it!"*

Kelly felt his arousal against her upper thigh. Feeling its massive size constrained so close to her lady friend made her kitty purr. She began to writhe and moan softly. Admiral stepped back towards the grill. His eyes remained locked on Kelly. He placed his hands on the top of his head. Breathing heavily, Admiral needed a moment to catch himself. He wanted to be in control the first time he made love to Kelly. He shook his head as he loosened his locks. Kelly watched as his hair fell wildly to his shoulders. She took in all of his sexiness. Admiral's stare intensified. His heat caused her breathing to quicken. No longer considered nibbling, Kelly bit down on her bottom lip. Admiral reached over and turned off the grill. He pulled his tattered shirt off and threw it to the ground.

"Inside, NOW!" he barked.

Kelly jumped. Her eyes danced with delight, but she didn't move. Admiral looked at her, then the back door. Kelly slowly began to stand up. If she didn't move faster, Admiral planned on having his way with her right in the backyard. They were surrounded by a privacy fence; however that wasn't what he had in mind. At least not for tonight.

Admiral moved to where Kelly stood. His brown eyes told a tale of the pleasures yet to come. His powerful arms cradled her curvy waist. He placed her body next to his. Kelly continued to bite her lip nervously. Admiral placed a single finger on her lips telling her, "No." When he pulled his finger away, he replaced it with his mouth. No longer holding back, Admiral kissed Kelly forcefully. Kelly's arms locked around him tightly as he walked her backwards to the door. He reached behind her to turn the knob. The heels of Kelly's feet fumbled their way up the short set of steps. Admiral backed Kelly into a wall once they were inside. His mouth tore away from hers. He kissed her chin. From there he kissed all the way down her jawbone and to her neck. Kelly's moans grew louder. His hands sought out her breast. Kelly's body tensed when he gently squeezed her top parts. His hands became frustrated with the fabric separating him from Kelly's naked body. He grabbed her hand without saying a word. He marched her upstairs to the bedroom.

Once there, Kelly decided to take control once again. She pushed Admiral down on the bed. She slowly removed one article of clothing at a time. With each piece, she enticed him even more. Admiral couldn't believe it. He couldn't believe that Kelly was standing before him naked. He took in all of her beauty. She was the image of a Goddess in his eyes.

"Take off your pants." Kelly said to Admiral.

Her Goddess like image instantly turned into a sexual creature.

Admiral loosened his belt and worked his way out of the loose jeans. The only thing concealing his solid shaft of manhood was his boxer briefs. The outline caught Kelly's attention. She anticipated it being big, just not that big. Admiral saw the look of panic written all over her face. He reached out and held her hand.

"Don't worry baby, we'll go slow. In fact, we don't have to do this if you don't want to." He reassured her.

Kelly smiled. She started to feel at ease. Admiral's words were honest and sincere. "I want to," she said quietly. "I want you." she told him.

Her comment, while it was directed towards Admiral, enticed Kelly even more. Her kitty became slick with her desire. She pushed him back on the bed once more. Kelly carefully placed her body on top of Admiral's. She steered clear of his powerful sword. Admiral's hands caressed her back slow and gentle. All of a sudden, he grips Kelly's ass tightly. She was caught off guard by the intense mix of sensual pleasure with pain.

Once again, the roles reverse. Admiral flipped Kelly on to her back. Staring into her eyes, he raised both of her legs. Kelly screamed deep in her mind. *"This is really happening."* she told herself. At the same time, Admiral wondered how things had gone from her hating his guts to being on the verge of making love. Admiral kissed Kelly's shoulder.

"Are you okay, baby?" he asked.

Too nervous to answer, Kelly smiled.

"We can stop if you want." he reassured her.

"NO!" Kelly blurted out loud.

"As you wish." Admiral assaulted her with kisses. He slowly worked his way lower. Tenderly, Admiral circled around her breast. Kelly moaned. Admiral moved lower. When he reached her navel, she shut her eyes tight. "I can stop if you want me to." He blew lightly on her navel.

"Oh God, please don't stop, baby. I don't want you to stop."

Admiral was glad Kelly begged him not to stop. He didn't think he could without exploding. Before he could fully dive in and feast on her nectar, fate intervened, yet again. "Knock, knock, knock." was the sound attempting to break up the moment.

"Ignore it." moaned Kelly.

Admiral lowered his head attempting to do just that. "KNOCK, KNOCK, KNOCK!!" The pounding increased. Not wanting to disturb his neighbors, Admiral reluctantly pulled away from Kelly.

"I have to get it. Don't move." He warned her as he struggled to hide his displeased member in a pair of sweats.

The pounding continued. "WHO IS IT!" he barked before swinging the door open.

The last person he expected stood on the other side. Before he could get an answer, he grabbed the handle and flung the door wide open.

"What the hell do...." stopping mid-sentence Admiral stood face to face with Sal.

"I want my wife!"

Kelly's mouth dropped when she came face to face with the person at the door.

"What are you doing here? Is something wrong?" she asked. Once a reply of 'no' was given Kelly started to breathe again. But she still didn't understand the visit. "Why are you here, Sal?"

Using all of the courage left in his body Sal blurted, "I want you back, Kelly baby, I need you."

Kelly stepped back shaking her head no.

"Sal, you can't be serious! I've told you before our marriage is over. There is no us. The papers are filed. I've officially ended this back and forth with us." Kelly air quoted. "The only us we will be is the us as parents to our kids." Kelly's thoughts instantly flew to her daughters. "Oh my God, Sal, where are the girls? Did you bring them here?" Kelly looked outside in a panic.

"No, I didn't, Kelly I'm begging you to let me make things right with you. I don't care about the things you've done and when you finish with this one." Sal pointed to Admiral who had remained quiet during this confrontation.

Admiral's body begin to tense. Kelly sensed the change and placed a hand on his chest to calm him.

"This one here," She questioned Sal's words.

"Yes," he replied, "Your little toy, plaything, or whatever you care to call him. He used you to get to me and now you're using him. I get it, I don't like it, but I get it."

Once again Kelly stepped in before Admiral could respond. "This MAN that you are so rudely referring to cares about me more than you ever could as my husband. By the way, which you were sorry at. Now don't you EVER show up here again."

Kelly slammed the door in Sal's face. Sal was fuming when he returned to his car. He couldn't believe that Kelly was choosing Admiral over him.

"I'm your husband!" He slammed his fists against the steering wheel.

Admiral, too, was filled with rage. "How could you let him talk to you that way," he barked. "He comes to MY house and talks about me as if I'm not standing there and you let him Kelly."

Kelly didn't like to see Admiral like this.

"I'm sorry for all of this." she replied.

Kelly headed back upstairs to get her things. "What are you doing?" Admiral asked as she began dressing.

"Every time I'm around you, I cause drama. I shouldn't have come here." Kelly fought to hold back the tears pooling in her eyes.

"No, no baby, I'm glad you came here. I missed you so much."

Kelly continued gathering her belongings. She willed herself to leave before her body betrayed her.

"I love you Kelly, please don't walk out on me again." Admiral pleaded.

His words fell on Kelly's back. No matter how many times he asked her to stay, her answer was still no. "Damn it!" Admiral cursed and banged as she drove away.

***

"What's wrong, Sal Pal," his sister asked.

Still fuming, Sal replied, "I showed up to that mother fucker's house to get my wife back. Can you believe he answered the door half naked and Kelly came downstairs in HIS ROBE!"

Kim's mouth dropped mocking Sal. Her attempt to laugh at his pain was unnoticed.

"She was in his robe! They were fucking!" He steamed.

"Hold up Sal let me go get something before you go any further." Kim ran off into the other room.

Sal paced until she returned. "You went to get popcorn," Asked Sal.

Kim responds, "You darn right, and I brought back some wine. This is about to get good."

"You think it's funny?" Kim wanted to tell her brother it was beyond funny. She felt it was payback for everything that he had put Kelly through, but she wouldn't kick him while he was so far down. "No! Not at all. So, he was half naked and she was in his robe? That's crazy. Keep going," she egged her brother on.

"I poured my heart to her. I told her I would wait for her to finish her little fling before we worked things out," Sal told Kim.

"Are you serious? Her lil fling? Brother, that man is far more than her fling. Those two are in love, but won't admit it. Come sit down. We need to put all the jokes aside and really talk," Said Kim.

Sal did as she asked. Kim could see the pain written all over his face.

"You know I love you, Kelly and the girls. I want nothing but the best for you and your family, but you need to be honest and see things as they really are. Do you think you had a healthy marriage?"

Sal thought about it for a moment. "Yes, I do. We had a few problems. Some ups and downs, but through it all we had a great marriage."

Kim shook her head. "I wouldn't say great. Kelly did everything she could to make you happy. Yet you still grumbled. The harder she tried, the more you grumbled. As time went on, I watched Kelly give up everything she loved to make it better."

"So, I didn't try to do anything to make her happy? I worked my ass off building that company to take care of her and the girls." Sal became very upset.

"Calm down," Kim said, "No one said that you didn't love your family. Yes, you take excellent care of them. But at some point, you and Kelly lost your way. She became focused on making you happy and you focused on being the best provider possible. Somewhere along the way you guys forgot to love each other."

Sal agreed with his sister to an extent. "I can see what you're saying, but I still love her. And I know she still loves me. Why can't we work this out?" Sal questioned.

"Yeah there is love between the two of you but there is also so much drama mixed in. Honestly speaking, things could never go back to the way they were before. Sal, you have a baby on the way by another woman. You will always love Kelly and after the pain heals, she might love you back. You will always be the father of her two beautiful daughters. I promise you she will love you for that. But loving you as her husband, lover, life partner, hell whatever you want to call it...NO! And to be honest I don't blame her. You took her through hell and back. Before you can even say anything...yes, she took you to hell and back as well. Even more reason why you guys won't be together."

Sal lowered his head and let his sister's words sink in. Her words were true. His marriage was over. "What am I supposed to do with Selena, Miss Know It All?"

Kim laughed, "Now that psycho bitch, she's your problem. You know how I am with the kids so this one will get the same treatment, but I refuse to deal with her. I'm telling you now. Don't look for me to get buddy with her. Any contact I have with the baby will go through you, Sal," Kim said firmly.

Sal responds "She's called me for the past week. I'm not ready to talk to her. I'll sit down with my lawyer before I talk to her again."

Kim chuckled, "Maybe I need to meet your lawyer. As much business you're given him, he's got to be rich. Tell me he's single."

***

Selena listened as another call went to his voicemail. Tears covered her face. Without Sal, she was out there alone. Left with no one else, she dialed the number unsure of what the outcome would be.

"Hello," the voice answered. Selena froze. "Hell...I know you're there. I can hear you breathing."

Selena hesitated before responding with a weak, "Hello."

Just as she thought, the voice on the other side of the phone wasn't pleased to hear from her.

"You have some nerve calling me. You do know they are after you?" The voice warned her.

"I wouldn't call you if I had any other choice," says Selena.

Silence came from the other end of the phone. "If they find me, they will kill my baby," Selena pleaded.

"If he finds out I helped you, my baby will kill me." The voice warned he, "I'll let Nancy know you're coming.

NOTHING LASTS FOREVER

Life or Death

Admiral wanted to curse himself for how things turned out with Kelly. Once again, he opened himself up to the thought of being with her. And just like every other time something, more like someone, got in the way. Needing to clear his head, he dialed Sam. Relieved when Sam answered, Admiral immediately began to apologize.

"Hey Sam, man I'm sorry to call you with this, but you know there's no one else I can talk to."

Sam knew right away what his brother-in-law was talking about.

"Look A, I've told you before I understand the situation with my sister, Michelle. We are doing everything in our power to make those bastards pay for what they did to her. I don't want you hanging on to what use to be. She's never coming back. Now tell me what's up?"

Admiral told Sam how Kelly showed up at his house to apologize and one thing lead to another. Before he could finish, Sam interrupted Admiral.

"It's about damn time bro!" Admiral let out a disapproving grunt, "Don't get excited. Once again something came up. This time her ex-husband showed up at my house! Can you believe he had the nerve to show up at my door begging her to take him back, AFTER she's done with me?"

Sam took a moment to take in what he heard. "Please tell me you didn't kill that fool?" Sam knew his brother-in-law/friend all too well.

"No sir, Kelly can hold her own."

Sam chuckled, "So, she shut you down, huh?"

"Yeah, yeah whatever," said Admiral. Sam became serious, "All jokes aside, talk to me." he told Admiral.

"Yeah, yeah whatever," said Admiral. Sam became serious, "All jokes aside, talk to me." he told Admiral.

"Sam, I feel like I should walk away from Kelly and just let her be. I'm tired of the back and forth. All I want is a normal relationship and everything with her is anything but normal."

Sam understood where his friend was coming from. This wasn't something you could talk to your everyday friends about. This could only be described as crazy by those not directly involved. "I ask the same thing every time and I'm going to say it again. Do you love her?"

Admiral did not have to think twice about his answer, "Yeah, I do. I love her."

"Then you know what you need to do. Stand by her, man. She's a good woman with a good heart. Help her out."

Admiral heard what Sam was saying, he just wished it was as easy to do. Stuck in his feelings of frustration and a bruised ego, Admiral resisted the urge to find Kelly. He dismissed the strange sense washing over his body. He convinced himself that it was just his natural desire to protect her. He needed a moment to reset his emotional state. Little did he know, Kelly was anything but safe.

The unanswered calls to Sal's phone triggered Selena to follow him right to Admiral's house. She watched from her car parked discretely down the street.

"How can he still beg her to take him back after I exposed how trifling she is?"

Selena didn't understand. She did everything possible to tear them apart. *"He should be mine,"* she cried softly. She touched her stomach as Sal's baby fluttered inside, *"you are his."*

There was only one-way Sal would get over Kelly. "I have to kill her," Selena said calmly. Selena was tired of watching Kelly take everyone and everything she cared about away from her. Starting from the bottom with BTB, working her way slowing to a position securing her future. Just when it was time to show the others, she was true BTB material, she met her mark. Sal was handsome. It was her job to charm him, she became enchanted with his ways. Thinking back to that very moment, Selena whispered "He's my everything." She called Sal one more time. She once again was greeted by his voicemail. Her last and final call could cost her, but it didn't matter.

***

Supreme barked from her chamber, "Be quiet!" She did not recognize the number on her caller ID. She told herself to let it go to voicemail. It was time to pick another mark. The group needed to move on from the 'Kelly Disaster', as they named it. Supreme convinced the group the failure was due to Selena's lack of experience, not her own obsession. Coming out of her trance, Supreme answered the call, "Hello." Selena was about to hang up. "Hello, is anyone there?" Supreme asked.

"I'm here," replied Selena. Supreme tried to alert the others without Selena hearing. They were too engulfed in their chatty conversations to notice.

"You should be dead. You and your bastard baby." The coldness oozed from her tone.

"Bitch, if you ever try to harm me or my baby again...mark my words, you'll be the one dead. Leave us alone and I'll leave you alone. Let me finish my business here with Kelly and I'm gone. You'll never see or hear from me again."

Supreme laughed and yelled into the phone, "You don't tell me what to do. This is MY show! You ungrateful bitch! I took your sorry ass in when you had nowhere to go. I found you lost in the streets, running away from your family. I gave you everything when you had nothing. I will hunt you down and kill you myself. I'm going to squeeze the last breath out of you."

Selena took Supreme's threat as a joke, "I'm not scared of you anymore. Like I said, stay out of my way. When I finished what I need to do, I'm gone."

Selena hung up before Supreme could open her mouth. Supreme decided not to tell the others about her call. They hated the way things turned out. She was to blame for everything gone wrong. Right now, everyone pointed fingers in the other direction. As long as they pointed away from her, she planned on keeping it that way.

Selena had to find Kelly. That was easy for her to do. When the group set its sights on Kelly, Selena was the one who staked her out. She had a good hunch where to find her. Selena picked one of the spots she followed Kelly to before. Just as she thought, Kelly showed up to her monthly dinner with her friends. "Time to get to work." Selena jumped right to it once Kelly went inside. She moved quick. One of Kelly's friends hadn't arrived yet. Selena didn't want to get caught in the act, so she slid under Kelly's car. Carefully, she sliced the brake lines. Not all the way, just enough to slowly drain the fluid. Selena said a silent prayer. She didn't want to hurt the twins, they were innocent in all of this. Selena really wasn't too concerned about them. Sal soon would have another baby. *"In the end, this is all for our baby."* she convinced herself.

Supreme left the compound without the other sisters noticing. From the car she called Admiral. She yelled at his answering machine, "A, I need to talk to you ASAP!" She dialed his number over and over again. "Please pick up," she cried this time into the machine, "I can't save her."

Seeing Supreme's number on his call log pissed Admiral off even more. He still was ticked off by Kelly's ex. *"Everyone involved with this chick is trouble."* he thought to himself. Sitting by the water to clear his head, Admiral wondered if a relationship with Kelly was in his best interest. He knew what his heart said, but this time he needed to think with his head.

Growing annoyed with the constant ringing and voicemail notifications, Admiral checked his phone. "You have 6 messages." the automated voice announced. The messages began to play back, Admiral hit delete once he heard the voice. He hit delete over and over again. As the made his way through, he noticed the callers voice became more and more frantic with each call. He listened to the whole message and dialed Supreme's number without hesitation.

"What do you mean you can't save her? What did you do!" he demanded.

"It's not me, I didn't do anything. But she's in trouble." Supreme told him.

Admiral was beyond furious. He hated talking to Supreme. She was one of the members that set Michelle up and now she was doing the same to Kelly. He hollered in to the receiver, "I told you to leave her alone!"

"A, I promised you that I would. That's exactly what I did. I walked away from Kelly completely. I tried to fix the whole situation, but Selena is out of control. She's after Kelly." She needed to tell him what Selena planned to do once she found Kelly. "I need you to stay calm. We have to stay in control if we are going to stop her."

"What the fuck are you talking about Supreme? TELL ME WHAT THE HELL IS GOING ON!" Supreme took a deep breath, "She's going to kill Kelly if we don't stop her." Admiral began to grow tired of Supreme's vagueness, "Who is trying to kill Kelly," he demanded to know. "Selena called me. She told me I better stay out of her way. If I know Selena, she's going to kill her. What are we going to do," she cried. Admiral didn't answer Supreme. He hung the phone up in her ear. He dialed Kelly's number as fast as his fingers would move. His call landed in her voicemail. He dialed her over and over again. "Damn it, Kelly!" he cursed.

"Sam!" Admiral yelled without giving his brother-in-law a chance to respond. He filled Sam in on the conversation he had with Supreme. "Calm down. I'll see what I can do." Sam hung up the phone knowing his brother-in-law wasn't going to take his advice. He called his wife, "Hey, Savannah," He said when she answered, "Things have spiraled out of control. Admiral just called me. Seems Selena is looking to kill Kelly. We've gotta do something." Savannah asked, "Does anyone know where Kelly is? Have they talked to her?" The answer to both of her questions were no. Sam hated feeling helpless. He couldn't bear to watch this happen to Admiral again. Savannah gave him a little bit of hope, "Hold on I think I still have that tracking device set up on her car. We set it up the first night she came to the party. Something told me not to take it off." She logged in and pulled up Kelly's location. "I'm sending you the info now, honey," Savannah said. Sam instantly forwarded the information to Admiral. He sped to Kelly's location only to find that he was too late. Selena had found Kelly. The two were engaged in a heated discussion. From his distance he couldn't hear what was being said, but he knew it was bad.

Kelly kept trying to walk away from Selena, who was hot on her heels. He called out Kelly's name. She turned to see who was calling her. "Can this day get any worse?" She threw her hands up. Kelly hopped in her car to get away from the two of them. Admiral continued screaming her name. She drove away as fast as possible to get away from them. Admiral followed to make sure she got away safely. Selena lingered back, just far enough to see her plan through.

Admiral continued dialing Kelly. She still wouldn't answer. Seeing his number pop up on her caller ID brought back feelings from their last conversation. Her heart told her Admiral was right for her. While her mind told her, she was all wrong for him. Seeing Selena, with Admiral running to her aid once again, just confirmed how things would be for the two of them. She convinced herself she would never be free from the reigns of BTB. She saw herself as forever ruined. Tears began to fall freely, Kelly struggled to see through them. She swerved in and out of traffic. Kelly fought to control both the car and her emotions. She continued to pick up speed as she rounded the windy turns. Admiral followed her in complete fear. "Stop Kelly!" he yelled out, hoping to will her to do so. Kelly continued to go faster and faster down the windy road. It was clear to him that she was in danger. He pulled up next to her, riding the shoulder of the road. The look on Kelly's face said it all. "Pull over!" he yelled at her. Through her tears she waved him away. This situation was getting dangerous. The last thing she wanted to do was harm Admiral.

She tried to slow down for the approaching red light. She pumped her breaks frantically. The more she pumped, the faster her car seemed to go. Admiral watched in horror as Kelly sped through the intersection. Fighting to avoid oncoming traffic Kelly forced her car off the road through a small break in the traffic. Admiral sighed in relief seeing her clear the other cars. Unfortunately, Kelly wasn't free from everything. She turned the steering wheel too far to the left. She tried to correct it by turning to the right. Her car started to spin out of control. Kelly screamed! Her car was moments away from stopping. The car spun completely off the side of the road and ran head on into a tree. Admiral watched in horror. *"How could this be happening again?"* He couldn't lose anyone else. He parked his car and ran to Kelly's. Smoke rose from under her smashed hood. He called her name repeatedly. Kelly did not respond. He opened the car door. Blood trickled down her forehead from a small gash. The sight made him cringe. "I'm here, baby." he said. Still, there was no response. Kelly was dazed. Her eyes were blank. When the paramedics arrived, they checked her vitals and determined that she was safe to transport. They rushed her to the nearest hospital where the doctors performed a number of tests. Slowly, Kelly started to come back. Seeing her change, the doctors updated Admiral with the good news. "The blow to the head caused a concussion. She's coming around and will be fine. We are going to keep her overnight for observation." Admiral sighed in relief. The doctor continued, "If she continues to show improvement, I will discharge her as long as she has someone with her at all times." Admiral nodded and shook the doctor's hand. "I won't let her out of my sight," he promised.

The doctor started walking away. He stopped and turned to Admiral, "The police want to talk to her. Something about her car being tampered with. I told them she would be up for it in a day or two. I don't want them hounding her before she's recovered. I know they need to investigate who sabotaged her vehicle, but my main concern is her health." Admiral agreed with the doctor. He immediately went to her room.

Kelly was awake but closed her eyes once Admiral walked in. "Why are you here?" she mumbled. Admiral chuckled, "Glad to see you didn't get the sass knocked out of you." Kelly pouted at his comment. "Awe, don't give me that look, baby. I was so worried about you." Admiral sat down next to her bed and held her hand as he continued, "I thought I had lost you, but now is not the time for that. Just rest." Kelly relaxed for a moment. She sprung up in slow motion. "Ow," she cried out in pain, "What about my girls?" Admiral frowned at her pain. "Woman, take it easy. I've taken care of that already. Sal's sister has the girls. She's keeping them until you're better." Kelly stared at Admiral in disbelief.

"Kelly, did you forget I was this close to being partners with your husband?"

She responded loud and clear, "You mean my ex!"

He smiled, "Call him what you want, but I reached out to him and let him know you were here." Her eyes widened as he continued, "He wanted to come up here. I didn't think you wanted that, so I told him you would call him when they finished checking you over."

Kelly sighed, "I'll call him when I get home. I'm ready to leave, how much longer til they finish? " she asked.

"Oh no," Admiral warned her, "You're not going anywhere. They're keeping you overnight."

She pouted again, but knew it was pointless. Admiral wasn't letting her leave. She closed her eyes and slept until the doctor came in. At least that was her plan. Kelly slept for hours. She heard voices conversing faintly. She slowly opened her eyes. Admiral was shaking hands with the doctor.

"No, wait," she called out before he left.

"Oh, well hello Sleeping Beauty. How are you feeling," the doctor asked. "I'm feeling much better." Kelly smiled sweetly.

Admiral watched her lay it on thick.

"In fact, the only thing that would make me feel better would be going home."

The doctor shifted his feet.

"If all stays the same, I don't see a problem with you going home tomorrow."

Kelly pouted, "Doc I really just want to go home and climb in my own bed. I'll even follow up with my doctor in the morning. It's just been a stressful day for me. Please," she begged.

The doctor sighed, "On one condition," Kelly smiled and agreed before he could finish his sentence, "Admiral remains by your side the entire time."

She shook her head "no". The doctor said, "Well, have it your way then, enjoy the rest of your stay here and I will check on you in the morning."

Kelly pounded the sheets in defeat, "Fine, I'll stay with him."

"Don't pout," the doctor told her, "This young man seems to care about you greatly. I know he'll do what's best for you. I'll have the nurse bring in your discharge papers." He turned to Admiral, "If things don't seem right, you rush her back in you hear me?"

Admiral replied, "I'll bring her back immediately if somethings wrong."

Once the doctor left Kelly started getting dressed. She told Admiral, "You can just drop me off at my place, I'll be fine."

He grabbed her shirt and pants out of her hands, "Are we going to do this the hard way or are you going to behave?"

She replied, "Fine."

Admiral kneeled and gently slid her pants on to her legs. His face lingered next to her skin. *"Not now."* he told himself. Then to Kelly, "We need to get your shirt on, I'll slip it over your head, once you pull it down, I can untie your gown." Admiral managed to get Kelly dressed and out of the hospital. They decided to go back to his house. Kelly was too tired to argue. Admiral settled her in and prepared a light meal while she rested. Kelly tossed and turned in his bed. Her mind recalled the last time she was here. She kicked the covers off. Laughter erupted from the doorway, "Not this again," Admiral teased.

"It's not nice to laugh at people," Kelly barked.

"I've never seen you so pouty. Talk to me, what can I do to make it better?"

Kelly wanted to tell him there was nothing he could do, it was all her fault but she couldn't will herself to.

"Eat," he told her, "you will feel better."

She did as he said and then took a shower. She raided his closet to find something that half way fit her. One look and Admiral blurted out, "I like that look on you." He cursed himself for saying it out loud. Still being somewhat defiant Kelly told him, "If we were at my house, I could find something a little more appropriate." She stuck out her tongue to add a little more sass. "You've got something coming once your better," he warned her.

"Can I have it now," she teased.

"Get in the bed and settle down." He says then sat across the room in a chair. "Come on so we can get some rest."

Kelly looked confused.

"You're not sleeping in that chair, are you?" Admiral nodded his head, "I'm fine. Just rest."

Kelly sat up, "Now you're just being silly. This is YOUR house, and I'm in YOUR bed. You can either get in this bed with me or we both are sitting up all night in chairs."

Admiral knew Kelly well enough to know she was serious. Reluctantly, he climbed in bed. He crawled to the far side, putting as much space as possible between them. Kelly laughed, "You look like you're scared." Admiral closed his eyes and spoke, "I'm tired. Good night." He turned over hoping Kelly would do the same. She turned away kicking and fussing at the sheets. He drifted off to sleep while Kelly continued with her battle.

Sometime later, Admiral woke to the sound of muffled crying.

"Baby, what's wrong? Are you in pain," Admiral asked.

Kelly shook her head side to side, afraid to talk. Admiral gently tugged her closer. Kelly resisted at first. He hated seeing her cry. He moved to her side. He stroked her face.

"Talk to me," he said.

Kelly closed her eyes, "I'm a horrible person. I dragged you in to all of this. Every time I try to walk away from you, things end up involving you." Tears trickled down her face. Admiral wiped them way, "No, baby you're wrong, I was involved in this well before you. I never told you my connection to BTB. It's time you stop punishing yourself about my connection." Kelly listened on intently. "BTB targeted my wife the same way they targeted you." Kelly jumped up, "OW," she cried out in pain.

"Take it easy," Admiral said holding her closer.

"What do you mean, your WIFE?" Kelly questioned.

"I never got a chance to tell you how I knew Supreme. I'm not going to have this conversation if you don't calm down. You need to take it easy," he warned. She turned and crossed her arms. "Talk," Kelly said.

"My wife or my ex-wife, I don't know what to call her anymore, was targeted just like you. BTB was set on destroying me, just like how they did with Sal. Michelle wouldn't let that happen. She fought BTB every step of the way trying to protect me. It became clear they wouldn't stop until I lost everything. She risked her life to save me from any of that. She ended up in an institution. She has the mind of a child after suffering from a complete and total breakdown. The doctors said she will never fully recover. I went to see her recently," Admiral paused before continuing on. Tears formed in the corner of his eyes, "I've never told anyone this story other than my Grandmom and Michelle's brother. They were the only family we had left." Kelly saw the pain written all over his face. "They took everything from me, until I met you. The day you walked into the shop was the happiest I felt in a long time." He leaned over and kissed her forehead again. "So, I'm involved in whatever it takes to keep them from hurting you anymore. Call me selfish, but I need you Kelly."

Kelly let his words sink in, "I love you," She blurted out. Admiral smiled, "I love you too." He closed his eyes and let her words sink in. She planted her lips softly against his. Admiral's body tensed up in reaction to her kiss. He wanted to kiss her back, but she was hurt. Once again, now was not the time for them to be together. "I can't," He told her, "you need to rest." Kelly grabbed his face, "I need this," she said as she put her mouth to his again. Admiral's beast stirred below. He resisted the urge to kiss Kelly back. He pulled away. Kelly didn't give up. She moved her kisses down to Admiral's jawline. Admiral groaned trying to fight the sensation.

"Kelly, don't do this," he pleaded.

Her hands moved to his chest.

"I love you," she said again.

Admiral turned his head away. He had to hide his emotions.

"Look at me," Kelly said softly. "I can't," Admiral replied. "I need you to look at me." Admiral turned his head back. His eyes were watery. A soft smile spread across Kelly's face. "I love you," He exhaled deeply. Kelly continued kissing Admiral's smooth chocolate skin. His conscious battled with his inner beast. *"If we do this, there's no turning back."* His inner beast roared loud and clear, *"From day one, there's been no turning back."* Admiral couldn't argue with that rational.

He positioned his body as his hands caressed her curves. Kelly's lips parted to moan, but her luscious lips were met by Admiral's. Kelly's body fluttered. Admiral lifted her shirt. He frowned at her bruises and cuts.

He reached his hand out to touch her. Kelly pulled his hand to her body. "It's okay." Admiral let Kelly place his hand on her bare skin. "I'm okay." Admiral groaned. She tenderly embraced his face. Fully giving in to the moment, his hands inched slowly up towards her breast. A tingly sensation ran through her body as Admiral's hands cupped her breast. He looked on, admiring how perfectly they fit his hands. He lowered his head, allowing his face to nuzzle her breast. Kelly's nipples reacted in anticipation of what was to come. He circled her darkened spots as if they were a road map to her mountain tops. Eventually, Admiral tore his mouth away from her mounds. He kissed his way down her body, making note of every scar and bruise. He placed a kiss on each one.

Kelly's hands disappeared between the individual coils of Admiral's locs. Admiral set a direct course for Kelly's honey spot. The route to her honey spot was blocked. Earlier he had loved the way his sweatpants hung from her sexy frame, right now they were an interference. His hands tore away from her breast. They locked on to the waistband and forcefully tugged them down. The curve of her hips caught his attention first. His lips connected with the bare skin near her soft mound. Kelly moaned as he inched closer to her sweetness. Admiral glanced up at Kelly before burying his face her lady garden. He inhaled her delectable scent. He parted her divide. He stared face to face with her kitty. Admiral flicked his tongue lightly against her clit. He repeated this, sending Kelly into a fit. He laughed knowing how worked up she was becoming.

Deciding to stop toying around, Admiral widened his tongue and placed it below her love hole. He licked his way back up to her clit. Admiral locked his lips on it tightly before, performing a rhythmic assault. Kelly moaned as Admiral brought her to the verge of climax and abruptly stopped. Kelly cried out, "NO, don't stop." Sitting up to adjust his member, Admiral's mouth was heavily coated with Kelly's delight. "We have to stop," she said. Admiral was puzzled, "Why?" Kelly sighed,

"Hello...PROTECTION!" Admiral put his finger up, "Hold that thought." He reached over to the nightstand. "Nothing's interfering with tonight." Admiral pulled out an arsenal of condoms. He tore open the packaging, keeping his eyes locked on Kelly. Her heart raced, "I don't know if I should be afraid or excited at this point." She played it off as if she was kidding around, but deep down she was serious.

Admiral read Kelly's expression. "Relax baby, I'm only going to do what you want me to. If you want me to stop, say it." He kissed her on her forehead. "You know I'd never hurt you."

Kelly smiled, "It's not you I'm worried about."

She nodded her head in the direction of his lower portion. She watched as he carefully rolled the condom over his dick. Once it was covered, he traced the tip around the lips of her vagina. Kelly hips began to move slowly.

"How does this feel," he asked.

Kelly parted her lips to moan, "Gooood."

He circled her clit, "How about now?"

Once again, her response was, "Gooood."

Admiral asked her again, only this time he said, "Look at me," Her eyes looked up at him, "How does this feel?" Admiral circled her opening.

Kelly blushed. She wanted to look away, but she knew better.

"You didn't answer my question, you don't like it?" Admiral pulled back.

"Don't stop," she begged.

Admiral put his dick back in to position and asks, "You want this?"

Kelly looked Admiral in the eyes. "I want it," she told him.

He slowly inserted his tip inside of her tight wet pussy. "You want this?" he asked. He asked one last time before fully making his way in to her core. Kelly gripped the sheets, she felt herself expanding around Admiral's dick. He started off with a slow pace, his dick slid in and out. Kelly's pussy coated it with a coating of her delight. Admiral went to thrust, but was stopped by Kelly. She pushed her hand against his chest.

"What's wrong, you want me to stop?"

Kelly replied, "No, it's my turn."

Admiral didn't want to stop. The look he was getting from Kelly confirmed that it was in his best interest. "I wanted to make love to you." He rolled over and gave Kelly a fake pouty face.

Kelly climbed on top of Admiral, "So, you like me being on top of you?" Admiral played along, he continued to pout. It was really hard for him pretend like he didn't want her on top. Kelly rested her clit up against his shaft. She trailed her fingertips around the head. "You didn't answer my question." Kelly used the pads of her fingers to gently squeeze the tip. Admiral couldn't hold out any longer. A low groan escaped from him. Kelly loved how sexy he sounded. "Mmmm, remember how you made me tell you how I wanted 'this'", she said referring to his dick, "I want YOU to tell me how bad you want me on top, riding you slowly. Tell me how bad you want to feel my walls sliding up and down on your big hard dick."

Admiral shook his head in disbelief, "You don't play fair."

Kelly pressed her body against his, she kissed his lips. "Tell me how you want to feel the inside of my wet pussy, baby." Kelly had Admiral right where she wanted him. He was close to caving. She motioned like she was about to climb off. Admiral grabbed on to her hips, "NO, I want you so bad!" Hearing the words she wanted to hear, Kelly squatted, placing her entrance over his tip.

The view from Admiral's position was amazing. Kelly's beautiful naked body lingered inches from his dick. The intense look on her face mesmerized him. "I want you, baby," he said again. Kelly inched her way down. Admiral watched as he disappears deep inside of Kelly. His hands held on to her hips. Kelly settled in to steady rhythm. Admiral was torn between the sight of her breast bouncing up and down and the disappearing act taking place between Kelly's legs. He dreamed of this very moment since they first met and so many times they tried, but life had a funny way of butting in. As much has he wanted to savor this moment, Kelly was in complete control. She circled her hips going faster and faster with each wind. It was a losing battle for Admiral. That sensation only known to his imagination was building down below. Every muscle in his body tensed up, Kelly moaned as she bounced harder on his manhood, "Are you gonna cum for me, baby," she asked.

Admiral wanted to respond but his mouth wouldn't cooperate. Kelly asked again, "Baby, I'm about to cum, are you gonna cum with me?" Admiral growled. Before he had a chance to answer, Kelly's face showed signs of imminent pleasure. Admiral growled again, "I'm cumming, baby!" He told Kelly just as she starting riding her own orgasmic wave. Kelly collapsed on top of Admiral. He closed his eyes and wrapped his arms tightly around her. Kelly giggled, "I can't believe we just did that." Admiral rolled her over to his side, "Are you okay with what we just did? I don't want you to do anything that you're not comfortable with." Kelly caressed his face, "I'm very comfortable with what we did. I haven't felt this way in a long time. I just can't believe it took us this long to get it together." Kelly kissed Admiral softly. "Don't get me started again," he warned her. "That's exactly what I'm trying to do." Admiral kissed her back one more time. "No more," he told her, "I've done enough damage for one night. Now, sleep." Kelly wanted to tell Admiral how he wasn't the boss of her, but the excitement of today had taken its toll. She laid her head on his chest and closed her eyes. Admiral watched as she drifted off to sleep. He sighed heavily. At this very moment everything was perfect. If things could stay this way he could finally start to live again. Something deep down told him to enjoy it now, because nothing lasts forever.

ALL EYES ON THE PRIZE

Signs of Opportunity

Selena couldn't believe Kelly survived the crash. Admiral got in the way of things turning out the way she planned. Selena arrived at the hospital with hopes of finishing what she started, but, Admiral was there playing hero again. *"I'm never going to get her as long as he's around."* she thought to herself. Selena came up with another plan. This one would require calling in one of her favors.

"It's been a while since I've heard from you, Dana."

Doctor Reynolds said into the receiver. Dana was the name Selena was born with. When she took her under her wing, Supreme insisted that Dana change her name to something more desirable. It took a long time for BTB to give Selena a chance. They considered her to be the group pet. They passed her around and around for their personal pleasure. It didn't take long for her to grow tired of the degrading routine. She started branching out on her own and building a clientele of her own.

"Hi, Doctor Reynolds," she purred.

"I've missed my time with you." he told her.

Selena recalled how she and the 'Good Doctor' used to spend time together.

"Why don't we meet up and do what you like since I'm in your area. In fact, I'm visiting someone in the hospital if you're working."

This was music to the doctor's ears.

"I'm with a patient who was in a car crash, maybe we can meet tonight." he suggested.

"That's not going to work, I need to see you now!" Selena caught herself getting worked up.

"But, I have a patient right now. It has to be later," he told her.

"I'll meet you at our special spot in about twenty minutes. That should give you enough time to get her situated. Don't keep me waiting, doc, I really need to see you," Selena said calmly.

"How do you know my patient is a she?" Doctor Reynolds asked.

Selena had to think quick before she got herself caught up. "Most women are terrible drivers, and I take it so was your patient." she laughed.

Dr. Reynolds fell for her explanation and met Selena a little later than she expected. The look on her face told him she was pissed. "I told you not to keep me waiting. I wait for no one!" Doctor Reynolds apologized for keeping Selena waiting.

"I'm sorry my patient wasn't doing too well when they first brought her in."

This peaked her interest. "So, it was a bad accident?"

Dr Reynolds sighed, "It was one, but I was able to get her fixed up. She's stable for now."

Selena pressed further, "What do you mean by for now?"

She removed the doctor's lab coat. His heart raced, "She took on a pretty nasty blow to the head. She sustained a serious concussion and a laceration to the forehead."

"Have you already discharged her?" Selena asked as she opened her coat.

"You're not wearing any clothes!" The doctor blurted out in surprise.

"Lucky for you, I keep a fun bag with me at all times. Now get on your knees," she demanded.

The "Good Doctor" did as he was told.

"Just like a good lil boy. Now tell me how much you've missed this." Selena spread her legs apart exposing her kitty.

Doctor Reynolds inhaled her scent, "Can I taste you Mistress?"

Selena shoo'ed him away. "Don't you have a patient to tend to?"

Doctor Reynolds didn't want to focus on his patient right now. "I want to tend to you right now."

Selena played him right along into her trap. "So, what's the deal with her anyway?" Selena asks. Doctor Reynolds told Selena how his patient wanted to go home, but she needed to stay for observation. Selena convinced him to let her go. "If you go back to the hospital and send her home you'd be free to taste me all night."

Doctor Reynolds laid his head on Selena's thigh. He loved the way her kitty smelled. Just the thought of her scented desire flowing through his nostrils was enough to make him shoot a load off.

"She could go home with the guy who brought her in." he thought out loud.

"She just needs someone to watch over her, right." she suggested.

He agreed to it and in return Selena let him lick the moist folds of her pussy. "Only a little bit baby, you have to save some for tonight." Selena moaned. She strung Doctor Reynolds along just far enough to get what she needed. Selena had no intention of seeing the good doctor after today. If everything went as she planned, she wouldn't see any of them after today.

She followed Kelly back to Admiral's house, after Doctor Reynolds discharged her. This would be easier if Kelly went back to her place, so Selena was determined to wait it out. Admiral wouldn't be able to protect her all the time. She sat in her car and watched. She watched the house for signs of opportunity. Several cars ahead of Selena, Supreme sat slumped behind the wheel of a minivan. Both completely unaware of the others' presence. While Supreme wanted to protect and love Kelly, Selena was the one who intended to harm her.

Also watching from afar was Sal. When Admiral called and informed him that his wife was injured in the hospital, Sal immediately jumped in his car. Admiral told him that he didn't think it was a good idea for him to come out because Kelly was very upset.

"That's MY wife not yours!" he barked at Admiral.

Still Admiral wouldn't let him see her. Sal drove circles around the hospital. He went back and forth about going inside. *"Was Kelly ok? Was it really her who didn't want him there or was it all Sal?"* So many questions rolled around in his head. Sal completely lost track of time. On his last circle around the block, something caught his eye. It was more like someone. "It's her!" he exclaimed. He spotted Kelly as Admiral helped wheel her out to his car. Sal pounded the steering wheel. He was tired of watching Admiral play the role that he took vows for. He followed the pair back to Admiral's house where he kept watch until he received a call from Selena. He couldn't believe things went this far. He lost his family because of her and now she was carrying his child. He would have to deal with her for the rest of his life. He sat in the car and waited for a chance to sneak a face-to- face conversation with Kelly. When his phone rang, it was the last person he wanted to talk to. Selena wanted to become this instant family, but the only family Sal wanted was with Kelly.

Sal sat in his car steaming. Between Admiral and Selena, he wasn't sure who pissed him off the most. Admiral was the man who took his wife from him and Selena was the woman who took him away from his wife. Together they both were the reason for Sal's divorce, or at least that's what he thought. Sal started his car and left. He decided to go pick his girls up from Kim's, they were the only thing that could take away the pain in his heart. Speeding off with a loud commotion, Sal whizzed past Selena. He didn't see him, however, Supreme saw him fly by. "Idiot," she said out loud. A few minutes later, Selena pulled past Supreme unnoticed. Supreme shifted in her seat. She settled in, prepared to wait for the perfect opportunity to take back what was to be hers.

Unaware of the chaos building outside of Admiral's front door. Kelly woke up a few hours later wrapped in Admiral's arms, "I could wake up like this every day," she told him. Admiral kissed her softly on the forehead. "Your wish is my command." he replied.

"That's not what I'm wishing for right now," Kelly teased him. She wiggled her body against his as he spoke, "Like I said before, your every wish is my command." Kelly knew there was more behind his sexual innuendo. He started kissing Kelly all over.

"Baby, you know if you want this every day, you can have me every day. I love you and will give everything to be there for you and the girls." Admiral tried to read the tense look on her face, "Now if that's not what you want or need, I understand and will respect that."

Kelly sighed, "That's not what I want."

This time Admiral was the one with the tensed look on his face.

"I want you in my life, I'm just not sure how to make it happen. I want to...."

Admiral cut her off, "Being happy is all that you should want and if I can do that for you and the girls, I will. If you let me, of course."

Kelly beamed from ear to ear, "I don't deserve you."

"Finally, something we can agree on," Admiral said. Kelly punched him lightly on his arm. He held on to her hands and kissed them, "You deserve so much more than me." He let go of her hands and ran his over the soft curves of her body. Kelly loved the way her body felt under his touch. His mouth grazed her shoulder. Kelly moaned. Admiral moved his kisses towards her neck. Her hands reached out for the back of his head. She pulled him closer, "Yes," she moaned. Admiral pulled back. Taking a deep breath, he replied, "Your wish is my command."

Just in time to ruin the perfect moment, Admiral's work phone rang. Kelly pounded the sheets in disgust.

"Just ignore it," he said to Kelly.

The phone rang again. "Answer it," she said as she moved away.

"WHAT?" Admiral barked in to his cell phone.

The voice on the other end spoke, "This is Secure Alert Security Systems, whom am I speaking with?" Admiral didn't want to be questioned right now, but he knew they were protecting his business.

"This Admiral Brown, how may I help you?"

"Sir, the alarm was triggered at The Brown Spot. We are sending an officer to this location. Is there someone at this location or will you meet them there?" the caller asked.

"Yes, I'm on my way," huffed Admiral. "I gotta go to the cafe, someone tripped the alarm," he told Kelly as he hung up the phone.

He quickly dressed. Before he left, he states sternly, "Stay here! Do not leave this house, Kelly."

Kelly's face crossed, he responded to her look, "I'm sorry baby, I just want you to be safe and to rest."

Kelly pouted, he smiled and promised, "If you stay put, I promise to pick up where I left off at." He tucked the blankets snuggly around her, he then turned on the t.v. before kissing her goodbye.

The moment Admiral walked out the door, Supreme knew her plan was close to working. If all went as planned, Kelly would do exactly what she needed her to do. Moments later, Kelly headed out the door and got into one of Admiral's spare cars. *"I'll be back before he even knows I left."* she assured herself. Kelly just wanted to go home and feel like she was half way normal. Happy to see her own driveway, she ran into the house. "It feels so good to be home. I can't wait to shower and get comfortable." Kelly kicked off Admiral's slides heading straight for her room. She blared smooth R&B tunes from her radio. Kelly undressed and hopped in the shower. The hot water stung at first. She cringed at the painful sensation until the warmth started to soothe her body. Kelly let the water wash away all of her tension. She was so relaxed, a little too relaxed to hear her front door close. Tip toeing her way up the stairs, Supreme shed her clothes. Placing a hand on the door, she pushed it open slowly. Steam billowed into the hallway. Gently stepping into the bathroom allowed Supreme to enter unnoticed. She admired Kelly's silhouette behind the curtain. *"How did she get me like this?"* Supreme asked her inner self. She partially peeled back the curtain before she could think of the answer.

With her eyes closed, Kelly found her mind wandering back to the way Admiral made her body feel. His hands covered every inch of her body. *"I have to go back."* She told herself. She really missed him. It was the only way she could explain why the sensation of his fingers lingered on her skin. Supreme stood behind Kelly, far enough back so that only her fingers could reach. When Kelly didn't react, she moved slightly closer. She wrapped Kelly in her arms, "I've missed this so much." Supreme said out loud instead of in her head.

Kelly screamed and jumped, realizing she was not alone, "What are you doing here? How did you get in here? Get out!" She yelled at the top of her lungs.

Admiral pulled up in the driveway, noticing that there were two cars in Kelly's driveway. He recognized both, one was his and the other belonged to Supreme. He wondered why Kelly would sneak off to meet up with her. Every time he takes a step forward with this girl, he takes a million back. Once he reached the door, he noticed it was a jar. Suddenly Kelly's scream pierced his ears. Darting in the house, he climbed the steps two at a time. He headed towards the commotion coming out of the bathroom. Admiral nearly loses it when he sees the Kelly entwined in Supreme's arms inside of the shower.

"This is why you left me? You want to be with her?"

Admiral pounded the wall. How could he be this stupid? He questioned himself.

"It's not what you think," Kelly yelled, fighting to get away from Supreme.

Seeing how livid Admiral is, Supreme keys in on his Admiral's emotions. "No, it's not what you think at all." She says slyly as she pins Kelly against the wall. Kelly continues to fight back. She pushes her way free. She jumps out of the shower and forcefully pulls the towel off of the rack. Realizing that she is in hysterics, it becomes clear to him that Kelly didn't want any of this. Admirals booming voice pierces the room, "Why didn't you stay at my house like I told you to?" Admiral was losing it at this point.

Kelly started to reply, "I didn't think."

Admiral cut her off, "That's just it, you never think about listening to anyone other than yourself! Did you forget what happened to you yesterday? I'm supposed to be taking care of you and what about what this bitch did to Michelle?"

"You still don't know, do you?" Supreme asked Admiral, "You can blame me all you want, but your beloved Michelle knew exactly what she was doing. Don't let her fool you."

Admiral looks at Kelly who is in the corner crying and shivering uncontrollably. His rage was boiling over, but all he could think about was comforting Kelly. He grabbed her up and buried her head in his chest. He reached into his pocket and dialed 911. Keeping his eyes focused on Supreme, he spoke into the handset, "I'd like to report an intruder."

It didn't take the officers long to arrive. Admiral was surprised Supreme didn't try to flee. She appeared to be calm until the officers arrived and she didn't recognize one of them. Admiral and Kelly watched as Supreme was handcuffed and carried away naked. Screaming at the top of her lungs, "It's not over! Michelle knew what she was doing just like this one here. No matter what you do, she's mine!" A violent shudder ran through Kelly. Supreme was right. She owned her and there was nothing she could do about it. After everything was settled, Admiral waited for Kelly to get her things. He followed her back to his house. Once inside, Kelly remained distant. He reached out to hug her but she pulled away.

"Baby, I'm sorry I flew off on you like that."

Admiral leaned back against the wall. His head hung low, his locs hung loose around his face. "I was scared Kelly," he said softly, "I was afraid I'd lost you."

It hurt Kelly to hear his pain. It hurt even more knowing that she was the cause of it all.

"I'm fine," she reassured him, "I just need to go lay down."

LEAVING IT ALL BEHIND

Bringing Down The House

While Kelly sorted through her options, Selena kept trying to get through to Sal. He needed to understand that they were going to be a family. She followed him to his house. She jumped out of her car and raced up to him. *"Beat him to the door."* she told herself.

"Sal, wait," she cried out.

"What the hell are you doing here," he questioned, "I told you I didn't want to see you anymore."

Tears streaked Selena's face, "Let me explain, baby," she pleaded.

Sal didn't want to hear anything else from Selena, "If it's not about the baby then leave me the fuck alone. Now leave before my girls get here." Sal slammed the door in her face. Selena begged once again, "Let me explain." No matter how hard she tried Sal wouldn't listen. Thoughts ran through her head. Thoughts she didn't want to hear, *"Make him listen. Make him pay. He left you no choice."*

Sal waited for Kim to drop the girls off. After letting Selena work his last nerve, the girls were just who he needed to see. They piled into his arms and smothered him with kisses. For a moment, everything wrong in his life was right.

"Daddy can we watch our movie? Aunt Kim brought us a new movie."

Sal hugged them a little tighter and replied, "Of course, we can. Who wants Daddy's special popcorn?"

The girls cried out in unison, "MEEEE!"

They snuggled on the couch and started watching the girls' latest repeat movie. By the time they reached the halfway point, Sal and his ladies were fast asleep. Selena waited until nightfall to peak into the windows. She found them in a dead sleep. She thought twice about what she was about to do. The way Sal held on to his daughters was all she wanted for her and the baby.

"You made me do this," she cried. She apologized silently over and over to Sal. She poured gasoline around the house's entire perimeter.

Selena coughed violently, inhaling the fumes was harmful for the baby. She started to feel lightheaded. *"Come on."* she pushed herself as she poured out the last drop. Pulling out the matches made her hands tremble. Tears filled her eyes. Selena wasn't sure if they were from the fumes or what she was about to do to the man she loved. Taking a few steps back, Selena put distance between her and the house. She took the fire bomb out of the small bag she was carrying. "Goodbye, Sal baby."she said before lighting the tip and throwing it towards the house. As if in slow motion, the house became engulfed in a sea of flames. Selena snuck off before anyone could see her. She was certain there was no way for them to escape.

Calls rang out over every emergency signal. The call came over the airways: All units report to 1242 Dawson Place for reports of a fire." Supreme called out from the back seat, "JERRY ENOUGH WITH THE GAMES! LET ME LOOSE SO WE CAN GO TO THAT HOUSE!" Jerry tried to ignore her. He didn't want to give off the wrong impression to his new partner, more importantly he did want his partner to know about his connection to Supreme.

"Quiet down back there," he ordered.

"GOD DAMN IT, JERRY, THAT'S KELLY'S PLACE!"

Jerry ignored her once again. Supreme banged on the metal cage, "IT'S KELLY'S PLACE!"

Jerry shook his head.

"We just left Kelly's house, I'm not buying it!"

Supreme kicked the back of the seat," Jerry, you don't understand. Kelly's family lives in that house, her ex-husband and her children. Do you think it's a coincidence that it's on fire? Please you've gotta take me there," she pleaded, "You're in this as much as me," she reminded him.

His rookie sat in silence as Jerry responded to the call, "Yeah, Dispatch, this is Car 4639 we are in route to 1242 Dawson Place."

Jerry didn't know how to explain it to his Rookie. "We'll just swing by and check things out." he said nonchalantly to him.

"Oh, no worries Sir. Whatever you say."

The Rookie didn't want to cause any trouble, nor did he want to be a part of whatever was going on. This was his first day on patrol.

"Oh my God!"

Supreme gasped when they turned the corner. The house was engulfed in flames. The street was filled with firetrucks attempting to control the beast destroying Kelly's old home. *"Selena."* she said under her breath. Jerry brought the car to a sudden stop. He jumped out of the car and went to check in with another officer. He was only gone for a few minutes. He found his rookie with a strange look on his face. He peered into the back seat.

"She's gone?" he questioned.

Slowly the rookie nodded.

"Dayum," Jerry said as he slumped in to the seat.

He remembered the first time Supreme pulled his card. "She owns everyone." he said trying to ease his guilt.

"Did the family at least make it out okay," asked the rookie.

"Yeah, they made it out. The two girls made it out safe, however the dad was badly burned trying to save them. "They are notifying the next of kin as we speak."

 Kelly's phone rang and rang.

"Kel, Kel, wake up." Admiral shook Kelly awake. She reached over and grabbed her phone. "Hello," she answered in a groggy voice, "WHAT," she yelled in to the receiver.

The caller repeated what he was saying before Kelly interrupted.

"There has been a fire at 1242 Dawson Place, you are listed as next of kin for Sal, Hailey and Harper James."

She cut him off again, "What happened? What do you mean next of kin?"

Kelly became visibly upset and this worried Admiral.

"Baby, what's going on?"

"Please what's happened to my girls?" Kelly pleaded.

Tears began to flow.

"Ma'am they are safe. They are being taken First National Memorial." She breathed a sigh of relief. "And what about my husband?"

The word husband escaped her mouth before she could even process the fact that they were no longer husband and wife.

"Sal James did not escape unharmed. We need you to meet the ambulance at First National Memorial."

Kelly jumped out of bed and got dressed.

"Baby what's going on," Admiral asked.

Kelly trembled, "The girls and Sal, the house, there was a fire."

Kelly barely made sense at this point.

"Stop!." Admiral held her, "Stop for a minute, baby. Slow down and let me help you."

Kelly shook her head, "NO, I have to go! It's my girls, Admiral."

"I know," he told her "Let me take you. You are in no condition to drive," he begged.

Kelly agreed to let him drive. She remained quiet on the drive over.

"Are you okay," Admiral asked.

Kelly quietly responded, "I can't keep living like this."

Admiral tried to hold her hand. Kelly quickly jerked her hand away. Admiral didn't push any further. They pulled up to the hospital.

"You go ahead in, I'll park the car and meet up with you."

Kelly raced to the information desk. She located the floor her girls were on. The girls cried out when they saw her. "Mommy!" Kelly hugged them tight, she cried her heart out. "My babies." Kelly checked every inch of their bodies. From head to toe, they were nothing short of a miracle. They were a little shook up and worried about Sal.

"Mommy, they won't let us see daddy. They said we had to wait for you." They cried.

"Stay here for mommy. I need to go talk to the doctors."

The girls held onto their mom, begging her to allow them to come along.

"I need you to wait here for me. I promise, I'm coming right back."

They clung on to her for dear life.

"I need to check on daddy, please let go girls."

She knew they were scared, but what if Sal wasn't in the same condition as them. So many questions ran through her head.

As usual, Admiral shows up at the right moment to divert their attention, "Hi, ladies." The girls softly replied, "Hi." He figured they might not be too receptive to him considering the situation, so he stopped by the gift shop as a precaution.

"I bought these for two little girls who had boo-boos." A small smile tempted their angelic faces. "But, I don't see anyone who needs these."

He held out two cuddly teddy bears. Each bear held a get-well balloon in each hand. The girls released Kelly from their clutches.

"I have a boo-boo," they chimed almost in unison.

"Why don't you come tell me about it while your mommy goes and talks to your dad and his doctors." The girls sat down next to Admiral, "But it hurts right here." pointing to elbows, fingertips, eyebrows and everywhere else. Kelly thanked him before she snuck off to Sal's room. She caught the doctor as he was coming out of Sal's room.

"Excuse me, are you his doctor," Kelly asked pointing to Sal.

"Yes. Are you his wife?" the doctor questioned. Kelly immediately replied, "Yes," out of habit, "I mean, I'm his ex-wife, Kelly James," she corrected herself.

The doctor was relieved to see her, "I've been expecting you. Sal listed you as his next of kin. Let's sit over here and discuss his injuries."

The doctor guided Kelly to one of the nearby Family Consultation rooms. He cut straight to the point.

"Your husband, I apologize your ex-husband was brought in with severe burns to 50% of his body,"

Kelly formed her mouth to ask how, but the doctor answered her question before she had a chance to ask it, "The residence caught on fire. He rescued your daughters, but wasn't able to escape the fire without injury. It's a miracle that your daughters escaped unharmed. We are treating his burns. Right now, he is sedated to help relieve the pain." Her heart was torn, as much as she wanted to end things with Sal, she would never wish this on him.

"Can I see him?" The doctor reached out for her hand.

"Of course, you can. I just want you to brace yourself for what you are about to see."

Those words echoed in her mind. They did not make it any easier to view Sal's partially charred body. She ran to the side of the bed. She stopped herself from reaching out to touch him.

"Oh, Sal," she cried, "I'm here honey, I'm here."

Sal moaned in response. His painful whine sent chills up her spine. She lowered her head, "Don't try to talk; I just wanted to thank you for saving our babies." She wept softly. "We will do whatever we need to. Just get better." Kelly sat by his side until the medication took over his body. She stopped by the Nurses Station to give them her contact information. They informed her that Sal was due for another treatment. She decided to take the girls home. She knew they were driving Admiral crazy by now.

She returned to the floor she left them on. The sitting area was filled with a crowd of nurses. Seeing so many nurses gathered together alarmed her. She made her way to the front. Greeted by giggle after giggle, Kelly found the girls still trying to win Admiral over with their boo-boos.

"Girls, why are you driving Mr. Admiral crazy with your silliness."

Admiral chuckled, "It's okay, I don't mind. They are trying to show me all of their boo-boos. If they find them all then they can have the balloons."

The girls turned their attention away from Kelly, "What about the bears?" they cried in unison.

"And the bears." he said.

"How about we talk about this in the car?" They gathered the girls' belongings and signed the required paperwork to release them.

"Where do you want to take them?" Admiral asked.

Kelly looked confused, "What do you mean where?" she asked.

"Do you want to go back to my place or do you feel safe enough to go back to yours?"

Admiral wanted to answer the question for her, but he didn't want to come off pushy. The thought of her house took her back to the confrontation with Supreme. Softly she replied, "Your place." She couldn't risk anything happening to her kids. They were all she had left.

Once they arrived at Admiral's, he showed the girls around while Kelly called Kim. The call didn't go well. Kim bombarded her with questions, "Why didn't you call me? How is he? Where are you? The girls...what about the girls? Why didn't you come here..." Kim tried to go on and on.

Kelly stopped her, "Kim, the girls are fine. They were sedating Sal when we left. He was in a lot of pain."

Kim sobbed, "Who would do this to him? First mom and dad...not him too." she said softly.

Kelly's heart ached, Sal and Kim became inseparable after the death of their parents.

"Kim calm down, he's going to pull through just fine. I'm sorry I didn't call you sooner. I wanted to get the girls out of there as soon as I could. They are allowing immediate family to visit with him for short periods of time."

Kim sighed, "I have to get myself together before I go see him."

Kelly agreed.

"Who would want to hurt him like this Kel?" Kim asked again and again.

Kelly lied, "I'm not sure Kim, I'm not sure at all."

Kelly hung up and went to find the girls. Once again, they were trying to win over Admiral. "Girls are you TRYING to drive him crazy?" she asked.

"It's fine mom, he said we could."

Admiral stopped her before she answered, "You know I'm a pushover when it comes to the ladies."

This time there wasn't anyone to stop her, "You wouldn't be caught up in my mess." The words rolled so easily off her tongue as she left the room.

Admiral chased after her. "I'm not caught up in any of your mess. I was in this way before you, so stop thinking like that."

Nothing Admiral said would change her mind. "I'm going to get the girls settled for bed. Where do you want them to sleep," she asked.

"You can have the two bedrooms; I'll stay in my office." Once again, he cut Kelly off before she could say anything, "I have a bed in there, so I'll be fine." Kelly didn't want to put him out like that in his own home. Admiral read her like a book. "It's okay. I promise." He kissed her on the forehead and walked away. Kelly settled the girls in the second bedroom. It didn't take long for them to fall fast asleep.

All of the excitement of today caught up with her as well, yet she couldn't sleep. She wanted to tell Admiral goodnight but she wanted to distance herself from him a little. She climbed in bed and hoped the blankets could wrap her as tight as his arms could. As the hands on the clock spun out of control, Kelly found herself fighting with the blankets once again. *"It looks like you're losing."* She heard his teasing in her mind. *"Maybe I should just tell him goodnight."* She threw the blankets off and tip-toed her way to the office. She prayed the girls didn't wake up and catch her in the act. She knocked softly on his door. No answer. So, she tried one more time. Still, no answer. Disappointed, she turned and started walking back to the bedroom. Suddenly, the door creaked open.

"Kelly, is everything okay?" he asked.

"Oh yes, I just, I just um." she stumbled on her words.

"What's wrong with you?" She asked herself.

"I just, just wanted to say good night."

Admiral smiled. He watched her shift back and forth on her tippy toes. "Mmmm ok, good night to you too, Kelly."

She stood there unsure of what to say next. He didn't give the response she expected. "Oh, I'll um, I guess I'll see you in the morning then," she said nervously as she turned to walk away.

Admiral reached out and caught her hand. "Come here," he said as he pulled her close. "You're cute when you pout." Continuing in her true nature, she sassed him back, "I'm not pouting! I came to tell you goodnight." Her breathing struggled to remain calm. Every time she was close to him, he sent her senses into an overload.

"It looks like this lip right here is pouting." He nudged her bottom lip with his.

She trembled, "Well it isn't, 'cuz I don't pout."

He toyed with her bottom lip. "So, you're going to bed?" he asked.

Kelly continued to act as if she didn't care. "Yes. I just wanted to come and say good night. So, I guess this is good night." Kelly pulled herself slightly away.

"Are you going somewhere?"

Kelly crossed her arms, "Back to bed."

Admiral turned towards his bed, "How about you snuggle with me for a while?"

Kelly looked at his bed. "Just for a little bit, then I have to go back to the other room. I don't want the girls to wake up and find me in here."

Admiral pulled her in, "Just a little bit is fine with me." He pulled back the sheets and climbed in first. He patted the empty spot next to him. "Lay with me."

Kelly climbed in next to him. She melted the moment her body was near his. He caressed her curves. He had the same conversation he had with himself every time he was near Kelly. "We're not going to do anything. Just hold her."

Kelly laughed, "You should keep your private conversations to yourself."

Admiral was so tired he didn't realize that he spoke his thoughts out loud. He was completely embarrassed, "Just because I said it out loud doesn't mean it's not true. I just want to hold you. You don't need me putting anything else on you. You're dealing with enough."

Kelly turned to face Admiral. "You are the one person who doesn't want anything from me. You are always in my corner and besides, you like putting "IT" on me." Kelly kissed his chest.

"Kelly, don't," Admiral warned her, "You know what's going to happen if you don't stop."

Kelly stopped kissing on Admiral. She sighed in disappointment, "I'll stop." Kelly moved away and eased her way out of the bed. "I'll go back to the other room."

Admiral abruptly grabbed her hand. "Don't." he growled. He looked up at Kelly with eyes full of intention. Her breathing quickened.

She pushed his hand off of her arm and teased, "We're not going to do anything, remember?"

"Kelly." he said with a deepening growl.

Her body shivered. His desire ran through her body. It was as if Kelly was under his command when she slowly started removing her pajama bottoms. Admiral followed the bottoms as they fell from her hips. Her exposed skin excited his manhood. Knowing that she had his full attention, her fingers danced around her kitty. Every time she neared her pleasure zone, Admiral's eyes widened. He reached out to pull her back in to bed.

"No, no, no my friend," She chided him.

Admiral jumped up and wrapped her tightly, "Is that all I am to you?" he asked.

Kelly looked puzzled, "What do you mean?"

He repeated the question, "Is that all I am to you?"

Kelly saw how her comment struck him. "I mean we are..." she stopped herself. She had to choose her words carefully, hurting him was the last thing she wanted to do. "Admiral, yes you are my friend."

Admiral tried to pull away. Kelly wouldn't let him.

"But you are SO much more than that to me." She paused, "I love you. I don't know exactly where things stand between us; I just know that I am happy when I'm with you."

She removed her shirt. Standing before him vulnerable and naked, she repeated herself, "I love you."

Admiral lost what little restraint he had left. His mouth sought out the first area of exposed skin. He loved the way she tasted.

"Say it again," he told her.

"Say, what?"

He kissed his way up between her breasts. "Say it again."

Kelly placed her hand on his forehead and his head back slightly. She looked deep into his eyes, "I love you Admiral. I loved you from the start, just as you love me. Now I need you to make love to me, baby."

Admiral growled. Kelly turned him on with her words. "You know I'd do anything for you." Admiral laid her down on the bed. He drank in her wonderful body. He placed himself at her feet. He massaged her tiny feet. He kept his eyes locked on her. Bringing the arch of her foot to his lips, he kissed his way up her thigh. He paused for a moment to take in the scent of her essence. Kelly's fingers mingled between Admiral's locks. He continued up past her navel.

"Admiral, baby," she moaned. He kept smothering her body in kisses, pushing her emotions into overdrive. "I love you so much," she cried out.

"Again," he said.

Kelly said it over and over again. Hearing Kelly say those three words was worth everything Admiral was fighting for. He planted a sensual kiss on her lips before diving down towards her treasure.

"I love you, Kelly."

Before she had a chance to respond, his mouth covered her clit. The warm sensation caused a sharp scream to escape her lips. Not wanting to wake the girls she tried to push his head away. But Admiral was determined to finish his feast. He parted her swollen lips. Her juices were already starting to flow. He used the tip of his finger and outlined a trail. His tongue followed the same path. Kelly tried to push him off again. He grabbed both of her hands tightly.

Kelly moaned, "Admiral."

He buried his face in her divide. He devoured her pussy, attempting to drink in every drop of her essence. Kelly moaned softly. He massaged her clit until she felt the pressure build, "Baby, I'm going to cum." Admiral immediately jumped up. "Not yet." He told her. Kelly pounded the sheets, "Are you serious?" Admiral sat between her legs. He spread her legs apart, exposing her pussy. Her lips were swollen a puffy pink and covered with her excitement. He teased the tip of his dick around the entrance of her core. He watched her squirm before he eased his way in. He leaned in and kissed her, "You are so beautiful." Just as Kelly exhaled, Admiral pushed his way in. Kelly muffled her scream. Admiral eased back. "Don't stop." Her trembling arms pulled him back in. He followed her wish. He thrust his member deep insider of her. He watched her tremble with each stroke. "Are you okay?" he whispered. Once again Kelly asked him not stop. Clearly something was up, but knowing Kelly she didn't want to talk about it. This was about a physical connection. Admiral made it just that. Flipping Kelly over, Admiral grabbed on to her hips. The forcefulness caused Kelly to moan, "I love you." He thrust harder and harder. Kelly began to tremble violently. "I love you, Kelly." he reassured her. She dug her nails into his muscles. He growled a deep moan. "Fuck me, baby." Admiral did exactly as Kelly wished. He fucked Kelly until her climax began to build. He hopped up, startling her. "What are you doing?" she yelled. He shhh'd her. Admiral flipped her over once again, then he dove in between her legs. Her clit was ready for the tongue lashing he was about to give.

Admiral sucked and licked her clit. He lapped up the juices flowing from Kelly's love hole. Her hands locked around the back of his head. It didn't take long for Kelly to reach her climax. She tightened her grip, locking Admiral on her magic spot. It was almost impossible to tell the difference between the violent trembles Kelly had before and the trembles caused by the orgasm. A soft whimper escaped her lips when the waved finished cursing through her body. Once he was free from her grasp, Admiral climbed back up to the top of the bed. He held Kelly in his arms. He tried to hold her until she stopped shaking.

"I'm always going to be here for you, Kelly."

As comforting as his words were, they had the opposite effect on her. Kelly closed her eyes. She felt safe when she was with him. But no matter how tight he held her, he couldn't stop the havoc BTB was causing in her life. She wrapped her arms around his. She kissed them once before she wiggled away from him.

"Goodnight." she whispered softly before she snuck back to the other bedroom.

She ran as fast as she could. She closed the door just as the tears rolled down her face. Kelly realized the best thing to do for her and the girls was going to be the hardest thing to do. She called her parents. Naturally they were startled by Kelly calling in the middle of the night.

"Mom, I'm okay. Yes, the girls are fine." Kelly's mom fired a series of questions. "Mom, calm down. I just need to talk to you." Her mom continued bombarding Kelly with questions. "Mom please, I need you!" Kelly's mom fell silent for a moment.

"I'm sorry Kelly, I get so worked up. What's going on?"

"I need to come home," she cried.

"You're always welcome here, you know that. But what's going on?"

Kelly took a deep breath before she told her mom the P.G. version of what led up to this point. She skimmed over the gritty details of the sex club, but admitted to being involved with Supreme.

"So, you're telling me this 'Supreme' girl wouldn't take no for an answer and set out to ruin your marriage?" Kelly's mom couldn't wrap her mind around someone being that scorned.

"I don't feel safe here anymore; they hurt Sal when the girls were there. I can't be here mom." she cried.

"Don't worry, I'll explain everything to your father. How soon can you get here?" her mom asked.

"Mom, EVERYTHING?" Kelly cried.

"Everything that he needs to know. When should I expect you?" she asked again.

"Let me make sure Sal is okay and the girls say goodbye. I'm thinking we should be there by the end of the week, Monday at the latest." Kelly felt relieved when she hung up. Sad, but relieved. Kelly wasn't sure how Admiral would take the news. She hugged her pillow tightly and cried herself to sleep.

That night Kelly wasn't the only one crying herself to sleep. Selena was safely hidden from everyone looking to find her. The last place anyone would look for her was at Mother Stella's.

Despite Admiral being her grandson, Mother Stella was the Grand Priestess of BTB. Protecting her fellow sisters came first before anything. "Selena, you know I love you as if you were my own child, but this has gone too far. I warned you just like I warned the others, this has gone too far. Look how many lives are ruined because you and Supreme couldn't focus on the mission."

Selena tried to defend herself, but the Grand Priestess wouldn't allow her.

"Letting all of your sinful pleasures cloud our true vision! Now I have to send you away. After tonight you are to never return here. Do you understand?" The Grand Priestess left Selena in tears before she could respond. True to her word, Selena was sent away the very next morning. She was sent to one of many hideouts only the Grand Priestess knew about. Now she had to deal with the issues Supreme created. It was time to reign in BTB and bring order back to her creation. She placed a call, "It's time to activate our back up plan."

When the dreaded call came in, Savannah looked at Sam. The look on her face said it all. "It's time," he said as he walked out of the room. Savannah didn't want things to end like this, but from the beginning that was always the last resort. They remained silent at the put the plan in motion. Savannah began sending out the coordinates to the rest of her team. It was time to take down BTB starting with the "Hive" as she called it. She kept her distance up arrival. In order to protect her connect with the authorities, she wouldn't enter the building until it was cleared. She watched as they raided the compound. One by one, they carried out her fellow BTB members. She didn't recognize any of the members coming

262 | T.J. LA RUE

out, but they all had the same look written all over their faces. Being new, the ladies didn't know what to expect, but for that very reason they were picked to be there that night. If and when they were interrogated, the information they were privy to was of no use to anyone. Savannah walked through the compound once the ladies were taken away. Seeing the empty rooms brought back memories. BTB might have gotten off track, but in the beginning, they helped so many women find their power. Walking through the halls Savannah dialed the Grand Priestess. She was short and to the point when she answered, "Is it done?" Savannah replied, "Yes." The was a brief silence, "I'll handle the rest." the Grand Priestess said before she abruptly hung up. *"Savannah did her part now it's time for me to handle Supreme."* the Grand Priestess said to herself. She summoned Supreme to her home. When the call came in Supreme wanted to send it right to voicemail.

"Hello Grand Priestess." she coo'ed into the phone.

"Cut the crap Supreme. We need to talk. I want you here NOW!"

Before she could respond, "Click" was all that Supreme heard. News of the raid hadn't reached Supreme yet. She thought the visit was just Grand Priestess in another mood to rant. She figured out how wrong she was the moment she arrived.

"Do you realize you and that lil flunky of yours cost me BTB?" Supreme was caught off guard.

"What do you mean cost you," she asked.

Grand Priestess shot her the dirtiest looks Supreme's ever seen. "Because you caught the hots for that girl, Selena was then ordered to take her husband down. Neither one of you could control your emotions and let this whole thing blow out of control. The police tore through our compound after your stunt at Kelly's house and Selena burned up Sal along with his home. What the hell were you two thinking?"

Supreme didn't know how to answer. "Selena did what?"

Priestess laughed sarcastically, "You had no control over your puppet, yet you reign *Supreme*. I blame myself for trusting you and for that it's cost me. But, I won't be the only one to pay. You're done with this Kelly mess. She needs to move on with her life as do you. I'm sending you away."

Supreme tried to cut in, "I'm sending you away, Supreme! Don't try to challenge my decision. Trust me on this one. The entire group wants you dead. If you want to take another breath you will leave in the car waiting for you out front."

Supreme hesitated but knew this decision was final. "I love her." she whispered softly, "No matter where you send me, my feelings for her won't change." Supreme did as she was ordered and left. Grand Priestess watched her car pull away. It would deliver Supreme to a secret location. All of the necessary measures were in place to help Supreme detox from her love addiction.

Some time had passed since the fall out of BTB and Sal's injury. He was making progress. The doctors were expecting him to make a full recovery. It would be painfully slow recovery, but everyone was thankful. Visits with Kelly, Kim and the girls kept him in good spirits. Once in a while the detectives would stop by to question Sal and Kelly. They searched high and low for Selena. She was nowhere to be found. The detectives told Sal, "It was as if she disappeared." It was better for Sal that she was gone. He thought about the baby, but maybe it was best this way. He could focus on making a better life for Kelly and the girls. He laid in his hospital bed heavily sedated. Kelly brought the girls by to see him.

"Girls, we are only staying for a minute. Daddy needs his rest." she told them. She stopped by today hoping to discuss her move with the girls. Clearly, he was in no condition to carry on a serious conversation.

Just as she said, the visit was quick. "Okay girls, let's let daddy rest."

Sal said goodbye to the girls. "Kelly, can I talk to you alone for a moment?"

Kelly situated the girls in the playroom nearby. "How are you feeling?" she asked Sal.

"Kelly don't make this about me. I can see it all over your face. Something is wrong. Talk to me." he told her.

"I'm fine Sal. Let's just let it be for now."

Sal refused to let it go. "What is it Kelly," he asked again. She took a deep breath before she blurted out, "I'm taking the girls and moving to my parents' house."

Sal tried to jump up, but he cried out in pain. "You can't take my girls! Not now."

Kelly tried to calm him down, "I'm not taking them, but you know as well as I do, we're not safe here. I don't want the girls to have to live in fear like we do."

Sal continued to fight her on this.

Fighting back her tears she begged, "Sal please, I need to do this to keep the girls safe."

As much as he hated to admit it, Kelly was right. The girls shouldn't pay for their sins. He tried not to cry in front of Kelly.

"It's okay, Sal," she reassured him. "We will get through this together no matter where we are. As time passes and all of this settles, we will visit."

Sal was hurt, "Go, Kelly."

She thanked him for understanding.

He yelled at her, "GO, KELLY!" She was startled. "Just leave me and GO! I want to be alone."

Kelly said her goodbyes. She picked up the girls from the playroom. "Ladies, can we go to the park? Mommy has something she wants to talk to you about. All the girls heard was more play time and no school for today.

"Yessss!" They cheered in unison.

Explaining the move to their grandparents' house to them was easier than she thought. Their only concern was about Sal. "What about daddy?" They asked. "Is he coming, too?"

Kelly explained how Sal needed to stay here so he can get better. She promised them that Sal would always be there for them. "Will you help me tell Auntie Kim so she won't be sad?" They agreed to help Kelly break the news, but wanted to have lunch first. The three of them headed back to Admiral's house. Kelly figured he would be at work. She would break the news to him when he got off tonight. The girls sprinted in the house.

"Admiral, Admiral! Guess what?" They jumped up and down.

"He's not here, I will tell him later. Don't worry about it." Kelly turned the corner to enter the kitchen. She collided with Admiral.

"Tell me what?"

A scream escaped Kelly's mouth, "What are you doing here?"

Admiral laughed, "I live here if that's okay with you. Now, what do you need to tell me?"

The girls blurted out the surprise before Kelly could say anything. "We are moving! We're going to our grandparents' far, far away."

Admiral was caught off guard. His eyes darted to Kelly. He tried to read her face. His eyes begged for her to say they were wrong. He eyes started to fill with anger when she didn't. "I'm sorry." she whispered. Admiral left the room before the girls saw him explode. Kelly grabbed his arm when he walked past her. "No." he said. He pulled himself away. "I'll be in my office alone," he told her. Admiral was mad, but he couldn't argue with Kelly. It was her decision if she wanted to leave. *"Who could blame her?"* he asked himself. Admiral wanted to be selfish. He wanted to keep her here, safe and sound with him. Kelly fed the girls dinner.

"Let's settle down early ladies." she said. "We've had a long day."

The girls showered and did as Kelly said. They climbed in bed with their favorite books. Kelly sat quietly in the front room with the T.V. on. She intended to sit down and watch anything that would take her mind off him. She knew he would be upset, but not like this. *"I'm only doing what's best for everyone."*she told herself. Admiral paced around in his office. He let his emotions get the best of him. He had gotten so wound up that he worked up an appetite. He tried to ignore it, but the rumbling in his stomach refused to let him. He peaked out in to the hallway. The doors to the girl's and Kelly's room were closed. Admiral figured it was safe to come out. He made a B-Line to the kitchen. He made his way down the hallway and rounded the corner. Thinking he was in the clear his mind blocked out the sounds coming from the T.V.

He turned to corner and found himself in the same room as Kelly. There was an awful silence between the two of them. He averted his eyes, too afraid to make eye contact. He let out a deep breath when he finally made it to the kitchen. He grabbed a pot and started rumbling around on the stove. He cooked up a quick meal and sat to the kitchen table. He sat there staring at his plate. He tried to force himself to eat, but his appetite was gone. He thought about how hurt Kelly looked sitting on the couch. *"You did that to her."* echoed through his mind. He pushed his plate away and decided to go talk to her. "Kelly can we talk?" he asked as his walked in to the front room. To his surprise the room was empty. He looked around the room. The T.V. was turned off and Kelly was gone.

Admiral went to her door and knocked softly, "Kelly." he whispered. She didn't answer. He knocked again, "Kelly, please." Still she didn't answer. Slowly he turned the knob. "I'm coming in," he announced. He found Kelly sitting on the bed with her face buried in her hands. He raced over and put his arms around her.

"Are you okay?" he asked.

Kelly pushed him away, "I'm so tired of people asking me if I'm okay. How the hell can I be okay with all of this shit going on?"

He was shocked to see Kelly explode.

"I'm sorry for being so selfish earlier. I know this is a lot for you."

Admiral could kill himself. "I shouldn't have acted like that."

Kelly stopped crying, "You acted really childish."

Admiral tried to explain, "Could you blame me? I was caught off guard by the girls jumping around like it was the best things ever. All I knew in that moment was that I was losing you. I didn't want to say anything around the girls, so I just wanted to be alone." Kelly was quiet as he continued, "It wasn't easy for me to come to terms with the fact that I was in love with someone other than my wife. Then you want to factor in all of the craziness that Selena and Supreme have been up to, I just want to keep you safe."

"And that's exactly why I decided to move!" Kelly exclaimed.

"You don't get it," he said, "I wanted to keep you safe. ME, Kelly! I wanted to do that. And then you come up with this decision without ever discussing it with me. We might not know exactly what this is between us is, but we know it's something."

Kelly told him the real reason why she waited to tell him. "I was afraid to tell you. I knew you wouldn't want me to go, but I can't be here anymore." she cried. "I'm so tired Admiral, I just want to live and be normal again."

He hugged her tight and kissed her forehead. "I know you do, you deserve to be happy. I won't lie and say that I want you to go because I don't. I can respect your reasons to go. I will help you with this anyway I can."

Kelly smiled. "Why are you so amazing," she asked.

Admiral answered from his heart, "Because of you baby, it's all because of you. Now it's your bedtime young lady. Let me tuck you in."

Admiral held Kelly while she drifted off to sleep. "I'm going to miss you." he whispered in her ear. He watched her sleep before he laid his head down next to hers. Admiral stayed with Kelly as long as he could. He didn't want the girls to wake up and find them lying in bed together. He kissed her forehead goodbye and peaked his head into the spare bedroom. The girls were sound asleep. Admiral had every intention of going to sleep after making sure everyone was safe. He laid down in his office to sleep. The more he tried the more frustrated he became. He banged on the pillow and jumped out of bed. "Fuck it," he said, "I might as well get some work done." He logged on to the computer and stared at page after page of spreadsheets. None of it made any sense to him. His mind couldn't wrap around crunching the numbers. All he could think about was her leaving. A million questions ran through his head. *"How was she getting there? What was she taking with her? How was she packing those things up?"* Then it hit him. Kelly would need a moving company. His fingers banged the keyboard. He searched local moving companies. He researched one after the other. He wasn't concerned with the pricing, just the quality of service. He prepared a list of reputable companies to show Kelly, but he selected the best and arranged for them to pack Kelly's belonging up tomorrow. "If she won't let me take care of her, at least I can make it easier for her." Admiral felt at ease looking at the list. He rested his head on the back of his chair. He closed his eyes for what he thought was a minute.

The next morning Kelly woke up to the ringing of her phone. Someone was calling her back to back. She read the name and instantly panicked, "Is everything ok?" she asked.

"I don't know, you tell me," the caller asked.

Kelly sat up in the bed, "Kim what's going on?" Suddenly it hit her. "You talked to the girls." she said.

"Yes, why do I have to hear from the girls that you are planning on moving out of town? Are you that boo'ed up that you forgot about me?"

Kelly tried to calm Kim down. "Kim it's not like that. Let me explain," she pleaded. "I talked to your brother yesterday about it and the girls and I were going to talk to you about it today. Kim with all that's been going on, it's just not safe for us to be here anymore." Kim started to calm down. "I know you're upset and don't want the girls to go, but

Kim I don't know any other way to keep them safe for now. You know I would never do anything to keep them from you." Kelly listened to Kim's silence. "Say something please," Kelly begged.

Finally, Kim broke her silence. "When are you planning on leaving," she asked.

"Monday," Kelly said quietly.

"MONDAY!" Kim yelled.

"I know, I know, but the sooner the better. My parents are waiting for me," Kelly told her.

"Well, can I at least see y'all before you leave?" Kim asked.

"Of course!" Kelly said. "I have a few things to get situated today so the girls can come over for a while. Then if you want, we can have lunch on Monday before we leave." Kim agreed before she hung up.

Kelly fell back in to bed. "That was harder than I thought." she said out loud.

"What was so hard mommy?" the girls asked as they climbed in to bed.

"Ohhhh you two are going to get it! I thought I asked you to help me with Auntie Kim?" asked Kelly.

The girls looked at each other for a moment. "That's what we did! We told her about our trip."

They jumped up and down on the bed. Kelly gently tackled them.

"You told her before I had a chance to, silly girls." Kelly tickled them both. "Well she called me and said she's going to miss you two. So, I thought today would be a perfect day for the three of you to have a girl's day."

The girls were excited about spending time with their aunt. They ate breakfast and got dressed as fast as possible. Kelly asked Admiral to ride with her to drop off the girls. "You could keep me company." She teased Admiral by kissing his neck. Admiral wanted to rip her clothes off right there, but he managed to ignore the throbbing below his belt. "Let's go," he said as he wiggled away. Admiral grabbed the list of movers and his keys. "I have something to discuss with you after we drop the girls off," he told her.

The girls didn't want to wait for the car to stop, when they pulled up to Kim's. "Bye, Mommy." they said jumping out the car. Once they were situated with their aunt, Admiral and Kelly decided to go to Kelly's house. He figured it would be the perfect place to discuss the moving company.

"This is the last time I'll pull in to this driveway for a while." Kelly climbed out of the car and looked around.

"There's something I wanted to talk to you about," Admiral blurted out, "It's actually about the house." Admiral showed Kelly the moving invoice. "Last night I was upset about your decision to leave. But, after we talked I.."

Kelly interrupted him, "You came to your senses."

Admiral laughed. "You're right. I came to my senses. Kelly you don't belong here, at least right now. So, to support your decision to go, I've hired a moving company to come in and pack everything up for you. They are going to deliver your house in one of those storage thingies."

Kelly smiled. "You didn't have to do that. I'll figure out a way to get our things there."

272 | T.J. LA RUE

Admiral gave her a stern look. "Please don't fight me on this. I want to be there for you and the girls. No, I am here for you and the girls. So, like I said, I've hired a moving company. They will be here shortly. All I'm asking you to do is to decide what you want to take. I will have them pack it up and deliver it to you."

Kelly knew when to push back. Clearly Admiral was standing his ground. "I love you." she said as she unlocked the front door. Admiral waited a few minutes before he followed her inside. He didn't want Kelly to see him blush. Kelly looked around at her things. Would she really miss or need anything here was the question she asked herself? Nothing jumped out right away. They were all just things. None of it really mattered to her. All she cared about was her family. She looked over at Admiral. He looked like a little lost puppy, who'd lost his best friend. "It won't be forever." she told him.

Admiral looked away. He wanted to tell her not to go so bad. "The movers will be here soon. We should get this figured out."

Kelly motioned for him to "Come here." He eased his way over. "That's not here." she teased.

"We have other things to deal with right now. And I don't want to make things harder than they need to be."

Kelly pointed to the spot in front of her. "Come here." she repeated.

"You're making this hard," he said.

Kelly smiled, "I'm not making it hard yet." she teased.

Admiral threw in the towel. He knew this battle was lost. He stood in front of Kelly. He lowered his head, letting his locs flow around her. "I'm here." he said. Kelly ran her hands up his chest. Her arms circled his neck. She nibbled on his bottom lip. His manhood stirred. He didn't fight the feeling. He went for her hips, pulling her closer. His manhood was hard and pressing against her thigh. Kelly felt her desire building. She dropped his pants and ordered him to sit down. Admiral happily obliged. Kelly slowly removed her top.

"You didn't wear a bra." he couldn't help but ask.

"Or these." Kelly said as she took off her pants.

That sent Admiral over the top. He reached out to grab her. Kelly pushed him away. "Sit back." she told him. She positioned herself to straddle him.

"Whooaa! Wait, wait, wait," he said. "I don't have anything here with me." He was referring to a condom. "I don't have any either. I didn't plan on doing this here, with you." Kelly kissed Admiral on his neck. "Kelly don't get me worked up. I swear I'll explode." That's exactly what Kelly wanted.

"Just one more time without one." she whispered in his ear. Kelly lowered herself onto his lap. His manhood slid in to her slick hole. Slowly, she eased him all the way in.

"Kelly." he said.

Everything in him wanted to tell her to stop, but the very thing inside of her refused to let him. Her walls massaged his shaft as she went up and down. He reached out to grab her hips. Once again, she smacked him away. "I got this." she told him. He watched her bounce on his lap like his dick was her favorite play toy. He reached out again. This time she didn't stop him. He held her tight. Her breast plopped against his head. His mouth sought out her globes. His mouth latched on to her nipples. He bit down gently. The sensation excited Kelly. She began to moan loudly. She begged him not to stop. Admiral looked up at Kelly. The look of pure pleasure was written all over her face. He pulled on the left nipple while he continued sucking on the right one. Kelly locked on to the back of his head. She was working up a fury. Admiral knew she was close.

"Cum for me, baby." He forced himself to meet every thrust Kelly made.

"Yesss." she cried out.

Admiral went harder and faster. Her juices coated his balls. "You're so wet," he told her. "I love how you make me feel." His words were the final touch.

Kelly exploded. "Admiral!" she called out as her face contorted.

He growled at the sight of her pleasure. He grabbed her hips. The sounds of flesh slamming against flesh mingled with moaning filled her home. Admiral's body tensed up. "Baby, you're gonna make me cum." Admiral warned Kelly. He tightened his grip. "Don't stop. Baby don't stop." Admiral's body took over. In his mind he knew he needed to pull out. But in this moment, the feeling of being wrapped in Kelly's soft warm pussy was all he could focus on.

Admiral pulled Kelly's face towards his.

"Kelly, I love you." he said as his load released.

Kelly collapsed on top of him. "I love you too." She said.

Kelly kissed Admiral until he playfully pushed her away.

"Keep it up and you're gonna start me up again."

Before Kelly had a chance to say or do anything, the doorbell rang. "Movers!" the voice said from the other side of the door. Kelly jumped up and grabbed her clothes. She turned a bright shade of red.

"I thought you said they were coming later!" she hit Admiral on the chest.

He laughed, "It is later." He gave her a kiss, then fixed his clothes. "Here I come." he told the voice on the other side of the door.

"NO,WAIT!" yelled Kelly. She sprayed the can of air freshener sitting on the coffee table.

"Are you serious?" he asked her.

"It smells like sex." she whispered.

"Your sex is my favorite scent." he sniffed the air.

Kelly ran upstairs promising to kill Admiral the very minute the movers left. By the time she returned, Admiral had instructed the movers to pack the entire house. Kelly looked around, still unsure of what she really wanted to bring.

"This way you can take your time to decide what's going to fit in your new life."

While Kelly thought he was talking about her belongings, Admiral was really talking about him. He had no clue where he stood with Kelly. Hopefully this time apart would answer that question soon. Once everything was taken care of with the moving company, he took her car to get serviced for the trip. "I have to find some things to keep the girls entertained on the car ride." They ran around town finishing up errands before picking up the girls. Kim fought back her tears when Kelly came to get the girls.

"I'm sorry," Kelly said. "

I'll be okay," Kim said. "I won't lie and say I'm happy about you going. But it has to be done."

Kelly made plans to meet with Kim for lunch before they hit the road. "Girls, why don't you stay with Aunt Kim tonight so she won't be sad?" The girls loved the idea. "Maybe Aunt Kim can take you to say bye to Daddy?"

Kim knew Kelly didn't want to face Sal. "I would love to." she hugged her nieces. "So, it's girls' night," she told the twins. "Who's picking the movie tonight?" Kim asked changing the subject. The girls ran for the remote and scrolled through the selections.

Kelly arranged to meet up for lunch with Kim at noon.

"You can have lunch at my shop, if you want." Admiral suggested. "My treat."

Kim looked Admiral up and down. "Kelly, I like him. He's a keeper." she told her.

"He's okay." Kelly teased.

Admiral flashed his pearly whites, "You should take my advice. Before I take him." Kim joked.

Admiral played along and gave Kim a bear hug.

"Alright enough, break it up." Kelly pulled the two apart.

Kim hugged Kelly before she let her out the door. "Kelly, all jokes aside. He's a good man." Kelly nodded her head in agreement.

She kissed the girls and walked out to Admiral, "Since it's just me and you tonight, let me take you out one last time."

The words one last time hit her hard.

"I wanted a nice quiet night at home, but spending time with a nice, handsome gentleman like yourself sounds wonderful."

It hit Kelly all of a sudden, "I don't have anything to wear. We just had everything packed up," she laughed.

"Let's hit the mall really quick." He told her.

Kelly protested.

He pulled her close, "It'll give me the chance to dress you for once."

Kelly flash backed to their moment on the couch. She started to tingle. *"Calm down."* she told herself. There was something about this man she couldn't get enough of. "I would love that." she told him. They raced to the mall making dinner reservations along the way.

True to his word, Admiral dressed Kelly and showed her an amazing night on the town. He wined and dined her. Savoring every minute they had together, he hung on to every word that flowed from her tongue. *"Tomorrow she'll be gone and you'll be alone again."* he told himself. They finished dessert and talked for a while.

"I need to get you home." he told her. "You need to rest before you hit the road tomorrow."

Kelly was tired. "Home would be perfect right about now."

Admiral settled the check. When they reached his house, Kelly was fast asleep. He gently stroked her face, "Baby, we're here," he said. Kelly didn't move. He leaned in and kissed her on the cheek. "Wake up, baby." Kelly started to stir. "Come on, let's put you to bed."

Kelly flashed a sleepy smile and she took off her seatbelt. Admiral got out the car and opened her door. "You're too good to me," she said softly.

"You deserve the world," he told her. "Come on, bed." he said.

"So bossy." Kelly said as she climbed the steps. He undressed her and ran a bath. Kelly crossed her arms. Admiral gave her a stern look. They were engaged in a silent battle. "You're my Queen tonight."

Kelly pouted, "How can I argue with that?"

Admiral bathed Kelly by candlelight. He dried her off when he was finished and carried her to the bedroom. He laid her down and covered her naked body with his blankets. He joined her in the bed but laid on top of the sheets. Kelly looked puzzled. "This way I can make sure you don't start anything." he said in a playful tone. "All jokes aside Kel, I just want to hold you tonight. These last moments with you I want them to be about you, and not your body. I remember the first time you walked in to my shop." Admiral talked about every moment he shared with Kelly and how special they were to him. His words helped ease Kelly to sleep. Admiral watched her all night. He studied every inch of her body, just in case he never laid eyes on her again.

The next morning, Kelly woke up feeling as if someone was staring at her. She rolled over, turning herself face to face with Admiral. "I thought I felt someone watching me." Kelly wiggled closer. "What's on your mind," she asked. Admiral gave her the usual 'Nothing' head shake. "We don't have much time, so I'm going to ask you again. What's on your mind?" Admiral gave in and spoke, "It's just that." Kelly looked puzzled.

"We don't have much time left together. What if this is the last time I'll ever get to see you again? How am I supposed to walk around every day knowing how I feel about you, but there's nothing I can do about it?" Admiral was getting worked up.

Kelly saw how strong his feeling for her really were. Her eyes watered. "Baby, I'm sorry. I feel the same way about you and our situation. Believe me, I wish it was another way."

Admiral kissed her lips. "I didn't mean to make you feel bad for making the best choice for you and the girls. It's just that you've given me a reason to love again. Now enough of talking about what we can't change. We'll deal with things as they come." He kissed her again. "Let me make you breakfast." Kelly fussed until he agreed to let her help. Afterwards, they prepared to meet Kim at the restaurant.

They arrived shortly before Kim. There was an awkward silence between the two. Admiral didn't want to upset her again. Kelly tried her best not to stir up any of Admiral's feeling. The conversation was short and to the point. Her face lit up for a split second when Kim's car pulled up. Then it hit her. She would have to say goodbye to Kim as well. Dealing with Admiral's emotions on top of Kim's left little room to process her own. *"Be a big girl."* she told herself. She smiled and hugged Kim and the girls.

"Is this really YOURS," the girls asked.

"All mine," he told them. He pulled two aprons from behind his back. "Let me put you two ladies to work." They giggled.

Kelly and Kim made small talk while they watched Admiral show the girls around.

"Look at the three of them together, Kelly." A smile warmed her heart. "They take to him naturally. I love my brother to death, but if there were ever to be another man in their life, I would hope it was him." Kelly sat in silence. Kim grabbed her hand. "Speaking of my brother, have you gone to see him?"

Kelly shook her head from side to side. "He asked me not to come back. He doesn't like my plan to move on with my life."

It wasn't a shock to Kim. "Sal will never get over what you guys had. You shared a life together as husband and wife. Before all of the bad, there was good. You have to admit when it was good, you two were great. Just give him time. I talked to him while we were at the hospital this morning. He'll come around. He knows you're only doing what needs to be done."

"Girls, come give Auntie a hug. It's almost time for us to hit the road." Hearing Kelly say those words made his heart sink. The girls tore away from Admiral and ran to Kim. She smothered them with hugs and kisses.

Kelly laughed. *"Goodbye isn't as bad as I thought."* Kelly felt better about it until she turned and saw the look on Admiral's face. She was wrong. Admiral tried to hide it, but Kelly saw right through him.

"I'll be in my office if you need me." he informed his staff. Halfway down the hallway Kelly caught up with him.

"Stop." she told him.

Admiral was startled. He stopped, but refused to turn around or say anything. He just hung his head down.

"I feel the same way too." Kelly whispered. Still he said nothing. She searched for words, "You were great with the girls,"

Admiral finally responded, "It was easy, you did a great job with them. You guys take all the time you need saying goodbye. I'm just going to go work on some paperwork."

Kelly grew tired of waiting for him to face her. She placed herself in front of him. "You don't want to see me off?" she asked.

In his mind he yelled, *"I don't want to see you go at all, why would I want to watch you drive out of my life?"* He told her, "I love you. I don't know if I can do this."

She threw her arms around him. "We'll figure this out. I don't know how or when, all I know is that I love you, too."

Admiral inhaled her scent. "I'm going to miss you so much."

He tangled his fingers in her hair. He tried to kiss every strand and every inch of her face. Kelly grabbed his face. She planted her lips on his. Torn between her emotions, Kelly moaned as tears welled up in her eyes.

"You have no idea what you do to me." she told him.

Before Admiral could respond the girls ran up, "OHHHHHH!" they sang. "Mommy's kissing Addie."

Kelly screamed, "OMG!"

She didn't want them to see the two of them together. At least not while the two of them were sorting things out.

"Mommy, Aunt Kim says it's time to go. Is it?"

Admiral laughed, "I love how they can complete the sentence together."

The girls put their hands on their hip. "It's a twin thing," they sassed.

"You two are going to get it," Kelly warned them.

"We were just playing," they whined.

"Let 'em be, Kelly, it was all in fun." Admiral came to their defense.

"Come on you two, your Aunt is right. It's time to go."

Before Admiral could get away, Kelly grabbed his hand.

"This way," she said guiding the girls.

Her comment was more so geared towards Admiral.

"I can't do this without you." she whispered in his ear.

Once they were all outside, Kelly hugged Kim.

"I'll call you as soon as we get there." she promised. "Forget that when we get there crap. You better call me on the hour; every hour!" Kim gave her a stern look. "Alright, sis. I'll call you," she laughed.

They waved bye as Kim pulled off. Admiral hugged and kissed the girls.

"I need you to promise me something." he told them.

They giggled, "Okayyyyy."

A smile broke out on his face. "Y'all are too cute. I need you to keep your mommy happy for me. Make her smile and give her lots of hugs. She likes hugs."

The girls looked at each other and nodded. "We can to that." they said together.

They hugged him one more time before climbing in to the back of Kelly's car. They squealed in delight.

"I think they like the travel packs we made." Kelly said nervously.

"I would say so. You know I'm expecting the same exact phone calls." he told her.

"Okay." she said softly. She placed her hand on his chest. Not realizing that her hand was on his heart. "Thank you, Admiral."

He shook his head no, "You don't have to thank me."

Kelly knew that she didn't have to thank him. "You're right. I don't have to thank you, but I want to. I walked in to your shop a woman who was completely unsure of who I was and afraid to find out. But, through everything that came my way, I could always count on you. You fought for me when I didn't know how to. I'm not afraid to stand on my own because of you. And for that, I am always going to be thankful."

Kelly hugged him one last time. He helped her to the car and closed the door.

"Make sure you call me." he begged her as she pulled off.

Kelly drove in silence. The girls were 'lost' in their new tablets. She appreciated the silence, as it allowed her to settle her emotions. It didn't take long for the twins to start in on their questions.

"Mommy do you like Addie?" Hailey asked.

"Yeah, Mommy do you like him, 'cuz we do." Harper said.

Kelly didn't have to think about it. "Yes, I do." she said proudly.

"Then why isn't he coming with us?"

Kelly wasn't prepared for that question. "I don't know, my angels. It's complicated." she told them.

"Well, maybe you will know when we get to Grandma and Grandpa's house." they told her.

"Maybe." Kelly said.

The girls went back to their tablets while Kelly went back to her thoughts. She wasn't sure when her girls became so wise, but she took their advice. The ride was long. Long enough to sort out where she needed to start her over at and who she wanted to start over with. She said farewell to all the drama and looked forward to what was to come, whatever that may be.

ABOUT THE AUTHOR

Falling in love with reading when she was only a Kindergartner, T. J. LaRue grew up with an unmatched ability to read a full-length novel in an hour while absorbing each detail between the lines. When her abilities blossomed into a full-fledge love for all things readable, she explored the wordsmith in her by birthing her debut novel, Sinful Pleasures--a sizzling novel on a cellular device at her son's little league game.

For so long a time she'd had to put her dreams of being a published author on hold to care for her family. She currently works in Corporate America, and has previously worked for a major Tech company.

Born and raised in Delaware, T. J. LaRue is a pet lover who runs a mini-zoo in her home. She loves watching superhero movies almost as much as she loves breathing life into the erotic storylines overcrowding her head.